FUMBLED

The Girls of Beachmont
Book 1

FUMBLED

The Girls of Beachmont
Book 1

a novel by T.K. Rapp

FUMBLED
The Girls of Beachmont ~ Book 1
by T.K. Rapp

Cover Design by Amy Queau & T.K. Rapp
Edited by Amy Jackson
Cover Images Courtesy ~ Krivosheev Vitaly & conrado/Bigstock.com
Copyright © 2015 T.K. Rapp
All rights reserved.

ISBN-13: 978-0-9896432-6-9
ISBN-10: 0-9896432-6-3

Dedication

Spence. I love you.
Always.

CHAPTER 1

DANI

"No no no no no!" I shouted as I twisted my hands on the steering wheel.

I hoped I had imagined the rumbling coming from the back end of my black 1957 Bel Air, but then the wobbling started. I pulled over in an old neighborhood and grumbled as I shut the door behind me with more force than necessary. I checked the back tires first, but found nothing. It wasn't until I examined the front passenger side that I noticed a large screw sticking out.

"Figures," I said aloud, kicking the flat tire as if that would actual help anything. It was the icing on the cake to an already shitty day.

My boss, the principal, had informed me thirty minutes before I I'd left for home that my after-school program, River's Kids, lacked the funding it needed for another school year. My entire summer was going to be spent finding backers and donations, which meant my "vacation" would likely be put on hold. That is, if I wanted the kids to have something to do the next year.

I stared at the screw protruding from the black rubber and willed it to disappear. Alas, I would not be a Jedi today. I'd have to fix the tire myself.

Fortunately, my dad taught my sister Grace and I how to

change a flat long before we were allowed to drive. My luck had run out, as I had never changed a flat until that moment.

"Dear God, please let me remember how to do this," I muttered as I gathered my hair into a messy ponytail.

I took a few deep breaths to calm my frayed nerves. But it didn't help. It was after five in the afternoon and the warm California sun caused my clothes to cling to me in the worst way. Or maybe it was my irritation with the circumstances I found myself in that made my temperature high.

The tools I needed were in a box in the trunk, prepared by my dad a long time ago. I removed the cotton shrug I wore over my thin white tank and tossed it into the back.

"All I wanted to do was go home, open a bottle of wine, and binge-watch *Cake Wars*. Is that too much to ask?" I grumbled to myself.

A blue sedan slowed as it passed by, but quickly sped off before offering to help.

I narrowed my eyes, resisting the urge to flip him off. "No. Really, it's fine. I've got this," I said sarcastically, as if the driver could hear me or even cared. "May your practical piece of shit overheat and die."

Funnily enough, being snarky and bitter toward a complete stranger made me smile, shifting my mood slightly. I kept up the charade as a few other cars continued to do the same, none stopping to help.

Fifteen minutes of fake reassurances that the lug nuts were getting looser didn't improve my situation. I knew I was screwed. The stupid bolts *had* to be welded in place. That was the only explanation for why I was unable to remove them. I worked out daily, could bench-press sixty pounds, seventy-five if I was spotted. It should have been easy.

"Come. On," I grunted, pulling one way and pushing another. "Stupid piece of shit!"

I threw the tire iron on the ground and jumped out of the way when it bounced. The last thing I needed was a bruise because I was a clumsy dumbass. I kicked the black rubber before wiping my hand across my face to move the stray auburn hair that clung to my forehead. My knees were blackened from the dirty asphalt and my hands were covered in brownish muck.

I was a complete mess.

I wiped my hands on my thighs and sat down on the curb, preparing to call my dad to drive over and save me.

"Do you need some help?" a low voice asked.

The sun blazed down, obstructing my view. Not even shielding my eyes seemed to help. All I could make out was a towering shadow a few feet away that was intimidating as hell. A gray Range Rover was parked behind him across the street, and I assumed it belonged to Mr. Tall-and-Helpful. He squatted down next to the tire, giving me an unobstructed view of him.

He wore gold-rimmed aviators and a baseball cap that hid his face well. But his full lips that were curved into a smirk had me entranced. I tried to avert my eyes to anywhere but his lips, knowing that he might be able to see exactly what I was thinking.

I cleared my throat and dropped my gaze, and it landed on the white T-shirt clinging to his chest. His pecs were straining beneath the thin material and it dawned on me as I continued to look him over that his muscles appeared to be bulging *everywhere*. Hell, his neck was probably the same size as one of my thighs.

After my breakup with Philip the year before, I'd sworn to myself that I would never rely on a man again—even for something as small as a tire change.

Don't get me wrong, I wasn't a man-hater by any means. I loved men. But I'd depended on Philip so heavily that I'd started to lose myself in the process. Once I'd found me again, I didn't want to let go.

But sometimes you need help, whether you want to admit it or not.

"I—I'll be fine," I lied, scrambling to my feet to give me some distance. I had a better view of the guy and I was unable to say anything more. Mr. Tall-Helpful-*and-Sexy* let out a disarming huff and it shook me from my perusal of his body.

"I'm sure you will," he said before stepping around me, picking up the tire iron, and pointing to the flat.

"Sure." I shrugged. "I've only been trying for the last fifteen minutes."

"I know." He smirked as he placed it over the lug nut. With one strong push, he loosened it.

"You know?" I questioned, laughing softly. "How long have

you been watching me?"

"Looked like you were determined to do it alone. Didn't want to step on your toes," he said without a hint of sarcasm.

"Oh," was all I could say in response.

His hands moved swiftly, removing the rest of the lug nuts and setting them aside. I was fascinated at how easy the whole thing was for him, and I was grateful for his help.

"I'm Tabor," he said as he put the car jack in place.

"Dani," I answered. "And thanks."

"No problem."

He flashed a smile over his shoulder before he turned back to the tire. I touched my hair and realized I probably looked like a frazzled mess. Sweat was running down my spine, my clothes were smudged with dirt and grime, and I was pretty sure my mascara was trudging into raccoon territory.

"So do you make it a daily ritual to scour the neighborhood for damsels in distress, or do you happen to live around here?" I asked, though it came out rude and not playful as I intended.

I was grateful for his help, but it wasn't coming through in my tone. My friends always told me my sarcastic, dry personality was off-putting, and when I wanted to rein it in, I failed miserably.

"Are you asking me if I come here often?" His eyebrow arched slightly over his sunglasses suggestively and he laughed as I stared at him feeling mortified.

My cheeks flushed at his response and I shook my head, thankful that he didn't seem to mind my tone. *I truly suck at flirting. Is that what I'm doing? Flirting?*

"Nope," he grunted, removing the tire completely and not embarrassing me further. "Just happened to be passing by." Wiping the sweat from his brow, he gave me a lopsided smile before rolling the spare into place.

I narrowed my eyes. "Have I met you before?" I asked before smacking my forehead with my hand.

Shut. Up. Dani. You sound like an idiot. He already insinuated that you were coming onto him.

"I mean, I don't think I have, I've never met anyone named Tabor before. That's an interesting name. I—I mean, you just look familiar," I said, wishing the verbal vomit would stop.

His shoulders shook in amusement and I wished I could see

his eyes. I didn't like that he was able to disguise himself so well, while everything I was thinking was painfully obvious.

"Is that a nice way of saying my name is weird?" he challenged.

"No. Not at all. I really like your name. It's just...different—good different—I mean, it's unique..." I said, shaking my head and smiling. "Forget it. I'm going to shut up now."

"I'm just kidding," he said, turning back to tire in front of him. "I'm pretty sure we haven't met before. I think I'd remember that face," he said with a tone that stole my breath.

Damn.

I tried not to watch the muscles in his back constrict with every tug and push on the lug nuts, and had to resist the urge to lean in closer.

Yep, flirting. Totally flirting.

"Well, thanks again for doing this. I really did have it," I added, hating that I was being "rescued" by some random guy who thought I was hitting on him. I wanted to explain that I didn't *need* help, that I could do it on my own. But before he'd walked up to help, I was seconds from calling Dad anyway.

"I think you loosened it for me," he finally said, looking up at me. His mouth quirked up on one side and I imagined there was a wink that went along with it.

He turned his hat backwards as he continued working. His short blond hair stuck out beneath the opening in the cap, contrasting against his light skin. I couldn't see the color of his eyes behind his sunglasses, but if they were blue, I was a goner.

"I'm pretty sure I did." I grinned.

This Tabor guy had the smirk and compliments down to a science—or maybe it had been too long since I'd been on the receiving end. Regardless, I was beginning to enjoy his attention, a fact that shocked me.

"So what do you do, Dani?"

"No way, you're a complete stranger, I'm not telling you that. What if you're a stalker or something, and then I'm the idiot who told you exactly how and where to find me?"

"I'm changing your tire. Pretty sure that means I'm a nice guy."

"You think...but Ted Bundy was pretty smooth too," I

answered, raising a brow. "What if you planted a line of nails six blocks that way and then hung out in your SUV, just waiting for your next victim?"

He smiled. "Was that a backhanded compliment? Smooth, but creepy?"

"I'm just saying," I said with a shrug.

"I promise, I'm not a murderer." He chuckled, and I died a little. That laugh flustered my inner sensibilities and made me want to say something funny to hear it again. Stupid, hot laugh.

"All right, point taken. You shouldn't trust me," he said. "You already know my name. What else do you want to know?"

I laughed and raised a brow. "Who said I wanted to know anything?"

"Ouch, my ego," he answered, placing a hand over his heart.

"I'm sure you'll be fine," I teased. "You have that whole big-muscle, tough-guy thing going for you."

I was only teasing him, but the longer the silence continued the more awkward it became. He picked up the tire and began working to fix it again.

He stayed silent, letting the quiet afternoon hang thickly in the air between us while he glanced back at me with a soft smile on his lips. I was the first to look away, with embarrassment flooding my cheeks. I felt like a jerk for wearing my emotions on my sleeve once again.

"So you're a teacher, huh?"

"How'd you guess?" I asked, stunned.

His muscles flexed as he slid the spare into place, but I quickly looked away before I could be caught ogling.

"My mom's a teacher, too. She's the only person I know that has that many papers in the back of her car. What grade do you teach?"

"Seventh," I said.

"You didn't just get off work, did you?"

"Sort of. I run an after-school program for at-risk teens. Today was our last day before the summer break."

"That's really cool," he said, flashing me another smile. It took only minutes for him to fasten the lug nuts and finish up. He wiped his hands on his jeans and I felt bad that he'd messed up a perfectly nice pair of pants. "So where do you teach?" he asked.

"I think I've already said too much," I said, my cheeks flaming hot as if he'd read my mind. "I have no idea who you are."

The moment the words came out of my mouth, he cocked his head to the side as if he knew something I didn't. Standing, he towered over me and I felt insignificant next to him. As I ran through a mental database to see if I'd ever met him before, I kept coming up blank. I wanted to see his eyes. You can tell a lot about a man by his eyes. But Tabor had yet to remove his sunglasses.

Finally, his smile returned. "Then let me take you out and you can get to know me."

My lips parted and I was a little stunned by the offer. But I kept my cool and straightened my posture, plastering a grin on my face. "Does that line really work?" I asked coyly.

"You're not gonna cut me any slack, are you?" He wiped his hands on his jeans once more and stuck out his hand. "Tabor Hunter. Nice to meet you."

Strange name.

I stared at his hand for longer than necessary and tried not to let my curiosity get to me, but it was pointless.

"Dani Miner, teacher. But you already knew that." I laughed softly as I stretched out my hand. His large hand enveloped mine in warmth and I felt a tingle run the length of my arm and straight to my chest. His fingers were rough, dirty, and in any other situation I probably would've tried to take my hand back as quickly as possible. But we both lingered a little too long, and by the warm smile on his face, he'd noticed too.

"So?" he asked, interrupting my thoughts.

"So what?"

"Are you going to let me take you out?"

He was still hanging onto my hand and I fought like hell to quell the screaming girlie hormones that were going crazy inside me. It was unreasonable to feel that sort of attraction to someone I'd just met.

Well not completely unreasonable. He was ridiculously gorgeous, after all. But the attraction didn't just have to do with looks, I could admit. It was something else.

"That depends."

"On?"

"Your eyes," I said.

"My eyes," he repeated slowly before finally releasing my hand and crossing his arms over his broad chest. His muscles strained beneath his T-shirt and he smirked at my request. I tugged at my lip, waiting.

"No eyes, no date," I added, crossing my arms and mimicking his posture.

Tabor exhaled and his smile faded slightly as he removed his sunglasses.

He cocked his head to the side and gave a small smile. "Did I pass?"

I tried to keep my face neutral and impassive as I cleared my throat and fought the urge to giggle. I was *never* that chick, and yet Barbie was about to burst from my psyche in the form of twirling my hair and batting my lashes—like my name was Mandi, and I always dotted my i's with little hearts and carried a tiny dog in my oversized Gucci bag.

I was so *that* chick.

My pulse was picking up pace and I wanted to slap myself. But I couldn't help it. His hazel eyes were breathtaking, and by the smug look on his face, he knew the effect he was having on me.

They're just eyes, I told myself. *Get a grip.*
Besides, he's just a guy.
Just a regular nice guy.
With a rippling chest.
Eyes that a girl could get lost in.
That knows how to change tires.
I wonder what else those hands can do?
He's hot.

Shit. He's staring.

"What did you say?" Tabor asked.
My eyes snapped to his and I felt my entire body warm.

Shit! Did I say something out loud?

"What?
"You said something."

"No I didn't," I argued, feeling as if someone cranked the heat up outside.

"Something about hot." He grinned knowingly.

I pursed my lips and tried to hide my grin. "It's June. In California, Tabor. It shouldn't be a new word for you," I said, fanning myself to help sell the lie.

His gaze wandered down to my collarbone, toward the apex of my V-neck tee, and back up to my eyes again. Thank god I really was sweating.

"So?" he asked.

"What?"

"You didn't say if I passed."

"Oh." I wiped my forehead. "*That.*" I sighed. "Yeah, I suppose." I shrugged, but couldn't hide my silly grin to save my life.

His smile returned in full and he looked down, scratching his jaw. With a nod, Tabor reached into his back pocket and pulled out his phone. "What's your number?"

I raised a brow and laughed. "Really?"

"What?"

"You don't waste any time, do you?" I teased. My cheeks flamed, and it had nothing to do with the heat of the day.

"Right, Ms. *Do I Come Here Often*. You know, I'm going to need that number so I can take you out," he said, his voice playful.

I chewed the inside of my cheek. "Give me your phone."

After creating a new contact and adding my number, I handed the phone back to him. He tucked it back into his pocket before looking at me again. He stared at me as if he was waiting for me to say or do something.

"Something wrong?" I asked.

Tabor reached out his hand, but stopped short of touching my face and pointed. "You have a little smudge on your cheek."

"Of course I do," I laughed, wiping at the spot. With a roll of my eyes, I mumbled, "Thanks."

"It was nice meeting you, Dani," he said and then lightly kicked at my tire. "Make sure you get that thing fixed."

"Isn't that what you just did?" I giggled. *Oh God, I'm giggling.*

"It's just a spare." He winked. "It won't last forever. But you already knew that."

"Yep." I saluted and laughed nervously. "On it."

"Would you happen to be free tomorrow?" Tabor asked.

"Can I get back to you?" I knew I had something going on, but with this man standing in front of me, all rational thought and memory seemed to be replaced with hormones and adrenaline.

"I'll text so you have my number," he said as he started walking away, "then you can call me when you know."

"Hey Tabor," I called.

He stopped walking and looked over his shoulder.

"You want the date, you call me."

He dug in his pocket, pulled out his keys, and his laugh went straight to my heart. "Bye, Dani," he said, sliding into his SUV.

"See ya."

I closed the trunk and watched from the corner of my eye as he sat in his SUV. He didn't drive off right away and I realized he was waiting for me to get in my car.

Who is this guy? Saint Tabor?

As I opened my car door, I looked over and waved before taking my place behind the wheel and closing the door. He finally drove off and I looked in the rearview mirror to see where he went, but I was distracted by my reflection and groaned.

Here I thought I'd glowed in a layer of pixie dust, my wit and charming personality shining through. But no, I wasn't that lucky. My forehead had one long black streak down the middle, and there was the smudge he'd referred to across my right cheek. I don't think I'd removed any of it when he'd pointed it out. My faded lip liner adhered to my top lip only and it wasn't remotely attractive. I hadn't realized that I'd worn a bright pink bra under my white tank that morning, and my sweat must've given Tabor a nice little peepshow, as I was pretty sure I could even see the lace. I looked like a cross between that chick from *Mean Girls* and a chimney sweep from *Mary Poppins*.

"Way to look gross, Dani," I muttered, annoyed at my lack of tidiness. Then getting annoyed for being annoyed.

"He wants to take me out," I mused. I was excited. Nervous. Hesitant. And all sorts of giddy.

Damn it.

CHAPTER 2

DANI

"So lemme guess…he was hot," Millie teased, her voice coy over the phone.

Just the mention of meeting a new guy had my best friend freaking out. I was trying to tell her about the flat tire and the subsequent handsome stranger that had helped me out—a.k.a. Hottiegate. Unfortunately, she made it nearly impossible to talk without interrupting with questions about his ass and whether or not his feet were bigger—or smaller—than a size eleven.

Granted, it was easier to focus on Tabor's hotness than my total geekiness during the entire exchange. No sense in mentioning my foray into damsel in distress territory or how I turned into a giant puddle of goo at his feet.

I'd keep those details to myself. Way too much ammunition for Millie.

"Tell me everything, Dani. Don't leave anything out," Millie demanded and I chuckled, wondering if I should make her suffer by delaying gratification.

"Well…" I began, taking my time.

"Ugh! Don't you dare, Dani Miner, or I will drive to your house and choke you with a pair of your yoga pants!"

"Did you just threaten me with death by Lycra?"

"You're still stalling!" she shouted, trying not to laugh.

"You brought it up. I was clarifying."

"Are you going to tell me about the hot guy or not?"

I snickered. "Hmmm. How much time should I spend describing his incredible forearms? What about his hazel eyes? Tell me what you want me to start with," I joked.

"Just start with something, damn it! I'm dying over here!"

My best friend was a total gossip, and it had gotten worse when she'd married. She kept me up to date on people we used to know and the things she saw in her neighborhood. She once called me at eleven o'clock at night just to tell me that TMZ was interviewing Joseph Gordon-Levitt. What? I had a thing for him. A short-lived micro-obsession. Don't judge. She was one of only a few people who never asked why, and just got me.

But the way Millie prattled and rambled was one of the many things I loved about her. All I had to do was hint at the fact that I'd spoken to a man, and she suddenly had a list of fifteen questions she needed answered immediately. The smallest things animated her, and her enthusiasm was contagious.

It was also incredibly easy to rattle her cage. And being the best friend that I was, I took full advantage of shaking her up as often as the opportunities presented themselves.

"He was charming," I began, "in that whole let-me-help-you-there-pretty-lady way."

"So did he just walk up behind you?"

"Yeah. I was trying to change the tire myself, but I couldn't get the lug nuts off."

"Mmmhmmm," she hummed.

"I'm not lying, I promise! I'd been there for fifteen minutes before he walked over."

"It just seems so cliché, Dani. Meeting a guy while changing a tire. Was it raining? Was 'In Your Eyes' playing in the background?" Millie laughed.

"Shut up," I grumbled, but I couldn't help snickering.

"You've never been the kind of chick to set women's rights back to the 1940s. You've always done everything yourself. Hell, *you* taught *me* how to change a tire when I first got my license," she huffed. "You totally planned this."

"What's that supposed to mean?"

"You saw an opportunity to score a bronze-bodied, green-eyed Cro-Magnon and you took it. Because otherwise I'm at a loss how Miss Independent would need *anyone* to help her to do anything."

"Ah, you found me out. Didn't you know? Roadsides are the new meat market. It's true, I read it last month in *Cosmo*," I snipped sarcastically.

"Huh, I must have missed that article," Millie quipped. "And here I thought hanging out in the frozen food section would be the place to find Cro-Magnon. Guess I was wrong." We both laughed. "Seriously though, spill it, Dani. What really happened?"

"I told you. I couldn't get the damn lug nuts loose. It was actually quite pathetic. I'm gonna have to up my gym game, apparently," I muttered. "He got out to help, but not before watching me struggle first. He may be hot, but I think he needs to work on the whole knight in shining armor thing."

"It's 2016, Dani. They don't wear armor anymore. Prince Alberts are the closest thing they get to wearing metal. Well, and other obvious means of protection… Bow-chicka-bow-wow."

"Oh my god, Millie, don't start with the porn music. And ewww."

"*Why hello there, big strapping piece of man, I'd love you to use your tire iron to loosen my lug nuts*," she mocked a high pitch voice.

"There was absolutely no porn music. Or Peter Gabriel. No cheesy rain montage. Just a hot, muscly guy helping out a woman in need. You know, there are people in this world who do things out of the kindness of their hearts," I remarked primly.

"This isn't 1955, McFly. Men these days don't usually fit in that category. The thing between their legs usually gets in the way of any good intentions," she professed.

"I'll be sure to let your husband know you said that," I snickered.

"He's the worst of them all! He thinks changing the lint trap means the panties are gonna drop—"

"Yuck! I get it, Mil, I don't need the visual!" I protested, making a gagging noise.

"Prude," she snapped.

"Exhibitionist."

"So does he have a girlfriend?" she asked, returning to the subject at hand.

"I don't think so," I muttered slowly. "He asked me out so I just assumed not, but I didn't ask either."

"Dani—" she began but I cut her off. I knew what she was going to say. And I didn't want to hear it.

"Sorry Mill, I gotta go, someone's calling. I'll be over in a bit."

"Maybe it's Mister I've-Gotta-Tool-Just-For-You," she singsonged. "Tell him that you've got some gears that need lube. Oh, or you could say that you've got a place he can put his spark plug—"

I hung up before she could say anything else, still laughing at the possibilities. I looked down at my phone, not recognizing the number on my screen.

"Maybe it is him," I told myself. I cleared my throat and tossed my hair over my shoulder as if he could see me.

"Hello?" I smiled, expecting to hear his voice.

"Yes. Hello. Is Danielle Miner available?"

Telemarketer.

I rolled my eyes and sighed as I hung up the phone, not even waiting to see who was calling and why. I was disappointed that it wasn't Tabor. Telling Millie about him had given me those stupid flutters in the pit of my stomach that I hadn't realized I missed.

***

"Someday you'll have one of these," Millie gushed as she looked down at her six-month-old baby, Colton.

Millie was almost back to her size-six self, and the extra curves of motherhood looked good on her. Her husband Nick had commented that she would look sexy with short hair, so I was with her when she chopped off her long brown locks and opted for a sassy pixie cut. I marveled at how much she'd changed, but was still my best friend.

"Whoa there, Mills. Missing a few steps, hon. And I'm in no rush for rug rats."

"But you're so good with kids," Millie gushed as I picked up the cutest baby I'd ever seen. He was even cuter than my niece,

Cleo, and that was saying something.

"Only because I'm in love with this one," I cooed into Colton's face. He reached his chubby hands out to me and I pretended to bite them when he shoved them in my mouth.

It was true: I was great with kids and they loved me. Mom always said it was a gift, and I believed it. My sister Grace had been the one who wanted the picket fence, dog running in the yard, and a *GQ* model for a husband.

I was always more practical. Perfection wasn't my endgame, and I was in no rush to get to the finish line. I was only twenty-four and I had years before I saw myself settled down with a ring on my finger. And kids? Yeah, definitely no rush in that department. I'd hit snooze on my biological clock a dozen times, so ignoring the telltale signs of a tick-tock was never a problem.

"Did I tell you Nick ran into Philip at the bar the other night?" Millie asked.

Gossip. Whore.

"You let Nick go to a bar? Without you?" I asked, feigning shock, intentionally ignoring the mention of my ex. I'd managed to avoid him since the breakup, and since I kept a lot to myself, I sidestepped the subject of him as well.

"It was a work thing," she said, waving her hand dismissively.

"Work, huh?"

"That's not the point. He saw Philip and he asked about you!"

"Great." I rolled my eyes. "And your point."

"I don't think he's seeing anyone. And if things don't work out with tire-guy, maybe you two…"

"Do *not* even finish that thought, Millie. I mean it." I set Colton back on the floor and walked into the kitchen, knowing Millie was hot on my tail. I grabbed a water bottle from her fridge, and when I turned around she was watching me expectantly.

"He really loved you, you know."

"You're supposed to be Team Dani." I set my hands on my hips. "So will you drop it? I haven't seen or talked to him in almost a year and I'd like to keep it that way."

"I *am* Team Dani. And I always will be. But is it so wrong for me to want to see my best friend finally settle down?"

"*Settle*. That's exactly what I'd be doing if I were still with Philip. I *settled* for the little time he was able to spend with me. I *settled* for the way he treated me, as if I wasn't good enough. I *settled* for a year with him, because he had me convinced he was the best I'd ever have. But he's not, and I don't want to go back."

"What? What do you mean? I thought you two were so good together."

"Yeah, well, looks can be deceiving," I reminded her.

"Why didn't you ever tell me all of this?"

"Because you and Nick liked him so much. And you know I'm not good with the whole sharing thing."

"But I'm your best friend. We've known each other for years—don't you think this is something you should have told me?"

"I've moved on, and I'm sure he has too."

"Maybe he's changed," Millie said timidly. She looked over her shoulder and started fidgeting with her wedding band. When she wouldn't make eye contact, I knew something was up.

"What's wrong?"

She finally looked at me, guilt written all over her face. "Nothing," she said quickly before turning to leave the room.

That time, I did the following, and stood with my arms crossed over my chest as she picked up Colton.

"That cute little Colton-shield isn't going to protect you," I warned. "What's up?"

She started bobbing up and down as if the baby was crying and I wanted to laugh, but something had her acting weirder than normal.

"Don't kill me." She flashed a toothy grin.

"Can't promise that," I said, shaking my head slowly. "Speak."

"I told Nick that you were coming over today and he should invite Philip over."

My jaw dropped open and I stared at her.

"Don't kill the baby mama. Don't kill the baby mama," I whispered to myself so she could hear. "It's not working, Millie, because I really want to strangle you right now."

"I'll have Nick call him as soon as he gets home," she pleaded. I would have laughed at the panic on her face had I not been completely livid with her.

"Who am I calling?" Nick asked as he strolled through the

back door.

"Philip. Now," I demanded.

"Easy," he said, raising his hands in the air. He walked over and kissed Millie and then Colton before turning back to me.

"Nick DeMarco...you better call him," I said as sternly as I could muster.

"Told you she didn't want to see the guy, babe," he said, ignoring the imaginary daggers I was shooting at him.

"So he's *not* coming," I stated, waiting for confirmation.

"Millie said you met some guy on the side of the road," Nick said, ignoring my statement.

"Yeah, had to give up the corner. Wasn't making any money there," I teased. I was certain it was his way of letting me know I was in the clear.

"Our hooker with a heart of gold," he quipped. "Keepin' it real."

"You know me." I shrugged. "A girl's gotta do..."

"Whatever her pimp tells her," he finished with a laugh. He raised his hand up and I gave him a high five.

Most people would probably be appalled by our banter, but Nick was the closest thing I had to a brother. Many even thought we were actually related because of our auburn hair and blue eyes, but that's where the similarities stopped. Nick was slightly taller than I was, and his olive complexion gave him an exotic appearance. But then again, his family was from Italy.

The moment he and Millie started dating, I adopted him. He was like the stray dog you couldn't get rid of, even if you wanted to.

They met our junior year at Beachmont University and were inseparable. I was a bridesmaid at their wedding, along with my other two roommates, Viola and Jolie. Our foursome welcomed Nick with open arms.

"So Philip is *not* coming over, right?"

Nick rubbed his hand across his forehead and looked at me like I had grown horns. "Do I have 'idiot' written across my face?"

I looked at Millie, who seemed to be irritated with her husband, and pointed at her angry scowl. "Aren't you afraid of *that*?"

"There are two things I know: one—you don't get involved in

other people's business."

"And two?" Millie asked with a raised brow.

"If you piss off your wife, you leave the kid with the best friend and take her anywhere she wants to go."

Millie smiled lovingly at her husband and all appeared right in their little world. I didn't envy their bubble. I'd always felt they married young, but who was I to stand in the way of their happiness? And it was clear they were happy.

I plucked Colton from Millie's arms and started making faces and weird noises to entertain him while his parents chatted. They were speaking in hushed tones, so I knew they were talking about me.

"So tell me about this guy," Nick pried, but I shook my head.

"Nothing to tell. He changed my tire and got my number. That's it."

"This was yesterday?"

"Yep."

"I bet he calls on Monday," he said with finality.

I turned to look at him and wanted to laugh at the confidence in his statement. While I was disappointed he hadn't called the day I met him, what Nick suggested was almost insulting.

"Monday, huh?"

"Yeah. Three-day rule. If he calls today, he's too eager. If he waits longer than three days, he's a player. My guess, he'll call on Monday. That way he looks busy, but not too busy. And interested, but not too interested."

I looked from Millie to Nick and back. "Is he serious?"

"Everyone knows the three-day rule, Dani."

"Clearly," I said, pointing to myself, "I must have been sick the day they handed out the memo."

"If I'm right, you owe me a kid-free night so I can be with my wife," Nick said, smirking at Millie.

"And if you're wrong?"

"I won't be wrong," he said.

I looked down at Colton, who was mesmerized by the necklace I was wearing, and kissed his chubby little cheeks. When I looked at my friends, they were exchanging looks that I'd rather they kept to themselves.

"Ew. Go. Now." I waved toward the door, shielding Colton's

eyes. "Go out and get that out of your system. This poor kid doesn't need to see that."

"Are you serious?" Millie asked, standing up hesitantly. "Because I will so take you up on the offer."

"Go. Colton and I have an exciting night of cartoons and sleeping planned."

Nick grabbed Millie's hand and pulled her behind him, waving as they left.

"You're the best, Dani," he said. "We won't be long."

"No worries. I have the better end of the deal," I teased.

I heard the door shut and I was alone with Colton, who seemed utterly content in my arms. I was swaying from side to side while he continued to grab whatever was catching his attention at the moment.

"Three-day rule, my ass," I muttered and Colton made a weird noise. I looked down at him and kissed his head. "You're not going to grow up to be a jerk like all the other guys, are you?"

His response was to drool, spit, and laugh.

"Typical," I laughed.

CHAPTER 3

DANI

My evening with Colton was uneventful…and that was a good thing. Millie was always going on about the lack of sleep she was getting, and how he constantly wanted to be held. That wasn't the case for me. He had a bottle and was asleep by nine, leaving me to channel surf until my eyes could no longer remain open.

I was certain that the issue wasn't Colton, but Millie. Something told me she probably kept waking him up to snuggle and kiss him all night. But who could blame her?

By the time she and Nick got home, I'd already tucked myself away in the guest bedroom, but not before checking my phone. I couldn't tell if I was disappointed or grateful that Tabor hadn't called.

Since I hadn't made it to Mom and Dad's the night before for the obligatory family dinner, I decided to make a surprise appearance after I left Millie's. Sundays in the Miner home were always reserved for church and family, so I knew they'd be happy to see me.

At least that's what I thought.

"What are you doing here?" Mom asked, giving me a quick hug when I opened the front door. "I'm heading to the mall, want to come with?"

I shuddered at the thought and shook my head. "Not even a little."

"Just like your dad," she scowled playfully.

"Is he here?"

"He's inside debating on whether or not he's going to get to the yard work. Head on in. Wanna stay for dinner?"

"We'll see," I answered. "Have fun in hell."

Mom swatted at my arm playfully and walked past, shutting the door behind me.

"Dad," I called out.

"Kitchen," he hollered in response.

I laughed when I saw him standing at the back door, his arms crossed as he stared at the yard. I figured maybe he was snacking on something, watching TV, but there he was simply observing.

"What's the verdict, Dad?"

"I think the lawn can wait," he chuckled, walking over and hugging me. "What brings you by?"

"Felt bad that I couldn't make it Friday night. Car troubles," I admitted.

"What's wrong with the Bel Air?"

"I got a flat tire when I got off work," I recalled, embarrassed.

"Good thing I taught you how to change a flat," he said, but his proud smile faded when he looked at me. "Right?"

"Yeah, not really," I scoffed. "Changing a flat on your own is great…if you can get the lug nuts off."

"You're joking."

"I wish. Nope, I was sweating like a pig, covered in grease, and this guy pulls over to help me fix it."

"You didn't let him help, did you?"

"What choice did I have?"

"Danielle, that's dangerous. What were you thinking?" Dad scolded. "You should have called me."

"I was about to, but then this guy swooped in and saved the day."

"Don't do that again," he warned. "I don't want to see my daughters' faces appearing on the news—missing—because they were caught off guard."

"Got it," I answered, and didn't say another word about the

stranger. Or that I had given him my phone number. That would have gone over about as well as the time I told them I was moving out. Not. Well.

Before he could say anything else, we heard the front door open and I looked back to see whom it was.

"Tessa?" Dad shouted.

"Not going to the mall," she answered.

I looked at Dad and laughed. "How'd you make that happen?"

Mom going to the mall spelled trouble for Dad. She was notorious for going to the store for one thing and coming back with armfuls of junk.

"Make what happen?" Mom repeated.

"Why are you back?" I asked, changing the subject.

"Can't I decide I want to see my daughter?" she smiled and hugged me.

"You could...but it's not true," I snarked. "So what's really going on?"

"Mimi!" the familiar shouts of little Cleo echoed throughout the house. Her footsteps pounded clumsily on the wood floor with my sister, Grace, trailing behind her. Grace smiled down at her daughter, who was in the middle of enjoying hearing her own voice.

"What about me?" I asked, scooping the blond-haired cutie when she tried to run past me. "Where's Aunt Dani's hug?"

Cleo looked at me with shock-filled eyes and I set her on the ground where she began looking around. Her palms were facing up while she walked around pretending not to see me. It was our game and she loved it.

"AuDani! AuDani hug! Whereyougo?"

Mom started laughing and Cleo kept up the charade.

"Where is it, Cleo?" I asked again.

"I no-no," she said with a silly smile.

"Is it...over there?" I asked, pointing to the pantry door.

Cleo ran over and tried to open the door, but turned and shook her head when she didn't get it opened.

"What about over there?" I asked, pointing to the couch, but she didn't budge. "Is it," I looked around and saw Cleo's face lit with the cutest smile, "here?"

I squatted down and opened my arms where my precious

niece ran into them and wrapped her chubby little arms around my neck. She placed a sloppy, wet kiss on my cheek and I set her back on her feet.

"She loves her Aunt Dani," Grace said, giving me a hug as Cleo ran between my parents.

"Who wouldn't love me?" I joked. "I'm amazing!"

Mom hoisted Cleo in her arms and walked off with Dad to let her play outside. When Grace and I were kids, they were always shoving us outside to run around in the yard and stay there until the sun went down. Unfortunately, where Grace lives there is very little yard to play in, so our parents make sure Cleo gets the full Mimi and Papi experience.

"Millie told me that Nick ran into Philip the other night," I said when our parents were gone.

"Don't even think of getting back with that one," she warned. "I never liked that guy."

"I know. Trust me, no plans there. I'm so much better off without him."

"Agreed. We need to find you someone who's not so controlling. I don't know what it was about him, but Philip gave me the creeps," she admitted.

Philip and I had ended dramatically—dramatic in that when I told him it was over I did it outside, in the rain, on the sidewalk in front of a popular restaurant. He was always so worried about appearances and I'd had enough. I hailed a cab and jumped in, but not before he grabbed me by my upper arm and I swear there was steam coming out of his ears.

"We'll finish this when we get back to my apartment," he *seethed and then pushed me into the back seat.*

Luckily, someone saw and pulled him away from the car, giving me time to slam the door shut and yell at the cab driver to leave. Of course Philip wasn't one to let things go, so he called my place a few times and then took to calling Grace.

"You know, you never said anything to me about not liking like him, but I guess I always knew," I told my sister.

We were close in so many ways, but it was always hard for me to someone when I was defeated. Especially when that someone was my sister, who I admired. And Philip had defeated me… For nearly six months, I was a mess. His verbal abuse was bad, but apparently not bad enough for me to leave. Fortunately, that changed when the physical abuse started. Therapy was the only thing that had seemed to help me get my life back.

"You seemed happy and it just wasn't my place to say anything," she admitted. "But I was damn glad to hear it was over."

"Yeah, well, tell Millie that. She was pushing for a Dani-Philip reunion. Hard. Trying to sell me on a happily-ever-after because it's worked out so well for her. But that's not what I'm looking for right now. I wish she could understand that."

"She just wants you to be happy."

"Millie acts as if I don't go out, but there's been a few dates. Let me tell you, Gracie, you are lucky. It's scary out there. Dating…no thank you. And then there's the whole apps thing to meet people," I said with a shudder.

"Apps?"

"Yeah, like dating websites." My mouth puckered. "I don't think so. What happened to meeting some nice guy by chance where it isn't so orchestrated? I want that old-fashioned lightning bolt, ya know?"

"It's not as hard as you think—just stop being so picky." She smirked.

"I'm not picky!" I defended. "Just because I prefer a guy who has a job, opens doors, treats his momma right, and you know—worships the ground I walk on doesn't mean I'm picky. Not all of us find *the one* right away."

"Trevor's a pretty good judge of character," she gushed about her husband. "Maybe he could set you up."

"No, thank you," I laughed. "No more setups."

"No *more*? When have you gone out on a blind date?"

The back door opened and Cleo ran through, jumping into her mom's arms.

"It was just one, but enough for me to swear off going on one ever again."

"What are we swearing off this week?" Dad asked. "Beef? Corporate America? Wine? Just, for the love of God, don't say beer! Tell me where to sign and how long we're boycotting."

Mom wrapped an arm around Dad's waist and rubbed his small beer belly. "I think it's beer."

"This isn't from beer," he bellowed. "This is from stress-eating because of all the estrogen in this house."

"Considering that I'm the only bit of estrogen left in this house on a daily basis, care to elaborate?" she challenged.

Dad's eyes shot up and he looked over at Grace and me for help, but I took a step back to avoid the fallout. Grace started laughing and I joined in.

"I didn't mean anything. You know I was kidding," he backpedaled. "Did I tell you how pretty you look today?"

"Pretty enough to take to the mall?" she asked, making me laugh a little harder.

Dad hung his head in defeat and started to walk out of the room. "I'll go get my shoes," he muttered with his head hung low.

"What are you two laughing about?" Mom asked, pointing between the two of us with a smirk on her face.

"You totally played him," I answered. "Well done, Mom."

"Hey, you don't stay married to a man for almost thirty years without learning a trick or two." She smiled.

Mom and Dad had the easiest relationship I'd ever seen. I'm sure it was tougher than they made it look, but they never had to pretend how much they loved each other. When they thought no one was looking, they'd blow kisses or grab each other's butts or some otherwise randomly embarrassing gesture. It was cute. Grace and I were always in awe.

"Mimi. Hungwee," Cleo said as Grace set her down. "Canny?"

"No, you can't have candy, Cleo," Grace warned. "You already had a piece."

"Pweese?" she asked, her little lip poking out sadly.

"No, ma'am," Grace said sternly.

"But Mom," Mom said to Grace, "she said *pweese*."

My sister glared at our mother before breaking. She could never say no to Cleo, and add Mom to the mix and it was game over. Someday that would bite her in the ass, but not yet.

"Fine," she conceded. "Just one, Cleo. I mean it."

"Yah, ma'am," Cleo answered, skipping off holding our mom's hand.

"You realize *you* were played, right? Cleo played both of you," I muttered under my breath.

"Yeah. I know," she answered in monotone.

I glanced at my watch and decided it was time to go. My date with the recorded television show and a bottle of wine would not wait. Okay, so it could wait, but I wanted climb into my yoga pants and oversized T-shirt and make myself comfortable for the rest of the night.

"Hey guys," I called out. "I'm gonna head home. Lots to do."

"Already?" Mom asked, wrapping me into a hug. "I barely got to see you."

"I know, and I'm sorry I missed dinner. But I'll be here next week. I promise."

"Okay, well be careful," she said, hugging me once more and kissing my cheek.

"I will. Gracie," I hollered, looking for my sister. "I'll see you Tuesday. Right?"

"Yeah. See you then."

"What's Tuesday?" Mom asked.

"I told her I'd go over and hang out. I was so busy during the school year that I didn't get over there much. She wants to show me how she's going to redecorate Cleo's room."

"Oh, it's adorable," Mom gushed. "You're going to love it."

Dad emerged and walked over to give me a hug before I left. I kissed his cheek and laughed at his mall-induced misery. "Sorry, Dad. You're on your own... All I can say is, better you than me."

"Help. Me," he mouthed dramatically, making me laugh.

CHAPTER 4

DANI

The school year officially ended for my students, but I still had to wrap up a few things and it would take a couple of trips to the school to complete. I wasn't in a rush to get anything done because I still had to figure out how to come up with the funding needed to continue River's Kids.

I sat down at my kitchen table and rifled through the pages of information I had amassed when I initially started the program. I was enthusiastic and idealistic when I got the ball rolling last year, but finding volunteers and donations had proved difficult. Still, I'd continued because I believed in the program and what it could do for the kids.

Watching their eyes light up when they walked in the first day it opened had warmed my heart, and I knew I had done the right thing. All the hours of work and pleading for help to get it off the ground had been worth the effort.

I closed the binder and sighed heavily as I rested my chin on my hands. "This sucks," I groaned.

Many of my students depended on River's Kids for activities and tutoring. Without it, they'd go home to empty houses where they were left to their own devices. Knowing I had the ability to do something is what drove me.

I grabbed my laptop and began doing a search on local foundations that might be willing to help out in some way. Mom always reminded me that it never hurt to ask, and she was right.

There were several Fortune 500 companies headquartered in San Diego, so I jotted a few names down and continued to look for others. It was going to be a long day, but I planned on speaking to the principal when I went to work; maybe he'd have some suggestions.

Just as I was about to call Millie to see if she had any ideas, my phone rang in my hand. I looked down and it was another unknown number.

I rolled my eyes and answered it gruffly, allowing my irritation to show.

I hate telemarketers.

"Da-Dani?" he questioned before clearing his throat. "Can I speak to Dani?"

When he finished speaking, I knew who it was and my stomach flopped nervously.

Nick was right: three days. I tried to play it cool.

"This is Dani," I answered, deciding to play dumb. "And this is?"

"Tabor. From the other day," he said.

My knees wobbled slightly and I started pacing my small living room. I wanted to laugh at how stupidly I reacted to his voice because it wasn't like me at all. I realized the silence had gone too long, and I desperately tried to find something witty to say but nothing came out. Truth be told, I'd never expected him to actually call.

"Hello?" he asked.

"Oh sorry," I said, tripping over a pillow that had fallen off my couch. I walked over to have a seat, figuring I'd be safer sitting still. "I'm here. Just…cleaning." I stumbled over my words.

"If you're busy I can call back," he said.

The room wasn't remotely dirty, but it was all I could come up with on short notice.

"No it's fine. I was just…finishing up," I lied and then scoffed.

His soft laugh filled the silence and I smiled at the sound.

"I wanted to make sure you got that tire fixed," he stated. "I mean, I'm sure it was fine, but you never know."

"You're good...I mean, *it's* good. The tire. The tire is fixed," I stuttered, running my hand over my face and laughing. "I took care of it the next day. Thank you again for helping."

"Not a problem."

The TV in my living room did little to fill the awkward silence that was taking over. I could hear Tabor breathing on the other end, but he didn't say anything.

"Well, it was nice of you to check on me," I finally said when I couldn't think of something better.

"So that's it?"

"What's it?"

"I thought you were going to let me take you out."

I smiled. "Well, you didn't ask."

I heard his laugh before he spoke. "So Dani, do you have any plans tonight?"

There was nothing on my calendar, but I didn't want to appear too available. He'd waited three days to call, just like Nick had predicted.

But if there was some kind of game to be played, I wasn't aware of the rules. *Am I supposed to wait three days before accepting? Damn.* The dating apps were looking better and better. All I had to do was click a box to tell them I was interested.

Plus, I didn't even know if Tabor had a girlfriend—or worse, a wife. I needed to know more before I agreed to anything.

"Actually, I'm going out with some friends tonight," I began, "but I was thinking that maybe I could take you out tomorrow...you know, as a thank you for helping me."

"But I called you," he said.

"What about your *girlfriend*?" I asked, my voice going up slightly at the mention of a partner, wincing as I awaited his response.

"I'm afraid my girlfriend can't make it," he said.

I slouched and my bottom lip jutted out, but he kept talking.

"Maybe I could bring her along next time though. I mean, if you're into that sort of thing."

I opened my mouth to say something, but with the disappointment simmering in my gut and my own mortification clouding my mind, I couldn't think of anything to say that wouldn't make me sound pathetic.

"Dani?" His deep voice echoed down the phone. "I'm kidding. I don't have a girlfriend."

"Oh!" I chirped. "Okay. Good to know," I said, playing off the rush of relief I felt.

"And just so you know, I'm not in the habit of asking women out when I'm dating someone else," he said.

"Great answer," I responded.

"Another test? Did I pass?"

"Yeah, I think you did." I smiled, even though he couldn't see it.

"Cool," he said confidently.

I couldn't stop grinning at the sound of his voice.

"So what time should I pick you up?"

And then the smile faded as I remembered what I was doing before he'd called.

"I'm actually going to my sister's tomorrow night."

"That's all right," he said, a hint of disappointment in his tone. "Maybe another time."

"Okay," I agreed, though it lacked any sort of enthusiasm. *Do not let this man hang up!* the voice in my head shouted.

"It was good talking to you. Have fun with your sister," he said.

No. No. No. I'm not going to wait around for him to call again! "Thanks." *Think, Dani!*

"Bye—" he started, but I cut him off.

"I'll be back around five," I blurted.

"Oh yeah? Okay, well, is seven good for you?"

"I think I can do seven." My heart slowed to a manageable level and I let out a breath.

"Sounds like a plan," he said. "What's your address?"

In a rare Dani display, I jumped up like a kid with a new toy and my smile threatened to split my face in two. And then in very Dani-fashion…I tripped and fell onto my ass. "Ow!"

"Dani?" he asked, his voice full of concern.

"Yeah, I'm okay," I replied. "I'm a bit of a klutz."

"Why don't you text me your address and I'll pick you up then."

"If it's easier, I can just meet you there," I offered.

"Call me old-fashioned, but I'd like to take you out the right way," he said.

"Oh. O...kay," I stammered and smiled.

It was if he were plucked from the description of what I'd told Grace I wanted in a guy. And since I was open to something new, someone old-fashioned was exactly what I wanted. And Tabor sweetly insisting on being a gentleman made my heart skip a beat.

"Well, now you have my number, so you can text me," he said. "Is that good for you?"

"Yeah, that sounds good," I answered.

"Then I'll see you tomorrow," he said.

"See you then," I replied evenly, though inside I was beyond giddy and I didn't understand the reaction.

We hung up and I sat on the floor where I'd landed moments before, immobile. It had been a while since I had looked forward to a date, despite Millie's numerous attempts at setups.

"I have a date," I said out loud, feeling excited and nervous at the same time.

I stood up and walked to my bedroom to get everything ready so I could go out with my friends, but then a surge of enthusiasm shot through me.

"I have a date!"

I turned into my bathroom and stared at my reflection in the mirror, seeing the spark of hope in my eyes. I pointed a finger at myself and narrowed my eyes.

"Do *not* look at me like that. For all you know, he's a world-class asshole who hides it well."

I shook my head at my words, knowing deep down he was a good guy. I wasn't sure why I was so quick to believe that, but something in me held tight to that notion. He was a handsome, sweet, and funny guy.

Crap! A guy I need to text!

Me: 333 Antigua Hills Dr
Tabor: Got it. See you at 7
Me: Where are we going?
Tabor: Have you been to Metropolis?

Is this guy serious? Metropolis was only one of the highest-

31

rated fine dining restaurants in the city, and that's where he suggested going. I'd never been, but I'd wanted to try it for some time.

> *Me: No. But I've heard of it*
> *Tabor: Do you like steak?*
> *Me: I do*
> *Tabor: Then you'll love it*
> *Me: Sounds good*

***

After I texted Tabor, I took a shower and got dressed so I could get over to the school. I had planned on spending a few hours there every day of the week, so I'd have the rest of the summer to myself.

Millie had her things taken care of a week before school ended. She needed to go back to turn in her keys and pick up a box or two, but she was otherwise done. I knew because I'd listened to her brag the other day.

By the time I got to River Valley Junior High, there were a few teachers tucked in their rooms taking inventory and putting things away in boxes. We were told that the school would be getting new paint and floors, so everything had to be packed up.

I visited with a few co-workers on my way to the classroom, and they told me of the plans they had with their kids. I didn't envy them much, because they were going to be busy entertaining while I was busy catching up on my reading and trying to enjoy some downtime.

As I walked out of my classroom with another box of books to turn in, I was stopped mid-delivery.

"Dani, can I see you in my office when you're done with that?" Principal Lopez asked.

I nodded and made my drop-off to the library, and then walked back to the main office.

"You ready for summer?" Linda, the secretary asked with a huge smile.

"I am," I answered. "You?"

She glanced up at the clock and nodded eagerly. "One more

hour."

"But who's counting, right?" I teased. She grinned sheepishly and I nodded toward the principal's office. "Is he in there?"

"Yeah. Go ahead, he's waiting for you," she said and I felt my heart race.

I had only been called into Mr. Lopez's office once since I'd worked with him, and that was once more than I had ever been called as a student growing up. Trips to the principal's office were something I dreaded more than visiting the gynecologist. At least with the doctor I knew what to expect. It wasn't pleasant, but there weren't any surprises. A visit with Mr. Lopez meant a lecture, a reprimand, or a request for help that entailed too much paperwork.

When I knocked on the door, Mr. Lopez waved at me and motioned for me to come in and close it behind me.

Not a good sign.

I took a seat across from his desk and tried not to fidget. His space was covered with pictures of nieces and nephews, brothers and sisters. Since he'd never had any children of his own, the students at River Valley Junior High were his kids.

"I know what you're going to say," I started, but he put a hand up to stop me from speaking.

"I don't know how you did it, but I have to say, I'm impressed." He smiled kindly.

Not what I thought he was going to say.

I shook my head slowly, not knowing what he was talking about, but he continued.

"I don't think I've known anyone as dedicated to these kids as you are, but I've already gotten two phone calls from companies who want to make donations to River's Kids. I'm proud of you," he beamed.

"Thank you, sir. But I just called them this morning," I said, recalling the runaround that at least four companies had given me.

"There's still a ways to go, but this is a great start. And you have the rest of the summer to figure out how to get another year from this program. I don't have to tell you what an asset it's been to our students."

"I'm going to do my best, Mr. Lopez," I said with sincerity. "I love these kids."

It was true. The students could be frustrating and mouthy, but at the end of the day they had one thing in common: they wanted something better.

"I know you do, Dani. And they love you."

"Sir, I've contacted so many companies today, but there's so much more to do and I'm at a loss. Who else can I contact?"

"Have you tried the Gulls? The Quakes? The Ballers? Sometimes the major league teams can donate items."

"Don't you think they get hit up all the time? Why would they take my call?"

"It never hurts to ask." He smiled.

"So I've heard," I responded. "Actually, I plan to go home today and look for more grants. Those served us well this past year—maybe we'll strike gold again."

"If anyone can do it, it's you, Ms. Miner. I have no doubt that River's Kids will live to see another year. Great job."

"Thank you." I smiled.

I got up from my chair and started to leave the office but turned to face him.

"Thank you for being so supportive of the program. I'm not sure many administrators would give their time and attention like you. So thank you," I told him, and waved as I left the office before he could say anything.

With a renewed sense of hope, I made my way to my classroom and closed it up. The rest could wait until the next day. I was eager to get home and research anything I could to get funding for my kids.

CHAPTER 5

DANI

Tabor: Are we still on for tonight?
Me: We're good :)
Tabor: Did you work today?
Me: From home
Tabor: Teachers can work from home now?
Me: When they're trying to get funding they can.
Tabor: Funding??
Me: My after-school program

When he didn't respond, I went back to my research. I had spent the better part of my day poring over website after website, looking at various foundations and sponsors for programs like mine. Between the two businesses that had contacted the school the day before, we had secured half the money needed. I still had a long way to go.

My phone rang and Tabor's name flashed on the screen.

"Hello?"
"Hey Dani, it's Tabor. Can you talk?"
"Yeah," I answered, surprised that he called. "What's up?"

35

"You mentioned funding for your after-school program and I was curious." He sounded like a businessman, not the flirtatious roadside hero from the other day.

I really liked *that* guy.

"Anything in particular?" I tried not to sound too disappointed about the reason he'd called. Not exactly something that gets you excited about a date later that day, but still nice that he took an interest.

"Can you tell me about it?"

I felt lightness in my chest and I smiled. Philip wasn't interested in my program when I was trying to get it off the ground, but Tabor was a complete stranger who had asked more about it in two simple questions. I tried to focus on that, and not the fact that he hadn't flirted with me at all.

I took a deep breath and began recalling how the after-school program came to be.

"I started teaching at River Valley two years ago, and noticed that many of my students came from single-parent homes. Others had two working parents, so the kids were going to empty homes for a couple of hours. Not the worst thing in the world, I know. But some of the kids were getting in trouble because they had too much idle time. So I went to my principal with the idea for River's Kids."

"So the program's been running for two years?" His intrigued tone was something I wasn't used to when I talked about the program.

"No. Unfortunately it took longer than I thought to get the grant money—a year, actually. But once we got it, it was only a matter of time until kids were lined up to participate. Several of my co-workers have given their time for an hour after school, which allowed us to open the door to more students."

"That's impressive," he said. "So did you apply for more grants?"

"I've been in the process of doing that and talking to several businesses to see if they'd be willing to sponsor us."

"That's great," he said, not elaborating further.

"So is this why you called me?" I asked coyly.

"Yes," he answered softly, adding, "and to make sure you weren't going to back out tonight."

There it is, the flirting I'm looking for.

"I told you we're still on," I laughed.

"Just wanted to hear your voice to make sure you weren't lying." I imagined his cute smile appearing at his words, and it made my heart flutter.

"Did I pass the test?" I asked him, using his words from the other day.

"Yeah. You did," he laughed. "We're going to have fun tonight. I promise."

"Are you always so sure of yourself?" I teased playfully.

"There are few places in my life where I'm not sure of myself," he quipped.

"And those would be?"

He sucked in a rush of air and tsked. "Maybe once I get to know you better I'll let you know."

"Good thing I agreed to go out with you then, huh?"

"I'm looking forward to seeing you," he said sweetly. "I don't go out very often."

"Oh? Why is that?" I asked, curious why the Greek god didn't date.

"Work," he said quickly. "Work has me traveling a lot, so my schedule is pretty tough."

"That sucks," I sympathized. "How are you going to meet anyone if you never get out?"

"I met you, didn't I?"

"You've got me there."

"But really, that's the least of my worries," he muttered under his breath. "Just too busy, I guess."

I found myself unable to respond to his words because I found them confusing. In the brief conversation we'd had, I'd learned that he traveled a lot and he was likely too busy for relationships.

I wasn't looking for an *ever after*, but what was the point in going out with him if it couldn't go anywhere?

"I'm in town for a while," he finally said, breaking me of my thoughts.

"What's that?" I asked, shaking the cobwebs from my mind.

"I just realized how all of that sounded." He chuckled lightly. "I'm not doing any traveling for the next couple of months."

"Oh, that's great," I said a little to eagerly. I didn't know

Tabor from the stranger on the street, but the idea of not getting a chance to get to know him had unsettled me.

"I better let you go so you can finish up before tonight. I'll see you at seven," he said.

"See you then," I said before hanging up the phone.

I sat at the kitchen table staring at my phone, wishing I had been more suave. Before Philip I had been outspoken and outgoing, but that had disappeared and I hated that I was missing that part of me. I had been fighting like hell to get back to my old self.

The old me would have flirted easily. She would have made sure that Tabor knew she was interested in him. More importantly, she wouldn't have needed to go to her sister to mentally prepare.

I grabbed my papers and laptop, stuffed them into my bag, and hurried out the door to head to Grace's. I needed her pep talk. I needed her to calm me.

***

"So you're going out with him tonight?" Grace asked from behind her couch when we finished the tour of Cleo's newly redecorated bedroom.

My sister was always worried about what I was doing with my free time. She'd met my brother-in-law, Trevor, in high school and they'd been together ever since. None of us were surprised when they married at twenty, before they finished college. They were in love and nothing would stop them. They'd waited until they graduated before starting their family. When little Cleo made her entrance two years ago, I don't think I'd seen either of them as happy as they were in that moment.

"Yep." I smiled at her before giving my full attention back to Cleo, who was running around the kitchen chasing the dog Skip.

"And he's taking you to Metropolis?" she asked, handing me a towel to dry the platter she washed.

"Yep." I grinned, setting it down before chasing after Cleo, who was laughing hysterically. I caught her and lifted her in the air, blowing on her tummy.

"Okay, what gives? You're holding out on me, I know it. Why didn't you tell me about this the other night? What does he look like?"

"He's pretty good-looking," I offered.

"Are we talking boy-next-door cute? Exotic hot? Model sexy? C'mon, Dani, fill me in," she whined.

"I don't know how to describe him. I tried telling Millie about him, but I couldn't find the words. He's just...beautiful," I sighed. "But not at all the type I'd typically go for."

"And that would be?"

"Suit-and-tie guy, I guess."

"Different is good." Grace sat on a barstool and angled her body to face me. "So what's he like?"

"In the brief time I talked with him, he's really nice. And funny. The guy doesn't know me at all, but he was so easy to joke around with and tease."

"Okay, okay, so he's got a great personality," she droned. "What does he *look* like?"

"Dude is built like a damn football player. He's huge! I mean, seriously has to be like six three or something. And then there's like muscles...everywhere," I told her, using my hands to describe his build.

"How would you know what a football player looks like?" she teased.

"Just because I don't follow the sport doesn't mean I don't know what one would look like."

"Okay, so the guy sounds pretty great," she sighed.

"Tabor," I said, returning my attention to Cleo.

"Tabor?" Grace repeated.

"Yeah. That's his name." I glanced up for a moment and saw this weird look on her face. "What?"

"Nothing." She shook her head and tried to play it off.

"Don't 'nothing' me, Gracie...I know that look!"

She stared at me blankly and panic surged through my body.

"Oh hell, did you date a Tabor or something? I don't remember a Tabor."

"No. It's just...well, you said he's built like a football player?"

"Yeah. Why?"

"And his name is Tabor?"

"Gracie! What the hell?" I all but shouted. Had Cleo not been right there, the language would have been more colorful. "You know, I came here for the old Gracie pep talk...but I have to say, you're failing miserably. I think I'm more nervous than when I got here. Thanks a lot."

"Give me one second. Okay?" She jumped up and disappeared from the kitchen, leaving me with Cleo.

"Your mommy's losing it," I whispered to my niece.

Cleo bobbed her head up and down as if she understood what I was saying, and I laughed. "Momma cwazey."

"Yeah, you know it too, don't you?" I answered.

"Mommy isn't that crazy," Gracie said as she entered the room with her laptop in hand. "His last name wouldn't happen to be Hunter, would it?"

My eyes widened at the name and she had my full attention. She waved me over and I scurried to my feet, sitting next to her with the computer on the counter. There were tons of tiny thumbnail pictures of football players, but I still wasn't following.

"Okay, just because I said he's built like a football player doesn't mean you and Trevor are going to get me to watch the damn sport, Gracie."

She ignored me and clicked on a link that brought up a larger image, and my heart stopped.

The eyes. The smile. The build. All of it was the man I'd met only days before and I was stunned into silence.

"That's Tabor," I whispered, unable use my full voice.

"*That's* JT Hunter, Dani. Star defensive lineman for the Quakes," she informed me.

"You have got to be kidding me," I said, shaking my head. "There's no way that Tabor is a professional football player. He would have said something," I said. "Wouldn't he?"

Gracie didn't respond. Instead she clicked on another link and biographical information about Tabor appeared on the screen.

Born Jordan Tabor Hunter on October 15, 1989 in Chicago, IL.

"How did you know it was the same guy?" I asked, still staring at the screen, my hand covering my mouth.

"You know JT is my favorite player and Tabor isn't exactly a common name, Dani," she answered. "Besides, you said he's built like a football player and it just clicked. Question is, how did you *not* know it was him?"

"You said it yourself: I'm not the football fan."

"*Everyone* knows who he is."

I stared at her blankly and she shook her head.

"Yeah, I know, look who I'm talking to: the woman who hates football."

"I don't hate it, I just don't watch it," I laughed.

"You're missing out. Tight uniforms, bulging muscles...do I need to go on?" She sighed, lost in her own world.

"You know how Dad is. During football season, nothing else exists. So yeah, sorry that I'm not a diehard like you," I teased.

"How are we even related?" Grace laughed. "We need to do a blood test or something."

"Agreed," I said straight-faced. "Or maybe I was born without the football gene."

Cleo started squealing loudly and banging her toys on the counter. I swooped down and picked her up, turning my back to the computer screen as I walked into the living room.

"You're going out with JT Hunter," Gracie said, her eyes glazing over.

"No, I'm going out with Tabor," I corrected and then gave Cleo my attention. "Isn't that right?" I said in a silly voice. She started laughing and I set her down at her play kitchen.

Gracie sat on the floor next to me and opened the screen, cycling through the various pictures of *JT Hunter—Football Star— Most Eligible Bachelor—Sexiest Man in the City*. "Do you see this?"

"I see it, but what's your point?"

"Dani, you freakin' met JT Hunter. JT Hunter changed your tire. And you gave your phone number to JT Hunter and now you are going out with JT Hunter," she shouted before jumping around excitedly.

"Say 'JT Hunter' again and maybe I'll get it," I joked.

"JT Hunter," she said and I laughed.

"Nope," I argued. "I met Tabor."

"Please don't act stupid right now," she said, rolling her eyes.

"For whatever reason, he introduced himself as Tabor. So

let's just leave it at that for now. Okay?"

"Fine," Gracie said, raising her hands in surrender.

"You know, it makes sense now," I offered.

"What does?"

"When I asked him to take his sunglasses off, he was hesitant. I guess now I know why."

"And that is?"

I shrugged. "He thought I'd recognize him."

"Um. Yeah! That's because *most* women in San Diego would. But then again, you're not most women." She smiled.

I grabbed her laptop and brought it to the couch where I scrolled through all of the images of Tabor.

Correction: *JT Hunter.*

JT Hunter with a group of kids.

JT Hunter shirtless.

JT Hunter at practice.

JT Hunter with a woman.

JT Hunter wearing sunglasses and smiling.

I couldn't help but grin when I saw that last one. Gracie nudged my leg, and I looked to see her watching me with amusement and I shrugged.

"Why do you think he introduced himself as Tabor?" I asked.

"Maybe you'll find out when he picks you up tonight." She smirked. "And I hate you, by the way."

"What am I supposed to do?" I asked. "I've never been on a date with anyone remotely famous. And now I'm going out with Tabor—JT Hunter? Maybe I should cancel."

I was fighting my own insecurities and I hated it. And I think I hated it more that I needed my big sister to assure me that I deserved to have some fun. It's amazing that one bad relationship can deplete your confidence. I grabbed my purse off the floor and pulled out my phone so I could scroll for his number, but Grace took it out of my hand.

"Gracie, give me that," I demanded, but she stood up to get distance from me.

"You need to calm down," she ordered. "You were excited about the date before you knew who he was, right?"

"Yeah," I replied.

"So you're going to hold his status against him? That's not fair, is it?"

"You are not fooling anyone." I lunged for my phone, but she moved. "You just want to live vicariously through me because he's on your list."

She crossed her arms and raised a brow. "So what if I am?"

I started laughing and jumped at her again, but she moved to the other side of Cleo.

"Don't use my niece as a shield," I laughed.

She held up my phone and started scrolling through the recent calls and turned the screen to face me.

"See! You already added his name to your contact list. You *want* to see this guy, regardless of who he is or who you *thought* he was. You owe it to yourself to go…you owe it to him," she said before handing me the device. "You used to be the bravest person I knew. What happened to that girl?"

Her words stung more than she realized. I never told Gracie how bad things had gotten with Philip. As far as everyone was concerned, I was the bad guy in the situation.

But I wanted to be brave.

I righted my posture and watched as she walked back to the floor and sat down with Cleo. I stood in the same place, staring at the screen and Tabor's name. I did want to see him. I liked talking with him and wanted to see if maybe there was something more.

At least I did before I knew who he was.

"You know I'm right," she said, staring at Cleo. And she was right.

"I guess one date won't hurt."

"Exactly," she answered.

I sat down on the couch and sighed. "Do I tell him that I know who he is?"

Gracie looked at me and shook her head. "That's up to you. But for whatever reason, he wanted to be Tabor with you. I'd just let it play out. From everything I've read, he's a really good guy, so I don't think he's trying to screw with you."

I nodded my head and took a deep breath. "I guess I'm going out with JT Hunter tonight," I muttered as a door shut.

Grace and I both turned our heads to see Trevor standing in

the doorway with his mouth hung open.

"You're going out with Hunter?" His eyes were so wide and I think he might have started to twitch at the mention of Tabor's name. He was a huge fan. "What the hell is going on? I come home from work and the world ends?"

"Get this," Gracie snorted and waved Trevor over.

Cleo started clapping at the sight of her dad, who picked her up and tossed her into the air.

"She didn't even know it was him."

"Are you surprised? She hates football," Trevor answered and Grace simply laughed.

"See, I told you." She pointed at me. "I think you might be the one person in this city who hasn't jumped on the *I love JT* bandwagon."

"Whatever," I said, picking up my purse and heading to the door. "But *I'm* the one who has a date with him."

I wiggled my fingers at Cleo, who was still smiling and running all over the place, and blew a kiss to Grace. She and Trevor were standing side by side, watching my departure.

"Call me," she called out as I closed the door behind me.

CHAPTER 6

TABOR

The afternoon I saw Dani, I had no idea what possessed me to turn down that street. It wasn't my normal route home, but I'd been distracted after a conversation I'd had with my agent. He was pushing me to endorse a clothing line that my sister Abbi had told me about. It would take me a while to sort through the endorsements being thrown my way, and at the time I hadn't wanted to think about it. Though I couldn't think of anything else.

And then I saw her.

I thought nothing of the classic car on the side of the road; after all, people have flats all the time.

But as I got closer I spotted the attractive woman bent on the ground next to it, changing the tire. I slowed my speed and watched this messy, determined woman as she used all of her weight to loosen the bolts on the tire, and I couldn't help but smile at her tenacity.

I felt like an ass as I sat in my car, watching her work the tire iron. But I couldn't take my eyes off of her. Her wavy auburn hair was falling into her face, strands no longer contained in her small ponytail.

At that moment I just wanted to meet her, and if helping her change that tire got me the introduction, I was all for it.

Then came the lie…or half-truth.

I don't know why I told her my name was Tabor. I kept that name exclusive to close family and friends. But seeing her, I didn't want to be *JT Hunter, football player*, and everything that went with the name. Funny enough, though, she didn't seem to know who I was—or if she did, she hid it well.

Her jeans were covered in dirt from her attempts at changing the tire, and when she argued that she had it, I didn't doubt she would have been fine without my help.

I could have walked away then and left her alone. But I didn't want to. The moment those blue eyes stared up into mine, I knew that I was where I needed to be.

"Hey," Abbi all but shouted over the phone when I answered. She had successfully stopped me from thinking about Dani— though in truth, I didn't mind thinking about her at all.

"What's up?"

"Can't I just call my brother up to talk?"

"Yeah, you could," I laughed, "but I can tell something's going on."

"You haven't talked to Mom, have you?"

"No. Why? Is everything okay?" I asked, momentarily alarmed.

"Yeah, she's fine. Sorry. I just meant, has she said anything to you?" She sounded nervous, her voice shaky, and I didn't understand why.

"About what, Abbi? What's going on?" I pushed, not liking the tone the conversation had taken.

"I sorta hoped she did call, even though I wanted to be the one to tell you myself." She was quiet and I was beginning to regret taking the call.

"Abbi, just say it already!" I tried to laugh, but it sounded strangled.

"It's about Marshall," she said quietly.

"What about him? Did you two break up?" I asked.

Of all the guys she'd ever dated, he was the one I hated the least. He was a decent guy, but I'd only met him a few times. He was good to Abbi, and that was all that mattered.

"Not exactly," she laughed and then the phone went quiet

again. "He proposed. Last night."

"Proposed what?" I stupidly asked, certain it wasn't what I was thinking.

"What do you think, dumbass? He asked me to marry him," she said, her voice rising in excitement.

"Are you serious? You've been dating, what—four months?" I asked, trying to figure out when I'd first heard of him. "You barely know the guy."

"Wow, you really suck. We've been together for almost a year, so thanks for paying attention," she said, amused with my questions. "And yes, I'm very serious. We want to get married next spring. Football will be over and you'll be able to give me away."

I sat down on the edge of my bed as I let the new information sink in. My sister—my *little* sister—was getting married?

"Are you still there?" she asked timidly. "You're happy for me, right?"

It was as if there was a delay from her question to my brain and then to my mouth as I tried to formulate a response.

"Is this what you want?" I finally asked as I tried to leave my own concerns aside.

"It is," she said, and I could almost hear her cheesy smile.

"Then yeah, I'm happy for you," I told her truthfully.

"And you'll give me away?"

There was a picture on my dresser of Abbi and me with Mom. It was taken the day I'd signed with the Quakes. Those two women were the most important people in my life, and even though they lived thousands of miles away, some things would never change.

"No," I said.

"What?" she asked stunned. Abbi wasn't used to me telling her no, and her disappointment was noticeable.

"I won't give you away. You're my little sister, and I'll never give you away. But I will walk you down the aisle."

"Thank you!" she practically shouted into the phone. "I love you, Tabor."

"You too," I said with a smile.

"Now we just need to find you someone who isn't a gold-digging whore," she said in that serious way of hers.

"Don't start with that again," I warned, hoping to avoid the list of potential dates. "You don't need to worry about me."

"Why?" Her voice was hushed. "Did you meet someone?"

"Not really."

"What kind of answer is that? You either met someone or you didn't," she stated with finality.

Abbi could always read me like a book—a boring, plain, stale book that had no plot whatsoever, yet she was always interested. Stupidly, I remained quiet too long and she jumped on it.

"Okay, you better start talking now," she barked, leaving little room for argument.

"Nothing to tell," I admitted. "I met someone the other day and don't know much about her."

"Not even her name?" she questioned, surprise registering in her tone.

"Dani," I answered simply. Just saying her name made me smile.

"So what else do you know about her?" she asked.

"She's a school teacher. Runs an after-school program. And…I told her my name is Tabor," I confessed, feeling like an idiot. I sat back, pinching the bridge of my nose, and closed my eyes as I recalled the panic I felt when her blue eyes landed on me.

"You're joking, right?"

"Nope."

"Do you think this Dani chick is for real?"

"I think she might be," I said, smirking to myself.

"Be careful," she said, sounding a lot like Mom at that moment. "You don't want to end up with someone like Natasha again. That woman was pure evil."

"You know me," I scoffed.

"Yeah. I do. So I repeat: be careful."

"What's that supposed to mean?" I asked.

"You wear your heart on your sleeve and you're so quick to believe the good in people. Promise me you'll play it cool—at least until you get to know her."

"I promise. But look, I need to go. I'm supposed to pick her up in an hour."

"You're seeing her tonight?" Her gasp made me laugh. "Where does she live? Is it far from you?"

"About thirty minutes, I guess," I said. "So I need to get

going."

"Are you nervous?" she teased.

"Abbi," I groaned, frustrated with her giddy tone.

"You *are* nervous," she laughed.

"Goodbye, Abs," I groaned, hanging up the phone before she could argue.

It was typically how our phone calls ended: one of us would annoy the other until someone hung up the phone. And neither of us held grudges; it was part of our Hunter charm.

But truth be told, I didn't remember the last time I *was* nervous about picking someone up for a date.

My phone buzzed and I looked down to see a text.

> **Abbi: Call me later. I want more details on this girl**
> **Me: Will do**

***

As I made my way down Dani's street, I took notice of the string of townhomes along the way. It was an older neighborhood, but by the looks of some of the people out for an evening walk, the tenants were young.

My speed slowed as the street numbers got closer to hers, and I knew I was at the right place when I noticed a garage with Dani's Bel Air parked in front of it. I found it cool that she was into classics and wondered if it was something she had always loved or a passing fad.

I stepped out of my car and straightened my shirt as I walked to her front door. It had been a long time since I'd experienced the anonymity of dating—something I would have to explain before long. The only drawback to going out in public was the fact that there were limited places I could go and enjoy a quiet evening without being noticed.

Metropolis Grill was a thirty-minute drive, but well worth it for the anonymity alone

I rang the doorbell and stepped back while I waited for her to answer. A silhouette approached the door and she moved the fabric away from the window to look out. When she opened it I found myself speechless, staring at the woman from the side of the road in a simple black dress that showed off her legs. Her hair was down, thick waves resting on her shoulders, and a small amount of makeup on her face.

"Wow, you look…" I said, trying not to sound too eager. "…beautiful."

"Thank you." She grinned, glancing down at her feet. She looked up and I watched as she shifted nervously on her feet.

Dani wearing jeans and a T-shirt would be sexy; something told me that was her norm. Dani in a sexy black dress—gorgeous.

"You don't look so bad yourself," she said with a smirk.

The side of my mouth curved up in a smile and I cocked my head to the side. "You clean up nice."

"Yeah, thanks for pointing out that 'smudge' on my face," she laughed.

"I thought it was kind of sexy, actually," I defended.

"Is that so?" Her cheeks flushed and she turned, pointing behind her. "I just need to grab my purse."

"We have a few minutes," I said, hoping to get a look at her place. It was small, but seemed to fit her. I pointed to her living room when I noticed her walls covered with various framed pictures.

"Go ahead." She motioned to the black and white photos I showed interest in.

"These are cool," I said as I looked at the images. Some were of the beach, others of people—possibly strangers—in random places.

"Thanks. My sister Gracie loves taking pictures. I started framing them when I saw they were stuffed in a closet collecting dust at her place."

She sat on the arm of her oversized beige couch and I could tell she was watching me. I could see her reflection in one of the frames so I pretended to stare at it. In reality, I was looking at her, longer than necessary.

"Nice place," I said as I turned to look at her.

"Thanks," she answered easily, laughing. "It's only taken two years for it to feel like home."

"I've been in my place for about that long and it still feels pretty empty."

"Why is that?" she pried.

Because I'm really JT Hunter and I don't have time.

"When I'm home, I like to relax. Shopping for house stuff doesn't fall into the *relaxing* category for me."

I could have told her then, but I wanted to hold onto my secret a little longer. It was nice to just be a regular guy to someone besides myself.

I walked toward her, and she started to get to her feet but managed to stumble in her heels. I quickly reached out and caught her elbow, steadying her.

"Are you falling for me?" I teased with a wink.

Her cheeks were bright pink, and when I looked down where my hand was touching on her arm, goose bumps appeared. I liked that I had some effect on her.

A waft of her flowery perfume—or maybe it was her shampoo—hit me, and with our proximity, I'd never been so tempted to steal a kiss. But I tore my eyes away from her lips, remembering I was supposed to be a gentleman.

"I—I'm good," she finally said, swallowing hard as she gained her footing. "Like I said…klutz."

Dani walked over to grab her purse and turned off the lamp on the hallway table before we walked outside. I was waiting for her to lock up and extended my hand, something that took me by surprise.

"I don't want you falling down the stairs," I said playfully, attempting to alleviate the tension.

"You're so funny," she said. But she placed her hand in mine anyway.

I planned on letting go when we reached the bottom step, but I liked the way her hand felt in mine. It felt natural, as if it was supposed to be that way.

We walked to the passenger side of my Range Rover and I opened the door for her.

"Nice car," she said when I climbed into the driver's seat and turned on the ignition.

"Thanks." I grinned. "It's the one thing I splurged on when…"

Just say it, Tabor.

I started to back out of the driveway, my arm extended across the back of her seat. I should have said it, because it was the perfect opportunity to come clean. But the longer I paused, the more awkward the silence became.

"Sorry, I lost my train of thought," I lied as I started driving down the street.

"You were talking about when you got this car."

"Oh, that. Yeah, when I got my new job. I realize it's not exactly a classic like yours, but it's not a practical—how did you put it—piece of shit, either."

Dani covered her face with her hands as she laughed. "You heard that? Oh hell! How long were you there?"

"Long enough, Dani," I admitted with a smile.

"Are you some sort of stalker?" she challenged.

"Hardly. Like I said, you seemed determined to change that tire yourself."

"I was. And I have to say, I do know how to do it. My dad taught me. I could've changed it myself—five more minutes was all I needed."

"Yeah. I'm sure all the car needed was a stern talking to and another swift kick to the tire."

She laughed. "That's right."

"So how long have you had the Bel Air? That's a pretty sweet ride."

"It was a gift from my parents when I graduated college. My dad knows how much I love classic cars, so he did some research and found it relatively cheap. It needed some work, but nothing too expensive."

"What did you have before?"

"No way. You asked me a question, now it's my turn." She shifted in her seat to face me and her dress slid up her thigh. I blinked a couple of times to get my head back on the road and cleared my throat as I waited for her question.

"*Tabor*—that's an interesting name," she said.

"Yeah, you mentioned that in your rambling the other day." I smirked.

She looked up at the sunroof and closed her eyes, a smile

playing on her lips. It was fun teasing her, and seeing that she was embarrassed over her slip, I reached over and touched her knee gently. "I'm just kidding."

Her eyes looked at where my hand was and I quickly pulled it back, placing it on the wheel. I panicked a little until I saw the look of disappointment that I'd pulled it away, and felt a little better about my uncharacteristic move.

"I wasn't rambling," she defended. "I was just trying to think of where I've heard that name before."

"I've never met another Tabor," I answered. "I'm probably one of a kind."

"Please," she chuckled, "no one is original anymore."

"No?"

"Everyone thinks they're the first to do something, find something, or be something, when in reality they're just the latest incarnation. Hell, movies are being remade all the time. Originality no longer exists."

"I'm sure my mom will be disappointed that she wasn't as unique as she thought," I responded without a trace of humor.

"Oh damn," she covered her face again. "I'm sorry. My mouth always gets me into trouble."

I couldn't help it—I started laughing and she looked at me and narrowed her eyes, smiling playfully.

"I'm kidding. Honestly, I have no idea where she came up with the name. I almost think she meant to name me Table or something. Or maybe my parents were just drunk."

"Maybe she was just really creative." She glanced at the dashboard before meeting my eyes again and smiled.

"Are you from here?"

"Yeah, grew up an hour north of here. But I went to Beachmont for college. I actually didn't plan on coming back, but I guess I missed it more than I expected. Are *you* from around here?

"Is that a pickup line?" I teased.

"Oh my god! Get over yourself," she said sarcastically.

"It's okay, I don't mind."

"If I were using a pickup line, you'd know it." She smirked.

"See, that right there...you're flirting with me," I said with a grin.

"I'm not hitting on you," she defended weakly through her

laughter.

I clutched my chest and winced and she laughed harder.

"Not like that. I mean, you're cute and all, and I don't think I've stopped smiling since…yeah, I'm going to shut up now."

"So I'm cute, huh?"

I could have let her off the hook, but I was enjoying watching her blush and stammer over her words.

"Would you prefer *hot*? Maybe I should have said 'OMG, you're like so hot,'" she said, sounding how I imagined her students would sound.

"Much better." I nodded. "So I'm hot?"

"Shut up." She swatted at my arm and turned her attention to the road. She was still smiling and I knew that I needed more of those smiles.

"To answer your question, I'm originally from Chicago."

"What brought you out here?"

I pulled into the parking lot in front of Metropolis Grill and turned to face her as the valet opened my door. "Work," I said with a wink.

I stepped out of the SUV and met Dani on the other side. I let my hand rest at the small of her back as I guided her to toward the restaurant. She shivered slightly at my touch and I knew it had nothing to do with the temperature outside. I passed off the key to the valet and before I realized what I was doing, I took her hand in mine.

When we got to the entrance, I paused and waited for her to look at me. The moment her blue eyes met mine, something told me she was different from the others. Her breath hitched and she pulled her bottom lip between her teeth briefly. As much as I wanted to kiss her, it would have to wait. It was our first date, and I still hadn't told her the truth about who I was.

I dropped my face to her ear and whispered, "If I forget to tell you, thank you for coming with me tonight."

CHAPTER 7

DANI

I ran my free hand along the side of my go-to black cocktail dress. It skimmed the tops of my thighs, reminding me of how short it was, but I fought the urge to tug on the hem. My five-foot seven frame was made taller by the three-inch heels I'd shoved my feet into, but I felt sexy.

"Damn," I whispered to myself as I walked alongside him into the restaurant. He hadn't let go of my hand, and I desperately needed some space after being so close to him. I wondered if he could see my heart pounding through the thin fabric of my dress. This man was all sorts of sexy.

The hostess looked at Tabor and smiled without a word as she ushered us to a table in the back. The restaurant was dimly lit, with nothing more than candles to light each table. There was soft music playing overhead and people engaged in quiet conversations.

"I've never been here," I whispered as we sat down. "Hey, isn't that—"

He glanced over to where I was nodding. "Yeah, that's Cooper Tanner," he leaned in to whisper, seeing the pitcher for the San Diego Swingers.

"Crazy," I muttered.

The waiter walked over and introduced himself before taking our drink order and disappearing so we could continue our conversation.

"I take it you like baseball?" he asked.

"Yeah, love it," I admitted. "But the rest of my family are football fans."

Tabor's brows furrowed. "And you?"

"I just never got into it."

He scoffed nervously as he relaxed into his seat. "No?"

I shook my head. "Something about all those men just beating the crap out of each other seems barbaric."

My eyes widened slightly when I remembered I was talking to a football player. I should have tried to cover, but I didn't care that he was JT Hunter. He was fun and I liked being around him. To be honest, I hadn't even thought about *who* he was until that moment.

"My sister would like you," he said. He lifted his menu and began looking it over when I spoke again.

"Why is that?"

"Because you don't..." He trailed off and looked at his menu without finishing.

He wanted to say it, I was sure of it. But I couldn't figure out why it was so hard for him to admit the truth.

"Like football?" I asked, completing his sentence.

"Yeah, something like that," he said. "Can I tell you something?"

"Sure." I closed my menu and set it in front of me.

"I wasn't exactly honest with you the other day," he started. He took a sip of water and set the glass down, his eyes avoiding mine. "It's stupid, really."

"What were you not honest about?" I pried.

"About me. Who I am," he said in a rush. He tapped his fingers on the table and sat back, clearing his throat, but was still refusing to meet my eyes. He ran his hand across his forehead and appeared anxious.

"You're Tabor Hunter," I clarified and paused to take a sip of my water. "Or *JT*, as most people know you."

My gaze met his and I felt a tingle run down my spine. I hadn't planned on admitting the truth *for* him, but he looked so nervous and I just wanted to take the pressure off. He blinked rapidly and I could tell he was trying to piece together what I said.

I kept quiet while he thought about my confession. When I'd gotten home from Gracie's I'd started doing a few searches on Tabor, or rather JT Hunter. I was curious to see what kind of guy he was. Since I wasn't a football fan and couldn't even name a starting player on any team, I figured anything would help.

Except that everything I read made JT Hunter sound too good to be true. As much as I wanted to believe all the great things, I found myself searching for the flaws. After all, no one is perfect. Right?

"You knew?" he finally asked accusingly, his voice almost a whisper.

"Not at first," I admitted with a sigh. "I was telling my sister about this nice guy who helped me change a tire and asked me out. Long story short, she put it together and then pretty much ridiculed me for not recognizing you."

He sat quiet for a moment and I couldn't tell if he was irritated, angry, or shocked. His brows were pinched and he stared at the table as he processed my words. I waited for him to say something or explain it, maybe even lash out. His expression was hard to read until his eyes met mine and a small smile appeared.

"What?" I asked.

"You didn't know who I was," he repeated.

"Until today? No. But it's not like you were honest about it," I said, crossing my arms over my chest.

"And you were talking to your sister about me, huh?"

I looked at the ceiling and scoffed before looking at him again. He was watching me with an amused grin, waiting for my response. I'd talked about him to Grace and Trevor. And if my brother-in-law were a woman, I knew for a fact that he would be throwing himself at Tabor. That thought alone was enough to make me smile.

"That's what the take-away is here?" I asked before leaning forward and raising a brow. "Why did you introduce yourself as Tabor?"

He ran his hand along his jaw and inhaled like he was preparing to face a firing squad. I feigned a smile to lighten the mood because I wasn't angry when I found out, just confused.

"That's what my family and friends back home have always

called me. I wasn't even thinking when I said it. Most people around here recognize me, and I've just gotten used to it. But when you didn't, I guess I just went with it. But I was going to tell you the truth," he said.

"Oh yeah?" I challenged.

He sat back in his seat and watched me intently. His features were hard to see without the flickering of the candlelight so close to his face. Tabor leaned in again and rested his arms on the table, never allowing his gaze to leave mine.

"I was going to tell you later tonight."

"Are you saying I bailed you out? It was eating you up inside to find the right time to admit the truth and I just went and made it really easy for you?" I teased.

"Something like that," he admitted with a sly smile.

"Okay, go ahead then," I said, leaning back and taking a sip of the wine the waiter had placed in front of me.

"What are you talking about?"

"Show me the big reveal," I said with a smirk.

"Are you serious?" he questioned with a smile, clearly amused by my request.

"Yeah, why not? You shouldn't get off so easily," I said.

Tabor exhaled loudly and rubbed the back of his neck before looking at me again. He pursed his lips and leaned forward. "I have a confession to make," he started.

My mouth opened wide and I feigned shock. "You're married?" I teased.

He was quiet for a second too long and panic surged through my veins.

Shit! I didn't research much about him, so maybe he is married. But wait, he said that he isn't seeing anyone. And Gracie said he's the most eligible bachelor in town.

Sweat was beginning to dampen the back of my neck and my stomach churned until he cleared his throat and shook his head.

"Nah." He grinned. "My name is Tabor, but I'm known in town as JT Hunter."

"As in JT Hunter, *the* football star?" I clarified, playing along. I couldn't help but be charmed by his shyness at the admission.

"That would be me."

"So why the secrecy?"

"It wasn't supposed to be. Like I said, when you didn't recognize me, I wanted to be that guy. The one that no one knows...a regular guy. It's hard going places where everyone is calling your name and asking for a piece of you. I knew I had to tell you the truth, but I liked how you saw me...as Tabor."

"Your family calls you Tabor?"

"When I was growing up and getting in trouble, Mom would scream out my full name—*Jordan Tabor Hunter, get your ass in here now!*—and I knew she meant business. I hated being called Jordan, and I'd never met another Tabor. So in junior high, I started introducing myself as Tabor. The rest is history."

The waiter returned, interrupting our conversation, and we ordered our food. When he left, an uncomfortable silence had settled between Tabor and me. I didn't care for it at all.

I liked the easy flirtation and banter between me and the guy I'd met on the road. I didn't even know him, but it was refreshing. As it was, the evening was quickly turning into a disappointment with all the pretenses and awkward silences.

"What are you thinking?" he finally asked.

I shook my head and considered my words. "I'm a pretty secure woman. I'm not needy and never fish for compliments, but I have to ask...why me?"

Tabor didn't hesitate before responding. "When I was driving home the other day, I saw you on the ground next to your car, busting your ass to change that tire. I considered driving past, just like everyone else did, but I didn't. I was fascinated with your determination. For whatever reason, I got out to help and that was it."

"Okay," I answered, unable to think of anything better to say.

"Well, that wasn't really it." He smirked. "I did get out to help, but when you asked to see my eyes, I was waiting for you to recognize me. You had dirt on your face and were sweating like crazy, but you didn't seem to care that I was seeing this. It was sexy as hell. I was watching you, and you truly didn't know who I was and agreed to the date anyway. I didn't want you to go out with me because I'm JT Hunter. I wanted you to go out with me because I made you laugh. I'd forgotten what that felt like— someone laughing because of something I said and not because of some celebrity status."

His words hit me right in the heart. I couldn't imagine being in the spotlight and worrying about if people liked you for you or for who they thought you were. I gave him a reprieve, and that was all I needed to know.

"If you wanted to keep your anonymity, why did you bring me here? Not that I'm complaining."

"The food is great, but even better—the staff is under strict orders not to bother the customers, and the rest of the diners respect that, too. So I can come here and enjoy a meal without people walking up to me every five seconds while my food gets cold."

"That would get annoying."

"I love the fans, I really do. I wouldn't be where I am without them. But it's nice to get a break every once in a while."

"So what now?"

"Well, that depends on you."

"What about me?"

"I like you, Dani. You're beautiful, smart, and so far, you've kept it interesting."

"I like you, too," I replied shyly.

"Does that mean I can see you again?"

The silence grew between us and I weighed my options. Tabor was fun and charming. I liked the way he looked at me and how comfortable he seemed in my presence. But *who* he was was stopping me.

"I'm not sure I'm cut out for the life you lead," I admitted. "I'm a teacher, Tabor. I'm with little people all day long. I barely know how to deal with adults, let alone someone with an entire city of fans."

"I take it that's a no?" he questioned, and I couldn't ignore the disappointment in his voice.

"It's definitely not a *no*. It's a *let's hang out and get to know each other*—perhaps away from your career?"

He started to speak, but the waiter began setting our food in front of us.

"Does everything look okay?" the waiter asked.

I looked up from my food to see Tabor watching me.

"Everything looks perfect," he answered, never taking his eyes off of me.

CHAPTER 8

DANI

"Wait," I said, panting heavily. "I can't go again. I need a minute."

"Are you okay?" he asked, looking down at me as sweat beaded on his forehead.

I nodded and swallowed hard, unable to answer with words. When my heart rate finally, slowed I cleared my throat.

"That was crazy," I finally managed.

"You're pretty good," he complimented and I laughed.

"Don't patronize me. The next one is all mine," I said, narrowing my eyes playfully.

"If you say so."

For the last twenty minutes, Tabor and I had been in an intense game of *Just Dance*, and somehow he'd managed to beat me. Every. Single. Time.

For someone of his build, he had impressive dance moves. We took turns picking out the song to compete to, and inevitably I ended up standing behind him laughing so hard that I couldn't dance. He had every step down and even attempted to throw some sass into his moves. He was adorably awkward to watch dance, and I loved it. I couldn't remember the last time I had so much fun playing a video game or laughed so hard.

When we'd left Metropolis, the local fans had swarmed the

sidewalk outside of the restaurant. Apparently someone had Tweeted Tabor's whereabouts, and that was all it took. I stood back while he dutifully signed every piece of paper, picture, and jersey that was shoved in front of him. He would look over and give me an apologetic shrug, but I waved him off. He talked to all of them with a smile and asked them questions. It was easy to see why people liked him so much.

After nearly thirty minutes of signing, he wrapped his arm around my waist, pulling my body to his. I melted into him as if I belonged there, and I didn't want him to let me go. As he guided me toward his SUV, there were eyes watching us and whispers—something that was foreign to me.

Neither of us was ready for the night to end, so we went back to my place to hang out and get to know one another better. I had no idea he was a video game junkie too.

"I have to sit down," I sighed, fanning my face. "Why are you so good at this?"

"My sister," he answered simply, taking a seat near me on the couch.

His body seemed to take over the entire piece of furniture, demanding attention. His broad shoulders spanned an entire section of the couch, and his arms were thick, widening his frame. He had a strong, sharp jaw, but in the past half hour he hadn't seemed as intimidating in my living room as he had at the restaurant. I couldn't help but look at him and observe this man hanging out in my condo. The Tabor I was getting to know was down to earth and charming. I had really yet to experience JT Hunter.

Or maybe I have.

Maybe it's just my perception.

"Ah, the sister who would like me?" I clarified. "Or do you have others?"

"There's just Abbi and me. I don't think my mom could handle more than the two of us," he laughed.

"Are you two close?"

"Yeah. But she's back home in Chicago, so I don't see her often," he admitted. "She just took her last final and called earlier to tell me she's getting married."

"That's exciting," I said. "Do they have a date yet?"

"I don't know. I didn't have time to get the details, other than she wants me to walk her down the aisle."

"That's sweet," I gushed. "But what about your dad?"

Tabor shifted and angled his body toward me. "Dad passed away when I was fourteen, and it's been just the three of us ever since."

"I'm sorry."

"It was a long time ago, but I miss him. He was a great dad." He smiled to himself and I couldn't help but smile sadly.

"How did he die?"

"Cancer. He fought hard for year, but in the end he was too weak."

"I'm so sorry. I didn't mean to pry."

"You're fine," he answered sadly.

I didn't know what I'd do without either of my parents; they were my lifelines. Tabor looked up at me, his eyes pleading with me to change the subject.

"So how long has your sister been with her fiancé?"

"Longer than I thought," he laughed. "A year."

"Wow, that's great."

"Yeah. I mean, she's happy, so I guess that's all that matters."

"But?"

He leaned back and stared at the ceiling as if he could glean some wisdom from it. I didn't say anything, because he looked lost in his own head. When he finally looked at me, he shrugged.

"I'm happy for her, but I guess I'm worried, too. Ever since my dad died, it's just been Abs, Mom, and me. I've done everything I can to support them and be there for them."

"What's Abbi's boyfriend like?"

"Marshall? He's pretty cool. A little on the quiet side, and he was the first guy she brought around who didn't kiss my ass because of who I am. So there's that."

"What's your sister like?"

He placed his hand over mine and squeezed softly, a gesture reserved for people who actually knew each other. While it felt strange, I also liked it.

I liked him.

"Enough about my sister. Tell me about you," he said

sweetly.

"What about me?" I asked coyly. I didn't like having attention on myself; I was much happier to grant that spotlight to others. But since we were in the get-to-know-you phase, I had to participate.

"What made you get into teaching?"

"My roommates," I laughed. "Millie and I have known each other since high school and we met our roommates at freshman orientation. I was the only one who didn't know what I wanted to study. Jolie is a lawyer, though you'd never guess it from her tattoos and piercings. Viola is a musician—she actually gives music lessons to kids. And Millie is a teacher too."

"So you were general studies," he teased.

"Yeah, for the first year. But Millie always knew she wanted to teach, and talked so passionately about it that I got excited too. Honestly, I'm not sure if I really fell in love with the idea of it or her excitement for it. But in the end it was a perfect fit. I love what I do, and the kids I get to work with are incredible."

Tabor nodded and smiled, but soon, only the sounds of the paused video game and us breathing filled the room. He was still wearing the same thing he wore for our date, but had taken off his jacket and undone a few buttons. Since I was at home, I'd changed into jeans and a T-shirt, happy for the comfort.

I shifted in my seat and tucked my knees underneath me to get a better look at him.

"What about you?" I asked, taking the pressure off myself. "What's it like?"

"What's that?"

"You, being JT Hunter and all the fans and the schedule...what's that like for you? Did you always want to play football?"

He thought for a moment before speaking, and I'm not sure what I expected, but I was surprised by his answer.

"I've been with the Quakes now for two years. I finished up college and was drafted in one of the last rounds. No one expected much out of me in the way of performance, but I was determined to prove them wrong. My dad got me into it as a way to channel my aggression as a kid. Dad and I would throw the ball around when I was a kid, and I guess after he died, I just kept doing it."

"Doesn't sound like you like it that much," I said.

"When I started, it was about proving something, and I've done that. But I'm a part of a great team and I love it here." He scratched his head. "So what's it like being me? Most days it's pretty great. I've gotten to travel around the country, met some cool people along the way, and got to start my own charity. These are things I wouldn't have had the chance to do on my own. But there are days where it kinda sucks."

I raised my eyebrows, shocked by his candor, but he simply laughed.

"Don't get me wrong, I don't take a second of it for granted. I'm grateful for everything I have and I want to give back. But yeah, there are days where I wish I could just be me and not worry about people freaking out when I walk into a store. That's why it was refreshing when I met you. I was able to do exactly that: be me."

When he finished, he winced and looked toward the darkness outside the window. I didn't understand the true reality of his life, but it sounded too intrusive for my liking. Tabor turned back to look at me, his brow furrowed, and shook his head slowly before scoffing. "I sound like a little bitch, don't I?"

"Not at all," I answered honestly. "I can go anywhere I want, and no one knows who I am."

"It can get lonely sometimes," he admitted. "That's why I'm so close with my mom and sister. They keep me grounded. Ya know?"

"Yeah, totally." I smiled, thinking of my own family. "My parents live about thirty minutes away, and my sister is further than that. But we get together every weekend for dinner and catch up on life. It's nice having them around."

"You have dinner with them every weekend?" he asked, wide-eyed.

"Mom is a great cook—no one wants to miss her meals," I admitted. "I wish I could cook like her."

"Every time my sister comes to town, the media speculates as to whether or not she's my girlfriend. It's pretty fuckin' sick."

"Yeah, that's pretty nasty," I laughed. "But you're a celebrity, I guess, right? Part of the territory. I can't imagine what it's like for you."

"There's never a dull moment," he offered.

"What's the craziest thing a fan has done?"

He thought for a minute and smiled. "There was one time when a woman showed up to a charity event and started telling everyone there that I was her boyfriend."

"That's weird," I laughed.

"Not as weird as the valet chick at the airport."

"What did she do?"

"That's the thing—I can't be sure. This woman with blue hair comes over to take my keys. I can tell she's legit, she's in uniform. I could tell she recognized me, so when she asked if she could get a picture, I told her it was no problem. I was flying out to see my mom and it wasn't until I got inside the airport that I realized I forgot my ChapStick in my car."

"Sounds harmless," I said with a shrug.

"Yeah, except the ChapStick was missing when I got back from my trip."

"Do you think she took it?"

"I don't know, but can you picture some woman walking around telling people she has JT Hunter's ChapStick? It's weird, I mean, it's just ChapStick."

I laughed so hard, because it was totally something I could see happening. People adored this guy, and getting a piece of him was like winning the lottery.

"Just watch out—first it's your ChapStick, and next thing you know, she's pregnant," I teased and Tabor laughed, warming me deep inside.

"You know, Dani," he extended his hand to mine and when we touched, something ignited inside of me, "I'd really like to see you again, but you should know, if we go out, there's a chance that you'll see firsthand what it's really like to be with me. What you saw tonight was pretty tame."

"Can I get to know Tabor first, and see how that works, before jumping into the JT Hunter madness?"

"It's hard to separate the two."

"I know, it's your job, you have an image to uphold."

"It's not about image. I'm not two different people. I mean, what you see is what you get. But I can't say that football isn't always there. Interviews, practice, teammates, my manager— they're all a part of my daily life. If we go out to dinner or to a movie or whatever, people are going to look. They're going to talk. We haven't even discussed the paparazzi yet."

His words echoed in my ears as I tried to understand what his life was about. It made me sad for him, because he deserved to have a life, but all I heard was how much people wanted a piece of him. All. The. Time.

Tabor cocked his head to the side and waited for me to give him my attention. His lips curved up slightly, but it wasn't a full smile. This look was more reserved…almost sad. "I really want to see you again."

"Yeah?" I asked, drawing my bottom lip between my teeth.

"Yeah. But I understand if it's too much." He looked down at our entwined fingers and added, "Dani, I don't know much about you, but I really hope I get the chance to learn."

"You're a charmer, aren't you?" Tabor was really everything I liked in a guy, and I was completely smitten.

"No. Just honest," he replied. And I believed him.

He pulled his phone out of his pocket and showed me the screen alerting him to a call.

"See?" He stood up and walked to the sliding glass door as he answered it. "What's up, Daniels?"

I remained on the couch, watching him talk on the phone as he looked at the framed images again. He appeared comfortable in my place, something that made me relax, too. As attracted as I was to him, I wasn't sure I could handle being the girl that JT Hunter was dating. The thought of people being in my business was the stuff my nightmares were made of. Even when my principal tried to give me an award for the after-school program, I refused to accept it. I was doing something I loved, to help others.

But there was Tabor, and the football circus that followed him. According to the news articles I'd read, he would be training most of the summer leading up to preseason.

Training Camp?

Preseason?

Football?

All of those terms made me want to break out into hives. I had never been a football fan, yet there I was, holding the attention of one of the league's most popular athletes. I was lost in my own thoughts and didn't hear Tabor speaking until he called my name again.

"Oh, I'm sorry," I said, shaking my head and plastering a smile on my face. "What did you say?"

"Just apologizing," he said. "I've been trying to get ahold of one of my teammates all day and he finally calls me back at twelve. What's that about?"

"It's midnight?" I repeated. I had been enjoying our conversation and lost track of time. Not that I had anything going on the next day.

"Yeah," he laughed. "I should probably get going."

I stood up. "I'll walk you out."

He picked up his sport coat and followed me to the front door, but I was waging an internal battle. Regret flooded my mind because I wasn't ready for him to leave. And as much as I wanted to see where things could go between us, I was scared. I wasn't sure my heart could take the public rejection if I tried and we failed. As I unlocked the door and stepped aside, Tabor stood in front me and I had to look up to see his face.

Mistake number one.

As soon as our eyes met, he dipped his face down to mine and slowly leaned forward until there was little space between us. He was giving me a chance to back away, to stop him, but I didn't dare move. I lifted my chin, bringing my lips closer to his, and as Tabor's lips grazed my own, a wave of desire coursed through my veins. It wasn't rushed or messy; actually, it was sort of perfect. My lips parted as he deepened the kiss and I was lost to his touch.

His arm wrapped around my waist and I felt tiny in his embrace. Without thought, my hand skimmed up his arm until it was wrapped around his neck, holding him close to me.

I barely knew this man, and yet the kiss felt familiar and perfect at the same time. He was most definitely giving me something to think about. But before I knew it he released me from his hold and stepped away, and I hated the space. Every part of me wanted a redo, but as clarity began to settle, I was grateful he'd stopped when he did.

"Sorry," he muttered. His eyes looked surprised by his brazen action, and I'm sure mine reflected the same. "I wanted to do that all night."

"It's okay," I said breathlessly. "That was nice."

"Nice?" he repeated, his lips curving up slightly.

"Nice." I flashed a coy smile and as I was about to say something else, he kissed me. That time it was as if his life depended on it, and I returned in kind.

During the impromptu make-out session, my mind was on a loop with words like *football, fans, celebrity,* and *sexiest man* flooding it.

"Hold on," I gasped between kisses until he was standing across from me in the small entry. "I...I need a minute. I need to think."

I ran my fingers through my hair to give me a moment and exhaled loudly as I calmed myself. Tabor was watching me, no doubt curious what I was thinking, but I couldn't formulate a sentence.

"I need to think," I repeated, winded.

"You just said that," he answered with a knowing smile.

"Sorry," I muttered. I was embarrassed by my reaction, and when I touched my fingers to my lips, which still burned from his touch, I knew I was in trouble.

My pulse was still racing, and though my entire being was screaming at me to go with it, my head had already taken over.

Time, Dani. You need to think about what you're getting into.

"Can I see you tomorrow?" he asked quietly.

"Tabor," I started, but he interrupted.

"I have some equipment—for your program," he said in a rush, a playful grin fixed on his face.

"What are you talking about?" I asked, bemused by the change in the conversation.

"You said you were spending your days trying to get funding for your program, and it just so happens that my charity helps support groups like yours."

"Are you for real?" I asked, stunned as I walked past him and away from the door. "You're too much," I snorted.

"After we talked, I made a call and pulled some strings," he said, looking somewhat embarrassed. "I hope that's okay."

"It's bribery," I joked. "Now I *have* to see you again."

I shook my head slowly as clarity set in. This guy, this somewhat stranger, wanted to help my kids. He'd actually listened to me the other day when I'd told him about River's Kids, and then he did something?

He looked down to the floor and took a step back. "Seeing me again was in question?" he asked quietly. "Dani? I didn't mean to overstep."

"I'm sorry," I responded quickly. "No, that's incredible, I'm actually just in shock, I guess. You didn't have to do that."

"I know, but I wanted to. Anyone who's as dedicated to their students as you are deserves to catch a break," he said.

My nose burned and I was fighting back the tears that were stinging my eyes. No one had ever done something so selfless for me—for my kids. I was beyond moved, and I showed him by reaching for his hand and squeezing it softly when the words wouldn't come out past the lump in my throat.

"Are you okay?" he asked as he lowered himself to look into my eyes, and I nodded.

Tabor flashed a sweet smile and stood to his full height as I gathered myself together. I took a deep breath and looked up at him, hoping my gratitude showed through my smile.

"Thank you so much, Tabor. And yes, I would very much like to see you again," I was finally able to say. "But—"

He exhaled. "You're welcome, Dani," he answered, his voice a low rumble. "Would it be okay if I dropped some things off at your school tomorrow?"

"I'm sure that could be arranged."

"What time should I pick you up?" he asked.

"We're going together?"

He smirked. "I need you to show me where to put the stuff."

I nodded. "Right. Um, Nine?" I said timidly, as if it were a question.

"Nine it is," he said, rubbing his thumb over the back of my hand that he was still holding. I didn't want to let go. I loved the way my stomach fluttered when he touched me.

Tabor pointed at the door and I nodded as we walked back down the small corridor together. When he reached for the handle, he stepped closer to me, leaving little space between us, and I breathed him in. I was so scared to look into his eyes because I already knew from the first kiss that I wanted to spend more time with him, and despite my words, I'd give in. But I looked up anyway and this time it was me who initiated the kiss. But it was a simple, perfect kiss that I felt everywhere.

"Goodnight," I said.

He lifted his hand and grazed the side of my face before stepping out onto the patio.

I watched as he sauntered down the steps the same way I'd watched him come in earlier: Confident. Sure. Sexy. He neared his car, but turned back to look at me and raised an eyebrow.

"I think you should go inside," he said playfully. "You've got some thinking to do."

And just like that, Tabor was in his car and pulling out of my driveway. I hated the uncertainty waging a battle in my head, because if he were any other guy, I would have no doubts about pursuing something with him. But Tabor Hunter wasn't just any guy.

He was San Diego's hero.

CHAPTER 9

DANI

It was well after midnight as I watched him drive away, and there was no way I was getting sleep anytime soon. Tabor was right about one thing: I needed to do some thinking,

I walked inside and dialed Millie's number without questioning it. Gracie and Trevor were the only people who knew I had a date with Tabor, or rather JT Hunter. If Millie found out from someone other than me, I'd never live it down. I knew it was late, but I needed to talk to her. And truth be told, I needed her perspective on the situation.

"Hello?" Millie answered groggily.

"Hey, Mill, I'm sorry to call so late. I just needed to talk to someone," I whispered, as if I was going to wake up her family.

"Everything okay? What time is it?" she asked, her voice raspy.

I was the biggest jerk on the planet. I knew sleep was a commodity for my friend, with baby Colton around, but I was selfish and needed her.

"It's late, I'm sorry," I said, wincing. "But I really need to talk to you."

"Hold on," she whispered into the phone. I could hear her say something to Nick, and then there was a rustling noise. I waited patiently, because she was doing me a solid by giving up her sleep for me.

"What's going on?" she asked through a yawn.

"I went out with tire-guy."

"Dani, if you woke me up to tell me it was a crappy date, I'm going to kill you," she groaned.

"No, no, nothing like that," I said. "I just found some things out that I haven't gotten to tell you since I was at your place."

"He's married," she deadpanned.

I was quiet for a moment and decided to rip off the Band-Aid.

"He's JT Hunter," I said.

"Ha-Ha. Very funny, goodnight, Dani. Thanks for waking me up," she said.

"His name is Tabor Hunter," I almost shouted to keep her from hanging up.

"If you're playing a sick joke on me, I might have to hurt you," she warned. "Wait, did you really go out with JT Hunter?"

"I did."

"Why didn't you tell me you were going out with him?" she asked, her voice slightly strained.

"I didn't know who he was. You know me...the guy introduced himself as Tabor, and when I was talking to Grace about him..." I explained when she interrupted.

"*She* recognized the name," she finished.

"Yeah," I answered, smiling sheepishly to myself before smacking my forehead. "I'm an idiot, Millie."

"Pretty much," she answered.

"Thanks," I mumbled.

"Okay, so tell me all about it," she said in that familiar giddy tone. "I can't believe you went out with JT Hunter."

"We went to Metropolis Grill and then came back here and hung out for a while," I said.

"Uh-huh," she replied suggestively. "I'm sure you *hung out*."

"Millie! It was a first date," I laughed. "But he's such a sweet guy and an amazing kisser."

"What?" she all but shouted before her voice was muffled by something. When she spoke again, it was like a conspiratorial whisper. "You kissed him?"

I laughed and filled her in on the date details, all the way down to Tabor asking to see me again.

"You're going to see him again. Right? The way you talk, he sounds perfect for you. So what's the problem?"

"He's a professional football player. He's famous. He has fans."

"So?"

"Oh Millie," I muttered. "You are no help. You would love nothing more than for your best friend to date your athlete crush."

"I resent that," she laughed. "Is it a bad thing to want my best friend to be happy?"

"No."

"Look, call Vi—she knows what it's like to be with someone in the spotlight. Maybe she can give you some advice."

"Maybe you're right."

I was mulling it over when she spoke again.

"Dani?"

"Yeah?"

"On a scale of one to ten, how good of a kisser was he?"

"Millie…they haven't made a scale to measure his kisses on."

"I knew it!"

"Look, I gotta go. Love you, sorry to call so late."

"For JT Hunter gossip, you can call me anytime you want," she answered. "Love you."

I hung up the phone and decided that sleep was the answer. Perhaps I'd figure it all out in a dream and wake with a plan. As I headed up to my room, my phone vibrated in my hand and I was certain it was Millie with more "help." But it wasn't her.

Tabor: Have you thought about it yet?
Me: You left like thirty minutes ago
Tabor: Okay. Then I'll see you tomorrow
Me: Only because you tricked me
Tabor: But I get to see you again. So Tabor-1 Dani-0
Me: I think it's more like 1-1
Tabor: I like my odds here. Goodnight Dani

I didn't respond to his last text. I didn't know how to answer. Tabor had given me something to think about, and I was going to have to weigh out the pros and cons. But that kiss…it made the pro list.

Without another thought, I dialed Viola's number. That girl kept insane hours and I knew she'd be up. Vi and Will had married before we graduated and she had been by his side ever since. They were the perfect couple, both creative and madly in love. I think what I admired most about their relationship was how supportive she was of his dream of becoming a rock star.

"Danielle! What's up?" Will asked when he answered Vi's phone. I laughed when he used my full name. Aside from my parents, he was the only person that called me Danielle, but I didn't mind.

"Hey Will. Is Vi there? I need some advice."

"She's in the shower. What's up?"

"You two heading to the bar?" I asked, trying to change the subject. Will's band played the local bar scene, including the one where he worked.

"In a little."

"Can you just tell her I called?" I asked as I prepared to hang up the call.

"Why can't you talk to me about whatever's up?"

"Who said anything's up?"

"It's almost one in the morning," he fired back. "Why else would you be calling?"

"It's no big."

"Why can't you tell me?"

"Because…you're Will," I answered with a laugh.

"Ah, c'mon, hit me," he said.

I could hear Viola somewhere in the background and figured she was finishing up. It was only a matter of time before the story made its way through our circle of friends and Will heard about it anyway. I went ahead and told him all about meeting Tabor, our date, and my current dilemma.

"So what's the problem? He likes you. You like him," Will said.

Okay, sure, it made sense in theory, but there was so much more to consider. "But he's famous and shit."

"So?"

"Valid argument," I muttered, throwing myself onto my bed

with a huff.

"I'm being serious. You're wondering why he likes you...plain old Danielle."

"Thanks," I said, rolling my eyes.

"But he does. Maybe he likes that he doesn't have to be *someone* when he's with you. Are you really just going to hide because of who he is?"

I was quiet for a moment and then I heard him tsk.

"I always thought you were cooler than that, Danielle."

"If it doesn't work out, do you realize the level of public humiliation I'd be subjected to?"

"Damn girl, I can't even talk to you. Here's Vi," he said, handing the phone over. I heard him mutter something about me being chickenshit, but I was too wrapped up on the cons of dating Tabor to be irritated.

"You went out with JT Hunter?" Viola asked without so much as a *hello*.

"Yes. And he wants to see me again," I told her.

"And the problem is?"

"Did you *not* hear the name—JT Hunter," I said sarcastically.

"Oh," she said and I heard her call out to Will, "You're right babe. Total chickenshit!"

"You know me, Vi. I don't like attention. If I were to go out with him, I'd basically be inviting the entire city to scrutinize my every move."

Right then, I heard Viola's laugh that I knew so well. It was loud and made me smile, but I found myself rolling my eyes.

"Get over yourself. Trust me, they're way more interest in him than the junior high school teacher. If anything, you're just going to have thousands of women jealous that he's with you."

The line was quiet after she spoke as I considered her words.

She was right...and so was Will. Millie had already told me to go for it, but my stupid fears kept me from giving in. It's not like I was going to marry the guy. He wanted to get to know me better and I felt the same. He was no different from any other man I'd dated, and I needed to see what happened. But I also had to accept the fact that if I was going to date Tabor, it meant the end to my privacy.

"Let me know how it goes," Viola said before hanging up the

phone.

I knew Vi had no doubts that I was going to give it a shot with Tabor. But I still needed to convince myself to take a chance. I wished I had the faith in me that my friends seemed to have.

CHAPTER 10

DANI

The better part of my morning was spent trying to find the outfit that said *I'm interested, but not trying too hard.* In the end, I opted for a pair of shorts and a fitted button-down shirt with my Converse. I pulled my hair into a simple ponytail and decided to forego the makeup since the rest of my day would be spent in the gym sorting through equipment.

It was supposed to be a beautiful day, and despite my nerves I was ready to spend it with Tabor.

He'd surprised me when he mentioned his foundation and the donation. I wasn't sure what that would consist of, but I would gladly take just about anything. The kids needed this program to survive, and I wanted that for them.

After my conversation with Will and Viola, I had spent an hour writing up a list of the pros and cons of dating JT Hunter. When it was completed, I stared at the list, and the good far outweighed the bad, but I was still apprehensive.

The smell of coffee filled the condo and I poured another cup. I'd made more than usual, in case Tabor wanted some. I was both nervous and excited to see him again and hoped that he didn't mistake my apprehension for disinterest.

I startled when I heard the knock at my door, and checked myself in the hall mirror to make sure I looked okay. As I opened the door, he stood in front of me in a pair of beige cargo shorts and a light blue T-shirt that showed every muscle in his chest. He was grinning as he looked me up and down.

"Good morning," I said, stepping aside. He looked so much more handsome in person than the few pictures I'd seen online. He didn't look comfortable in the spotlight, but with me, he seemed himself. Or what I figured was the real him.

He walked inside and I closed the door behind him, but when I turned he was standing a short distance away from me. I cocked my head to the side and waited for him to say something, but when he didn't I spoke up.

"Did you have a good night?" I grinned.

He nodded, but still hadn't spoken a word.

"How 'bout some coffee before we go?"

He nodded again, his eyes glued to mine and a sweet smile playing on his lips. I wanted to know what he was thinking—hell, I wanted him to speak. His deep voice made my stomach flip and twist in ways I didn't know were possible. I started to move past him and bring him into the kitchen when his hand reached for mine. He leaned against the wall, making it evident the conversation was going to be had then and there.

I looked at our hands and then back at him and said nothing, figuring it was his turn to feel awkward. I'm not sure how long we stood like that—it could have been seconds or minutes before he spoke.

"I did some thinking of my own last night," he said.

I swallowed hard, fighting to not break the eye contact we were engaged in. I was afraid I would be lost forever, but being lost in him might not have been so bad. "And?"

"The fact that you're intimidated by the spotlight makes me like you even more. And if you want to see what's happening here without everyone knowing, then that's what I want too."

"You mean, like our own little secret?" I asked, intrigued by the offer.

"Yeah," he answered as his fingers threaded with mine. He tugged gently so I stepped toward him, forcing me to tip my head further back to look at him.

"People already saw us together last night," I said, barely audible.

"And you've already talked about me to your friend," he said.

"Friends—plural," I responded.

His brows pinched together and he pursed his lips.

"Yeah, I needed some help with my thinking," I admitted.

"What did you come up with?"

Instead of giving him an answer, I took another step closer so I was flush against his body, but I still had to stand on my toes. I rested my free hand against his chest, my mouth inches from his. Before I could talk myself out of it, I pressed my lips to Tabor's and felt his arms at my waist as he returned the kiss. It was a frenzied kiss, and when I felt his tongue graze mine I couldn't get enough of him. One hand held me firmly against him while the other traveled up to the nape of my neck.

It was the best answer I could give him at the moment. As the kiss slowed I felt my cheeks flush, and I knew he had questions. I tried to step away, but Tabor held me close and lifted my chin to look at him.

I was barely able to compute the action as he wrapped both arms around my waist, lifting me off the floor so I was looking into his eyes. My arms were around his neck, but I felt like a rag doll. As much as I wanted to wrap my legs around him and hold on for dear life, I had to pace myself.

He kissed me again before setting me on my feet but still holding my hand. I didn't know if he expected an answer then, and I wasn't sure I could give him one.

"As far as anyone knows, this is a working relationship. If you want to tell people that you wrote my foundation and we agreed to help sponsor your program, we can do that. I'm not sure how long people will buy it, because I like being around you and I like who I am with you."

"I like who you are too," I admitted. "Let's just give it a little time, see what happens before people find out?"

"Whatever you need," he agreed.

"Coffee," I answered, clearing my throat. "I need my coffee."

I walked into my tiny kitchen and poured a mug for Tabor, and grabbed mine before joining him at the table. The way he stared at me made me feel beautiful and wanted. I tried so hard to quell the way he electrified every sensation in my body, but it was no use. Despite myself, Tabor Hunter was someone I wanted to get to know, and he was someone worth taking the time to learn about.

"Tell me more about your program," Tabor said. He sounded like a businessman again and it was pretty sexy.

"It's something I started last year for kids who have no place to go after school. We do a lot of activities, arts, skills training, and whatever else the kids are interested in," I gushed proudly of what we'd been able to accomplish in one year.

"How do you get your funding?" he asked. "Sorry. I'm not trying to be nosy."

"I don't mind. Grants," I said simply. "Lots of grants and a few sponsors."

"But there weren't as many this year?" he asked.

"There were a few, but the corporate sponsors we had bailed at the end of the year. My boss waited until the then to tell me what was going on. We managed to get by with what we had, but the kids and I are so grateful, we accept whatever we can."

"Have you ever approached any local businesses to see if they'd be willing to help?"

"I tried several. But when you mention River Valley, they suddenly remember that they maxed out their charitable contributions for the year," I scoffed.

"Does your program have a wish list or a budget of what is needed to help it succeed?" Tabor asked.

"Honestly, I didn't know what I was getting into when I created it. I did some general searches online, but I really just wanted to give these kids something to do after school. The other teachers have been amazing. If I had to make a list of things we needed, it would be pretty scary."

"So why don't we start there?" he asked. "We can drop off what I have and see what else you need." Tabor stood up and extended his hand. "Come on, let's go."

***

We got to the school and I parked in the back lot nearest the gym where the activities took place. The athletic coach had given me access to the sports closet and said we could use anything we wanted. I unlocked the building and disarmed the alarm before we set foot inside. Our shoes echoed and squeaked on the wooden gym floor as we walked to the closet.

"Aside from this program, what do you teach?"

"American History," I said over my shoulder.

"Cool," he responded. "Was that your focus in college?"

"Actually, no." I smirked. "Spanish."

"Really?"

"Yep. It's helped me a lot," I admitted. "Someday, I want to go to Central America and really immerse myself in it."

He looked at me and raised a brow and pointed. "You realize Tijuana is *literally* right there."

"Yeah, I know." I shrugged and opened the closet door. "But I'm talking like Honduras or someplace like that."

I flipped the light switch and watched as Tabor looked through the items we had at our disposal. None of it was great and most of it needed updating, but the kids rarely complained. The grant money we'd received over the school year had been used to buy activity sets and supplies for a classroom that had gone unused the year before. We hadn't received much, but we were grateful just the same.

"It looks like you could use a lot of," he looked around and back at me, "well, everything."

"Pretty much," I sighed.

I walked over to the tattered equipment that had been donated to the school. Some of it looked like it had been around since the Reagan administration, but the kids never seemed to mind. I started picking up cones, bats, basketballs, and other odd pieces to inspect their shelf life when I felt Tabor watching me. I was too nervous to actually look and verify my suspicions, so I kept moving around, losing track of what I was doing.

He was beginning to have a way with distracting me—something I liked and hated.

"You really love what you do, don't you?" he asked from behind me.

I turned to face him and nodded. "These are some of the most amazing kids. They don't have much, and the school isn't able to offer much, but they have big dreams. I want them to have every chance of seeing them become reality."

Tabor strolled to where I stood and glanced at the soccer ball in my hands. It was worn and the stitching looked as if one more kick would shred it, but I held onto it for dear life.

I swallowed and tried to ignore the way my pulse accelerated, rapidly beating inside my chest and leaving me flushed. "I was lucky growing up. I had parents that were able to let me try whatever I wanted, and a school that had the means to encourage my dreams. This school might not have much, but it does have an army of teachers that would do anything for these kids."

Tabor reached for the ball in my hands, his fingers igniting a trail of goose bumps over my skin. He took the soccer ball out of my hands and put it back on the shelf. My hands were empty and I tried to keep myself from wringing them.

"That sounds pretty damn good to me," he said, lifting my chin so our eyes met.

"What's that?"

"A teacher who cares."

"You think?"

He nodded once and lowered his face so his lips were inches away from mine.

"I know," he said and sealed those words with a kiss that I felt all the way to my toes. I wrapped my arms around his neck as he wrapped his arm around my waist. It felt so cliché to be making out in a closet at school, but it was officially summer break and no one was there that day.

Tabor made me want things, things that I had never really considered, and it scared me. If he had been a regular guy and I'd felt about him the way I did, I would have been ecstatic. But he was so much more than a regular guy, and I was intimidated by what came as part of the package.

I slowed the kiss to give myself space and hopefully return to the task at hand, but damn if I didn't want to continue kissing him. Those full lips and deep hazel eyes could hypnotize me without my consent. I wasn't *that* girl, and yet, it appeared I *was*.

"Tabor," I murmured against his mouth as we parted.

"Don't think about it," he pleaded, as if he could read my mind. "It's just me."

"But you come with a lot," I admitted. I hated my own

indecisiveness on the situation. I could only imagine what was going through his mind, because mine was a muddled mess.

"And like I said, we'll take this at whatever pace you want," he said, brushing his thumb softly against my cheek.

"Let's start with friends?" I almost whispered, shocked that *that* was the offer I was putting on the table. My heart wanted to give it a try, but my stupid head seemed to be in control.

There was no denying the disappointment that flashed in his eyes, and regret flooded my veins. But I was too stubborn to take it back, to tell him what I really wanted. And Tabor was too much of a gentleman to push me into something I wasn't ready for.

"If that's what you want," he said quietly.

I nodded, unable to say anything else past the lump that formed in my throat. I don't think I had ever experienced such disappointment as I had in that moment. And then he placed one last chaste kiss to my temple before giving me some much-needed space. As he let go of my hand he stood next to me, staring at the shelves in front of us.

"I really like you, Tabor. A lot. And I *do* want to get to know you," I said before chancing a glimpse at him.

"Good." He smirked, not looking at me. "When I told Abbi about you, she said you sounded too good to be true. Maybe you are."

"You know, my sister would like you, too," I scoffed nervously.

He turned to face me, with wide eyes and his charming smile. "Is that your way of inviting me to dinner at your parents'?" he teased and my cheeks flamed hot.

"I…didn't…I mean," I stammered.

"I accept," he answered before I could argue and turned back to the shelves. "Let's start making that list."

"Well played, Mr. Hunter," I quipped. "Well played."

CHAPTER 11

DANI

"We need to talk," I said to my parents, taking a seat across from them in the living room of my childhood home. Dad closed his eyes briefly, as if preparing for the worst, and Mom's chin lifted slightly, making her appear stoic. I almost laughed when Dad reached over to Mom's hand and squeezed.

"What is it, baby?" Mom finally asked, her voice shaking slightly. "Are you sick?"

"No, of course not," I answered sympathetically. It wasn't something I had considered they would assume, and I realized I'd planned the reveal poorly.

"I met someone," I started out slowly. It was a delicate situation that needed to be handled as such.

"Is *she* good to you?" Dad asked sweetly.

I sat wide-eyed, unable to speak for a moment before I burst out laughing. Tears were streaming down my face as my parents exchanged confused looks and glanced at me again. All I could do was laugh and shake my head, adding to the confusion.

"I'm not coming out, Dad," I said through my laughter. "But it's nice to know I'd have your support if I was."

Mom's eyes narrowed slightly and she studied me while I tried to rein in my laughter. "Okay, you're not sick and you're not a lesbian...so why is this a conversation that requires us to sit down?"

"I just needed to tell you in person—and for the record, it's a guy," I said. "But there's more."

"You're scaring me," Mom finally admitted. "Are you pregnant?"

"No!" I laughed again. "Jeez, Mom! Will you let me get this out?"

I took a few deep breaths and sobered. My parents were growing impatient with me, and I closed my eyes in anticipation of what was to come. I exhaled and looked at both of them before speaking.

"His name is Tabor. But people around here just know him as JT Hunter."

Mom and Dad looked at each other and remained quiet for a second before rolling their eyes and sitting back in their seats.

"Tessa, can you believe this?" Dad asked Mom and then looked at me. "Did Gracie put you up to this? Do you even know who that is?" Dad teased and patted Mom's knee.

I sat in front of them quietly while they debated back and forth how I came up with the scheme. I was mildly amused, but also offended. Did they think it was out of the realm of possibility?

Probably.

Hell, I thought so too, until it happened.

"I know who he is," I finally said. "And for some crazy-ass reason, he likes me."

"Of course he does," Dad placated. "Are you hungry?" He stood up and walked to the kitchen with Mom hot on his heels. The child in me wanted to jump up and down in protest, but it would get me nowhere.

"You don't believe me," I said, walking after them.

"Honey, you hate football," he argued as he grabbed a beer from the fridge.

"Why does everyone keep saying that? I don't hate football, I just don't follow or worship it like you people do."

"Sundays are reserved for two things in this house," Mom said.

"I know—church and football," I finished as I rolled my eyes.

"Church and family," she corrected. "Your dad adds football, but it's a distant third to the others." She kissed my cheek and continued scurrying about the kitchen.

"So what brings you by on a Thursday?" Dad asked, as if he hadn't heard me moments ago.

I pulled out my phone and found a picture I had asked Tabor to take with me while we were at the school. I wasn't sure he still wanted to hang out when I put the *F* word out there. But then he made me fall for him a little more when he told me *"I'd rather have you as a friend than nothing at all."* It took every ounce of willpower not to throw myself at him and beg for a redo.

But if Tabor was really going to meet my family, I needed to prepare them. Anticipating their disbelief, I had come prepared. Luckily, Tabor had obliged, and I was glad to have the picture. He said that he abhorred "selfies," but willingly gave in when I explained.

"Dad—who is this?" I asked, handing him my phone.

He glanced at the screen and gave it back to me before looking at the kitchen television. I waited for recognition to hit him, and when it did, I didn't bother stifling my laughter. He turned to face me and looked at the device in my hand and back to me.

"Why do you have a picture with JT Hunter?"

"His name is Tabor," I answered.

"That's JT Hunter," he repeated, more for himself than for me.

"Yes."

"And you," he added, as if I didn't know.

"Yes."

"Dani…why are you with JT Hunter?"

"We're sort of friends," I answered with a small smile.

Dad snatched the phone from my hand and studied the image, and looked at me again in disbelief. Mom walked over to look at the picture too and grinned her approval.

"You….and…him. JT Hunter?" he questioned.

"Me. And Tabor," I corrected. "Look, he's just a regular guy," I regurgitated the lines my friends had spewed while trying to convince me to date Tabor.

"You're dating JT Hunter," he clarified. "My daughter is dating JT Hunter? But…how?"

"We're friends, Dad. Just friends," I defended. Admitting the truth out loud was like a punch to the gut and I hated it.

I began by telling Dad the true story of the flat tire.

"*He* was the stranger you mentioned?" he asked with a confused look.

"You knew about this?" Mom asked him, but he shook his head and she looked at me for answers.

"I didn't know who he was. He pulled over to help me and asked me out on a date. He was so nice and I just gave him my number," I admitted.

Mom's dreamy look likely matched my own, but then again, Dad looked like he might have a bigger crush on Tabor than I did. He sat back in his chair, winded, looking like he'd run a triathlon.

"Are you okay?" I finally asked.

"I always knew he was good guy," Dad beamed. "And now my daughter is dating him?"

"Friends," I repeated. I knew it was something I was going to remind him of again and again, and every time I did, it was going to sting a little. I looked up to the ceiling, bracing myself for the next hurdle. I took a deep, steadying breath and bit my lip before speaking.

"Which brings me back to your question about why I'm here. I...sort of invited him over for dinner tomorrow night," I admitted.

Mom's back went rigid and I knew she'd heard me. It was only a matter of time until she lost her mind and ran around frantically.

"JT Hunter is coming here?" Dad asked. "Dani, if you're joking with me, I might die of a broken heart."

"Mom. Dad. I'm serious, you have to treat him like any other guy," I demanded. "Tabor is really sweet and we're still getting to know each other. I just need you to be cool. Can you do that?"

The kitchen faucet was running, but Mom hadn't moved since I'd mentioned Tabor being a guest. I walked over and shut the water off for her and leaned my back against the counter to see her face.

"You okay?" I asked, taking in her shocked state. Mom was always prepared and readily opened the home to anyone and everyone, but I knew I'd thrown her for a loop. "Mom?"

"Tomorrow?" she finally asked as she turned to face me.

"You're bringing him here tomorrow and I'm just finding out about this now?"

I wrapped an arm around her shoulder and gave her a squeeze as I kissed her cheek.

"If it makes you feel any better, it was his idea. Not mine."

She turned to face me and crossed her arms over her chest. I knew that stance. It was the interrogator coming out, and as much as I wished I were prepared for the inquisition, there was never really a way *to* prepare.

"You're telling me you just met him the other day?"

"Yes."

"And you're already bringing him over to meet your family?"

"Yes. But honestly, I think he's sort of homesick or something."

"What's really going on between you two?" she asked, concern lacing her tone. She reached for my hand and gave it a squeeze. "You like him, don't you?"

"He's a nice guy," I answered nonchalantly. "We're friends."

"If you say 'friends' one more time, maybe I'll believe you." She smirked.

"We had a date and we really hit it off, but I can't be that girl," I said, thinking about that evening. I walked around the counter and sat on the barstool across from my mom and waited. I knew it was coming—the motherly advice.

"I guess I'm confused," she said, resting her forearms on the counter. "You can't be that girl that meets a nice man? You can't be that girl who gets to know him? Or you can't be that girl who discovers that he might be the one?"

"Are you crazy?" I scoffed and leaned back in my seat. "I just met the guy, like a week ago. Don't go marrying me off just yet."

"At your pace, you're never getting down the aisle, because you won't open the damn door. That's a great way to meet someone, Dani."

My temper was beginning to flare, but I knew she was just being Mom. She always had my best interests at heart, but she didn't know what it was like. I had barely experienced the Tabor Circus, and it was crazy enough. If I could just date Tabor, the guy who changed my tire, sure—it would be a no-brainer. But he'd said so himself: he couldn't separate the two.

"Is it okay if he comes with me tomorrow night?" I asked. "Or should I tell him that someone's sick?"

"Neil, are you sick?"

"Nope," he answered quickly. "Are you sick, honey?"

"Can't say I am." She grinned at my dad.

I rolled my eyes and smiled. "You just want to meet JT Hunter."

I stood up to grab my things so I could get home. I had things I needed to take care of, and mentally preparing to bring Tabor around my family was one of them.

"No," Dad spoke up, his eyes still trained on the TV. "We want to meet this Tabor person who seems to have you acting like a scared little girl."

"Goodnight," I called out, ignoring his comment, though it hit a little closer to the truth than I let on.

The entire drive home, I kept thinking about Tabor and the way he'd looked at me when I'd told him I could only offer him friendship. It was possibly the worst lie I'd ever told, and I sold it with such conviction that he didn't seem to notice.

The rest of the afternoon with Tabor had been spent taking inventory of what we had, and making a wish list of what we needed. It had been on the tip of my tongue to say something, but I hadn't. And the few times that his arm brushed against mine while we were working, all I'd wanted to do was take it back and kiss him. At one point, I could feel his eyes on me while he was standing near the door, but I'd refused to look at him because the moment I had, I would have lost all my resolve.

He had been so patient and sweet while we worked tirelessly for two hours. When it was time to put everything away, we'd looked at the list...the very long list. Tabor wrapped one arm around my shoulder in a friendly embrace and given me a squeeze. I leaned my head into his chest and closed my eyes as I breathed him in.

Before I knew it, I was pulling into my driveway and wondering how I'd gotten there. Thanks to my Tabor-induced daydream, I was filled with regret once again, and eager to see him the next night. I pulled out my phone and sent him a text.

Me: Dinner at 6. Still on?

He didn't respond right away, so I gathered my things and went inside to change my clothes. I was in the middle of washing my face when a text came through, and I was happy to see it was him.

Tabor: Yes. I'll pick you up at 5:30.
Me: I'll pick you up.

I almost added a smiley face, but I didn't want to be too flirtatious.

Tabor: You don't know where I live
Me: Then I guess you need to give me your address.
Tabor: 1701 Greenbriar Ave

I set my phone down and finished getting ready for bed. When I was finally able to settle in for the night, exhaustion took over and I tried to succumb to it. But as soon as my eyes closed, Tabor was all I could see, and I wanted so much for my reality to be different.

Tabor: I was hoping to see you today

I was grinning like a teenager at his text.

Me: Oh yeah? Why?
Tabor: Dani…I thought you said you don't fish.
Me: Touché
Tabor: J/K
Me: Are you flirting with me?
Tabor: When have I NOT flirted with you?
Me: Can I ask you a question?
Tabor: Should I call?
Me: Okay

I answered the phone on the first ring and found myself

adjusting my clothes as if he could see me. He made me nervous in the best possible way, and yet it terrified me.

"So what do you want to ask me?" he said, his deep voice making me turn to mush.

"I've been thinking about this dating stuff," I admitted.

"And…"

"How does that whole thing work out? I mean, if we're trying to keep it secret and all, does that just mean lots of quiet nights in, just the two of us? I mean, we can't really go anywhere because people know you *everywhere*," I admitted.

"Do they?" Tabor challenged good-naturedly.

"Tabor, I was at the grocery store last night and wherever I looked, you were there," I laughed. "How did I not notice those ads before?"

His response was so perfect that I found it hard not to cave right then and there. "Because you weren't looking for JT Hunter."

I smiled and leaned against my headboard. What he said was the truth. Plain and simple. "I guess you're right."

"I know you're apprehensive about whatever this could be between us, but I'm not."

"How are you so sure?" I asked. "What makes you think I'm worth the effort?"

"What makes you think you're not?" he lobbed back.

"I think I might like you, Tabor," I said, despite my efforts to keep the word vomit from escaping.

"Good," he answered.

"I'll see you tomorrow," I said quietly, embarrassed at my earlier admission.

"Looking forward to it," he said. I began to hang up the phone when I heard him call my name.

"Yeah?" I asked.

"Can you send me that picture of us?"

I began laughing, because it was like pulling teeth to get him to take it in the first place. But I liked that he wanted it too, because when I looked at it, I couldn't help but smile.

"I think you like me, too," I teased.

"I thought that was pretty obvious," he answered without skipping a beat. "Goodnight, Dani."

"Goodnight," I said before hanging up.

I found the image of the two of us and sent it over, but kept staring at it with a smile on my face. I took the opportunity to really look at him and admire his physique. It was obvious that he worked out—hell, he was a football player. Even though his size was intimidating, he was nothing more than a teddy bear. I closed the image and was about to set my phone on the nightstand when it buzzed, alerting me to a text.

Tabor: Cute couple ;)

CHAPTER 12

DANI

The entire day, all I could think about was the evening ahead.

That and Tabor's use of the word "couple" to describe us. I hadn't committed to that title, or even dating, though I felt like I was close to caving. But those were put on the back burner to the questions plaguing me.

Are my parents going to act weird?
What are the chances they embarrass me?
Will Tabor behave?

I knew the answer to at least two of those questions, but the last one, I just needed to see how it played out. I texted my mom and told her we might be a little late because I wasn't sure where Tabor's house was. Since he was a famous athlete, I figured it would have been in a gated community with armed guards and the promise to give up your firstborn. At least that's the way everyone made it sound.

But as I turned down his street, I was pleasantly surprised. Modest but lovely homes lined both sides of the street, with trees all over the place. It was almost too picturesque, with dads playing catch with their kids in the lawn while other children ran between yards. I smiled, remembering my own childhood when Grace and I would run wildly all over the neighborhood.

My phone speaking directions dragged me back to the present. "The destination is on your right. 1701 Greenbriar Avenue."

I looked for the house and noticed a large home set back away from the street. It was a sprawling landscape with huge trees and modest gardens. I wondered if Tabor actually maintained them himself, or if he had a crew. Knowing who he was, it was hard to picture the man gardening, or pushing a lawn mower around. Not because he didn't seem the type to do it, but because he was larger than life in San Diego. Celebrities don't attend to their own personal stuff.

At least that's what I figured. But then again, Tabor, the athlete—*the celebrity*—had gotten dirty and changed my tire for me. So who was I to judge?

I pulled into the long driveway and leaned forward in my seat to take in the expanse of the home. It was larger than the home I grew up in, but not nearly as large as I thought people would assume he'd own.

I got out of my car and closed the door behind me. As I made my way up the sidewalk, butterflies began swimming in my stomach, causing me to exhale loudly to calm my nerves.

"Friends," I muttered to myself over and over. If I said it enough, maybe I'd believe it.

I lifted my fist to knock on the door, only to have it open before I could even make a sound. In front of me stood an overdressed Tabor. He took in my worn, fitted jeans, white T-shirt, and Converse, quickly realizing his mistake.

"You better come in." He grinned, stepping aside to let me pass.

He was wearing dress slacks and a button-down shirt, looking very much like he had on our date. He was very sexy, and would be *very* out of place dressed like that.

"Sorry," I chuckled. "You look nice, but yeah, a little overdressed."

"You think?" he said sarcastically.

"What made you think it was something to get dressed up

for?"

"I don't know," he laughed, disappearing around the corner.

I stayed in the entry until he peeked around.

"C'mere."

I followed his path and walked into a modern, beautiful kitchen.

"Nice digs," I teased, waving my hand at the state-of-the-art appliances. "Do you actually use this or is it for looks?"

He looked around, and when his eyes met mine he flashed me that adorable grin of his and I returned it easily.

"When I was drafted, my mom and Abbi flew out to help me find a place to live. Actually, I was burned out on day one, so I gave them the reins and this is what they found."

"You still didn't answer the question." I raised a brow.

"I didn't realize you really wanted an answer," he said. "But yeah, I'm actually a good cook."

"Okay," I said, throwing my hands up in surrender. "I believe you."

I looked at the time on the oven and he followed my gaze. "I'll just be a minute." He walked around the corner and called out, "Make yourself at home. There're drinks in the fridge, and the living room is across the hall."

When he was gone, I stood in the room feeling oddly comfortable in his place. I went into the living room, stepping onto the hardwood floors, and the first thing I noticed was how plain his walls were. Despite the few feminine touches, *hopefully done by his mom and sister*, the place screamed "bachelor pad." I leaned against the wide threshold, taking it all in, when I heard him walking back.

His cargo shorts were hung low on his hips and he was in the middle of pulling the shirt on, giving me front row seats to the gun show. And the abs show. And the holy shit he's ripped show.

I swallowed thickly, trying to avoid eye contact, but he'd already caught me looking. And if he didn't, he'd know by the redness in my face.

"I like your...couch," I said, pointing over my shoulder.

"Thanks."

Tabor walked toward me and I stood up straighter and raised my chin. He was close enough that I could reach out and touch him, but far enough that I could still breathe. Just his proximity had my pulse racing. When he stepped closer, my breath hitched and I noticed that he clenched his jaw.

"You know…you could use, your walls…" He stepped closer and I stammered through the rest of the sentence. "…they're plain."

Tabor nodded, remaining quiet as he stepped closer.

"Just some pictures," I whispered. "Or a clock."

He lowered his face, his lips dangerously close to finding their destination, and I was torn. Our breaths mingled in the space between us and I felt my resolve deteriorating. In that moment, the battle was over and I was about to give in as his breath tickled my ear.

"So what did your parents say?" he asked as his lips grazed my earlobe.

"About?" I mumbled.

"Us."

His one-word answer made my legs feel heavy and numb—not the response I expected.

"Us?" I repeated before reality smacked me in the gut.

There is no us.

"I told them we're friends," I answered, feeling disappointment wash over me at the words.

"Friends," he repeated, nodding his head. "I guess I was just hoping…" He trailed off.

"Hoping what?" I asked, a little too eager, even though I knew the answer.

He looked down at his watch. "Hey, we better go."

Tabor retreated across the hallway to the kitchen, the moment between us long gone.

Idiot! That was your chance, I mentally scolded.

I walked to the front door where Tabor joined me, wishing I could rewind ten minutes just to have all of those feelings again.

"Ready?" he asked cheerfully, as if completely unaffected by what had happened. I wasn't able to say anything, fearful my voice would crack with disappointment, so I nodded and walked out the door.

***

"Fair warning, my parents might freak out," I told him as we turned down the street. "I told them to act like you were any other guy, but I apologize in advance if my dad cries. He's a big fan."

"Are you sure it's okay that I'm here?" He smirked.

"I think Dad would disown me if I didn't bring you." I grinned. "Besides, you're old news."

Despite the pushes from my friends and family, I was still not prepared to take the leap with Tabor. And the almost-kiss would go down as one of my regrets. I'd kissed him already. I knew what I was missing. He hadn't pushed too hard since I'd said the dreaded F-word, and that both relieved and disappointed me.

Tabor insisted on bringing a bottle of wine, even though it wasn't necessary. There was no arguing with him, so I let it go. We met at the front of my car and walked the short distance to the front door, which Mom opened before we had a chance to knock.

"You're finally here," Mom gushed, waving us inside.

"Mom, Dad, this is Tabor," I said, stepping aside.

"Tabor, this is Tessa and Neil—my parents. And Grace is probably somewhere inside with Trevor and my niece, Cleo."

I had begged Grace to play it cool and not make a big deal about Tabor, but I saw her trying too hard sitting on the couch with Trevor next to her. Her leg was bouncing nervously and her toothy smile made her look creepy. Still beautiful, but creepy nonetheless.

"It's a pleasure to meet you," Tabor smiled, shaking my parents' hands. "Oh, I brought this for you."

He handed Mom the bottle of wine and she looked from Tabor to me with an impassive mask on her face.

"Dani, didn't you tell him that we don't drink in this house?"

I bit my lip, watching his reaction to the news, as if he'd just been told he smelled like shit. He looked down at me and Mom and I both burst into laughter.

"I'm just kidding."

Tabor's nervous laugh was the sweetest thing I'd heard all day, but his unease vanished quickly as he followed my dad inside.

"Ignore her," he scolded playfully. "She thinks she's funny."

"Dani laughed," Mom defended.

"You should have seen the look on your face," I said behind Tabor.

"Are you sure you want to be friends with this one?" Dad challenged, nudging his thumb in my direction.

Tabor looked over his shoulder, his eyes locking with mine. "No sir, I don't. But I'm not going anywhere."

I felt lightheaded at his words, my stomach flipping in a million different directions. He winked and turned around to follow my dad back into the living room, leaving me standing still. Mom walked past me, bumping my shoulder on her way, acknowledging the moment.

***

The initial awe of JT Hunter wore off after about an hour of "what's so-and-so like," followed up by a short round of "have you met this guy?" It was pretty impressive to watch Tabor handle the questions and not miss a beat. He was charming and sweet, and everyone quickly realized what I already had: he was just a really great guy.

My brother-in-law Trevor worked as a realtor and discussed the housing market, something that seemed to interest Tabor. The three men congregated around the grill, drinking beer and laughing at whatever lame jokes my dad managed to tell. Dad was cooking the burgers while Mom and Grace chatted inside.

And where was I? I was a floater.

I stayed with my niece, Cleo, who needed constant supervision. But my ears were alert, waiting for anything that might give me some insight into Tabor's life. I'm sure he would have told me anything I asked, but I was looking for some imperfection to justify my friend logic.

"Jeez, Dani," Grace gushed, interrupting my inspection of Tabor. "The way he looks at you...damn. It's no secret he likes you."

"No—especially since he told me so himself," I said to a squealing Grace.

"Then what are you waiting for?"

"Gracie, I don't know what to do. I told him that I'm not ready for his fandom."

"Then throw him back and let some other lucky girl have a chance at catching him," she teased. But when she saw the look on my face she quieted her voice. "Holy shit, you *do* like him—I mean, like-like him, and you want to date him. Don't you?"

"He's so sweet and funny. I like talking to him and spending time with him," I admitted.

"Then you should tell him that, sweetie," Mom said, joining the conversation.

"I just need a little time," I said truthfully.

Mom wrapped me in a hug and kissed my temple. "What happened to my daughter who isn't scared of anything? Have you seen her?"

"I'm right here, Mom," Grace waved. "But sadly, I'm already taken."

"You wish," I muttered.

"Then go get your man," Grace challenged.

I narrowed my eyes and wrinkled my nose before turning my back and heading outside to join my company. Dad and Trevor walked past me with the platter of burgers as they went inside. Cleo came running out the door with her doll, throwing herself against my leg while Tabor looked on. I'd never met anyone famous and wondered if they were all as down to earth as he was, or was he some sort of anomaly. It's funny—as a kid, you imagine your heroes being larger than life, and though Tabor wasn't a hero of mine in the traditional sense, he was still larger than life.

"How old is she?" he asked, walking over and squatting in front of Cleo.

"Fifteen months, I think," I answered, trying to recall the last month Grace had mentioned. I never understood the months-versus-year thing. "She turned one a few months ago."

"C'mere, Cleo," Tabor said sweetly.

She looked up at him and giggled, but clung to me as if her life depended on it.

"I hear ya, kid," I muttered.

Tabor was in front of her with his arms outstretched, but she was hesitant to take the leap.

He started making some weird sound, and she was intrigued enough to leave my leg and toddle over to him. Tabor hoisted her up in the air and started playing with her, causing her to laugh. She melted into a puddle of goo, so I stood up and walked over to the pair and kissed Cleo's cheek.

"Sellout," I muttered into her ear.

Cleo ignored me, opting instead to shower Tabor with all of her affection. He walked down the few steps to the grass, set her down, and followed behind as she ran around. She made it a habit of falling down and then laughing until he picked her up again.

He sat down on the grass and Cleo started using him as a human jungle gym, and he obliged. Tabor's hands were ready to catch her if she fell the short distance, and my heart began to warm.

"You're good with her."

Is that the sound of my biological clock actually *ticking? Down, girl!*

"Kids are easy," he answered.

"You think?"

"Well, I can't speak from a parent's perspective, but yeah. Kids are real. They don't know how to be fake."

"Yeah. I guess so."

"Hell—" He covered his mouth and grinned. "Sorry. *Heck,* I'm sure you know that from your program."

I nodded and walked over to sit next to him. Cleo ran into my arms and I fell back with her so that she was on top of me. I raised her in the air and moved her around in my arms, pretending she was an airplane, and then I set her so down so she was straddling my stomach. Before I could register the action, Tabor leaned down and kissed me. It wasn't passionate, but it was exactly the type of kiss to make me question the friends thing. He stood up and Cleo raised her arms in the air, so he picked her up and I quickly got to my feet as he walked away with her in his arms.

Tabor looked over his shoulder at me and smirked. "It's the adults you have to worry about."

CHAPTER 13

TABOR

For the rest of the night, all I could think about was that kiss. It wasn't the first time I'd kissed her, but this one was in the open where anyone in her family could have seen it. She was nervous about entering my life and what my sister dubbed the *JT Hunter Circus*. What Dani saw as an obstacle, I saw as a glimpse into who she was, and I liked it.

As we left the Miners' house, I said goodbye to her family and stifled my laughter when I spotted her dad giving her a thumbs-up. Her cheeks burned red and she shooed him off as she tried to get her poker face on. I had some work ahead of me with Dani, but something told me she was worth the effort.

She gave me a sideways glance when I asked if she'd let me drive her Bel Air. It was a nice car, and despite her reluctance, she gave in. Inside I was content knowing that she seemed to trust me.

As we made our way back to my place, I could feel her eyes on me. And all I could think about was the kiss I'd given her. I knew it had been ballsy, but I couldn't stop myself from doing it either. Seeing her with Cleo and laughing so freely had tugged at something inside me.

"Can you come inside for minute?" I asked as we pulled into my driveway.

"I should really get home," she said, opening the passenger door and shutting it behind her. We were standing in front of the car and I cocked my head to the side, gauging her mood.

"Ten minutes," I said, watching as she debated. "Please?"

We were in a silent standoff, me smirking and her with a furrowed brow. I wished like hell I could read her mind.

"What was that kiss about earlier?" she finally asked.

"Wait…do friends not kiss?" I asked, feigning shock.

"Not in my experience," she answered humorously.

"Look, please Dani, just come inside for a minute."

I reached out for her hand and she allowed me to guide her down the path that led to my back door. I still hadn't said anything and it began to feel awkward between us. I thought it would be easier to talk, and yet I found myself staring at her as if *she* was the one who asked to come in.

"So why did you want me to come inside?" she asked quietly.

Dani looked calm, crossing her arms over her chest, but it wasn't convincing. As I rested my arms on the countertop in front of me, I knew that she was someone worth putting myself out there for. We were separated by the massive granite island in the center and she looked grateful for the barrier.

I grabbed two beers and handed one to her, standing in front of her, but giving her enough space to think. She smiled nervously as she took a sip of her beer. I watched her run her finger along the condensation on the bottle, nervously avoiding me.

"So you kissed me earlier," she said casually, but kept her eyes on the beer label that she had started peeling off.

"Yeah. And if I recall, you kissed me back."

She shifted uncomfortably and brought her eyes to mine, a look of determination flooding her. "I didn't."

"Why are you lying?" I took a swig of beer and raised a brow.

"I'm not," she started to object, as she leaned back against the counter behind her. But I suppose it was farther than she realized because she stumbled backward. I stepped forward and reached out, catching her elbow, and held on until she stabilized. "Lying," she finished.

When I released Dani's arm, I brushed a stray hair from her face. Her body shivered as my fingers grazed her cheek.

"Why are you so adamant that we shouldn't at least try?"

"Why are you so adamant that we should?"

"Because...why not?"

It wasn't a sound argument, but with Dani mere inches away, it seemed good enough and she seemed to believe it too. She sighed and closed her eyes briefly before our eyes locked again.

"What is it you're so scared about?" I cocked my head to the side, genuinely intrigued by her reasoning.

"I hate that word," she huffed. "It's a helpless word...a weak word."

"I don't know you very well, but from what I've seen so far, you are neither helpless or weak."

"Honestly, I'm just not sure it's the right time for me to get involved with someone."

"With someone? Or with me?"

"Tabor," she started, but I interrupted.

"I have women sending me private messages, nude pictures, and throwing themselves at me," I told her, shaking my head as the words came out. "They have no idea who I am, they just want a piece of me because I'm relevant at the moment. How are you any different? You're holding who I am *against* me, just like it's a selling point for them. I *want* to get to know you. I don't care about the shit they do. I'm not stupid, I know what they're after. You can say whatever you want, but I know you like me, too. So if you're not scared, what is it?"

"Are you always so cocky?"

"When I know I'm right, I am."

Dani shook her head and set the beer down, bracing her hands on the granite behind her as she looked into my eyes. "What makes you so sure you're right?"

I didn't answer right away, instead setting my own beer down and sauntering the few steps it took to stand in front of her. I rested my hands on either side of her body, pinning her in, but leaned down to look into her eyes. As I began to speak, I wanted her to know every word coming from me was truth.

"Because, when I saw you the other day fixing your tire, you agreed to a date. Because you kissed me the other night and I know you felt something. Because you told your friends about me. Because whenever we're together, I can see it in your eyes," I said with a smirk. "Do I need to go on?"

Dani shook her head slowly, knowing I was right. Every bit of it. I'd put my cards on the table and wanted to get to know her, but she was the one who was slowing the pace.

"What if it doesn't work?"

"What if it does?" I fired back. "We may find out we have nothing in common and maybe we really are better off as friends. But the way I see it, we won't know until we try."

I leaned forward so I was close enough to smell her hair as she continued to talk.

"But I still don't want everyone to know—at least not yet. I'd like to keep this between us and the few people that know, because I like my privacy."

"Something else I like about you," I said, moving my lips to her cheek.

I leaned back and watched as her eyes fluttered closed. She slowly opened them and took a deep breath, but when she spoke I knew the game was over.

"What else do you like about me?" she asked, grinning up at me.

I leaned in and kissed her pink, full lips. "The first thing I liked, was how messy you were trying to change that damn tire," I said, kissing the corner of her mouth.

"And second?" she asked breathily.

"That you didn't seem impressed by me," I chuckled, kissing her cheek.

"I'm not." She laughed softly before closing her eyes as I trailed more kisses along her jaw. "What else?"

"You're not trying too hard," I answered, kissing just below her ear.

"You're just a guy," she murmured, unable to speak in her normal voice as I kissed her neck.

I brought my forehead to hers and closed my eyes. My arm was wrapped around her waist and I gently pulled her against me. Dani's hands were braced on my arms and I didn't want her to let go.

"That's right," I said as I stood up to my full height. "I'm just a guy. Take away the endorsements, agents, and teammates, and I'm just like any other guy."

She snaked her arm around my neck and pulled me to her,

finally kissing me the way I had hoped. Dani was one of the few women I'd met that I wanted to spend time getting to know, and I wanted her to feel the same.

Dani pulled away, ending the kiss, and narrowed her eyes playfully. "I hope you're not like any other guy. I'm going out on a limb here because I think you might be unlike anyone I've met before...all that stuff you mentioned aside. So don't break me. Okay?"

Those words held so much vulnerability in them, because this was her way of letting me know that she wanted to try. So I did the only thing I could think of: I kissed her—promising, with my touch, that I would do everything in my power not to hurt her. Because she deserved my best.

My free hand traveled up her back until it tangled in her hair, holding her to me. Her body responded to my touch and her soft moans as she let her guard down were all I wanted.

I released her from my arms as she separated from my lips, even though it was that last thing I wanted. We were breathing heavily, and as she took a step back I watched the beauty that was Dani Miner. She smiled up at me and I couldn't help but return it with my own when I saw her cheeks flush.

"I should go," she said hesitantly, but I got the feeling she wanted to stay. "You probably have a lot going on tomorrow."

I reached for her hand and smiled. "I have a late appointment, so no need to rush out...unless you want to go."

"I don't."

I grabbed our beers with my free hand and nodded my head toward the living room.

"Where are we going?" she asked, chuckling behind me.

"Thought maybe we can watch a movie or something."

"Or something?" she teased. "Smooth, Tabor."

"That's not what I meant, but I like where your mind is going," I answered quickly before walking toward the leather couch.

She watched as I tossed several pillows onto the floor. Abbi and Mom went overboard in decorating, despite my argument that men don't care about pillows.

When the space was cleared, I sat down in the spot I'd worn from my vegging and reclined the seat back. I patted the open spot next to me and casually draped my arm across the back.

Dani was still standing off to the side as I turned on the TV and began flipping channels, glancing in her direction a couple of times.

"I won't bite," I said teasingly as I patted the seat again.

"Good to know," she shot back. "I'm just waiting to see what you pick before I make the commitment."

I turned away, smirking and shaking my head, never stopping on any channel. I liked the playfulness in our banter. Dani had a dry personality, but that was something that made me laugh. It was hard to tell when she was serious or joking, and that kept me guessing. Every once in a while, I'd pause on a channel only to change it again.

She finally walked over and joined me on the couch, and when she did I dropped my arm over her shoulder as if she'd always been there. I handed her the remote and laughed at her reaction.

"Wow. You play well with others?" she asked, feigning shock before handing it back to me. "You pick."

"All right." I shrugged, flipping the channel a few more times before stopping and angling my body toward her. "It's too much pressure," I laughed.

"No movies then," she said, turning to face me so she could see my face. My finger ran lazy circles on her upper arm and I noticed a shiver as she tried to hide her reaction.

"Okay." I smirked, leaning in to kiss her, but she pressed her hand over my mouth.

"Not that either," she said. She gave a mocking scold and grinned. "Tell me something about you that most people don't know."

I leaned back and looked at the ceiling as I considered her question.

"I don't really like talking to people," I admitted.

Dani's face scrunched in confusion and I smiled, shaking my head.

"I like people. But I've never been completely at ease in front of a crowd. I hate press conferences, but we are obligated to do them after a game."

"Why do you hate it so much?" she asked.

I inhaled loudly and cleared my throat. "I don't *hate* it, but when I was a kid, I had a bit of a stutter. I was teased when I was in first grade by the other kids and I just got to the point where I so was embarrassed that I finally stopped talking altogether."

"Really? But I haven't heard you stutter," she observed, and she wasn't wrong.

"Remember how I said my mom was a teacher?"

She nodded and I continued.

"She worked at a different school from where Abbi and I went. The speech pathologist at her school was supposed to be the best in the area, so Mom moved us there. I was in speech therapy until I was in fifth grade."

"So you don't stutter anymore," she clarified.

"I still have my moments, but for the most part, I'm good. But that's why I hate talking to people, or in public," I said. "What about you?"

"I don't stutter," she quipped with a wink.

"Not that. Tell me something other people don't know about you," I prodded.

Dani looked deep in thought and I figured she was going to reveal a secret tattoo or odd piercing. But when she began speaking, I knew it was something deep and personal.

"You know, I've had a pretty easy, uneventful life. But my senior year in college, I started seeing someone. It was casual at first—no commitment—and we didn't get serious until I graduated. Everyone loved him. My roommates thought he was perfect. He was cute and funny, nice—only he wasn't like that when we were alone. He could be rude, mean, and terribly inconsiderate. We were together longer than we should have been, and I ended it when he hit me for the second time."

She said her words as if they had no effect on her. I suppose she had time to get over it and move on. But my entire body burned with a rage that I only felt on the gridiron, and it was a terrifying feeling. My hand that had been touching her froze, unable to do anything at all.

"And your friends did nothing?" I seethed, disgusted that no one helped her.

"They didn't know," she admitted. "I was always the quiet one of my roommates and I was too embarrassed to tell them I'd let it happen. So they were disappointed when we broke up."

"Why do they think you dumped him?" I asked, still pained at her admission.

She shrugged. "To focus on work. I didn't want to chance falling back into a relationship like that, so haven't dated for about a year. The girls keep trying to set me up, and I always have an excuse."

I felt my nostrils flare as I exhaled in an attempt to quell the anger inside. I gently pulled Dani to me so she was curved into my side, wrapping an arm securely around her. Her head was leaned against my chest, and knowing that she was in my arms was the only thing to settle my erratic heartbeat. She wrapped her arm around my waist and squeezed until I relaxed.

"I'm sorry you went through that," I admitted, kissing the top of her head.

"I've never told anyone that," she finally said. "Never."

"Why didn't you turn him in?" I asked. "Did you ever see him again?"

She pulled away slightly and looked up at me. "I just wanted him to stay away from me. I told him if he ever came near me again, I had pictures that I would take to the police."

"And that was enough to keep him away, huh?" I asked.

"Pretty much," she yawned through her words. "I saw him in passing a time or two and avoided him."

"What else do you want to know?" I asked, rubbing my hand up and down her arm. I could tell by the dismissive way she spoke that she didn't want to continue talking about the abusive asshole ex, so I changed the subject.

"What's your family like?" she asked, sounding miles away as her voice quieted.

"They're great," I started. "Similar to your family…I liked them, by the way."

"Me, too," she muttered sleepily and I chuckled.

"My dad was the best, but after he died, Mom had to take on the role of both. She never dated, just gave Abbi and me all of her attention. I don't think I'd be where I am today without her."

"That's nice," she responded quietly. Sleep was taking over, I could tell, but I didn't want to wake her and I didn't want her to leave.

"Would she approve?" she asked, soft and distant.

I didn't answer right away, because a cute snore escaped and I squeezed her softly to me.

"She would approve, Dani," I answered quietly, kissing the top of her head. "She just wants me to be happy."

I reached behind me and pulled a blanket from the back of the couch, laying it over both of us. Having Dani in my arms felt right; it was where she belonged. The thought should have alarmed me, but it didn't. I'd go at whatever pace she wanted to convince her that there was something happening between us.

I rested my cheek against her head as her breathing lulled me into my own peaceful sleep.

"Tabor," a whisper called out in the darkness.

"Hm?" I muttered groggily.

"I should…" she began to say, but I held her firmly in my grasp until she quieted.

My eyes were closed and I thought she was asleep until I felt her inching up further on the section of the recliner we shared. Dani placed a kiss against my neck.

"Thank you," she whispered before snuggling closer to me.

"'Night, baby," I whispered, kissing the top of her head without thinking.

My eyes shot open at the words and I worried that she'd freak out. But Dani didn't flinch or question the sentiment, instead curling into me.

It was the best sleep I'd had in a long time.

Because Dani was in my arms.

CHAPTER 14

DANI

After the night at my parents' house, Tabor and I spent as much time together as we could. It had been a month since we'd decided to make it official, dating in secret, but it worked.

He was busy making the rounds through his foundation, visiting sick kids and funding programs similar to mine. I was never one to pay attention to the news, but I found myself tuning in to catch glimpses of him in that world.

It wasn't something I did often, because that was the persona. I wanted the guy.

I had spent much of my day organizing the new equipment provided to us by Hunter's Heroes. My principal was excited that we had received the funding and commended me on the success. The goal was to have the program run year-round, for those kids who didn't have any place to go in the summer.

It was a long and exhausting day, and I was grateful for the volunteers who had shown up to help. When I got home, I showered and heated up some leftovers, taking them and a glass of wine to the couch. I flipped on the evening news, wondering if I'd see Tabor's face there because he'd been off doing his thing all day.

Reports of accidents, domestic violence, and politics led the news and I cringed. As a teacher, I should've been eager to stay current on all things news, but the human in me grew tired and sad by the constant bleak outlook. I muted it and opted to check my email instead.

When the sports highlights came on, I quickly turned up the volume and watched as if my existence depended on it. It reminded me of my dad and I laughed at the thought.

A video showing Tabor with a group of kids hanging all over him led the segment and I smiled at his comfort with them. He was a natural leader, and everyone rallied around his civic efforts.

"JT," a reporter asked while he was hanging out with a group of kids.

He looked up at the reporter and smiled before giving his attention back to the kids.

"There's a rumor going around that you're dating a swimsuit model."

I knew he was with me, but still there was an ache in my heart at the suggestion that he was with someone else—let alone a swimsuit model. I waited with bated breath for his response as he paused for an answer. During the last week, we had been debating about taking our relationship public. He wanted people to know about me and insisted it could be as subtle as us going out to dinner. But I was dragging my feet, wanting to remain in our bubble a little longer.

As he was opening his mouth to answer, Tabor was interrupted by one of the kids with him.

"You have a girlfriend?" a little girl asked with wide eyes before breaking out into giggles.

Tabor squatted down and whispered something in her ear, making her laugh even more. She gripped her stomach and drew the attention of the others around her. She said something to a few of the other kids, who started laughing as well while he watched with amusement.

How can I not fall for the guy? He is perfect.

"What's so funny?" the reporter asked hopefully.

Tabor looked at him and shook his head. "Inside joke."

"So are the rumors true?" the annoying man pushed.

"Today is about these kids here. They're amazing, right?"

Tabor countered, taking the attention off of his love life.

The reporter looked as though he'd been sucker punched and fumbled over his words. "Yeah...no, you're right. These are great kids."

Tabor barely spared the guy another glance, focusing on the tiny humans around him.

"How do you think the Quakes are going to do this year?" another reporter asked.

Tabor appeared to like that question better and shrugged. "We have a great team and coaching staff. We'll just have to see how everything pans out."

"Are you ready for training camp?"

He laughed and shook his head. "I still have a couple of weeks left, guys. Besides, I'm having too much fun with these kids here."

The story ended and Tabor gave a wave to the reporters before going back inside with the kids that surrounded him, shouting more of their own questions at him.

There was a knock at my door and I knew it was him. We'd agreed to see each other that night because his mom and sister were supposed to visit for the weekend and he wasn't sure how much I'd see of him.

It was strange to think that Tabor was the same guy everyone in the city admired—though it was easy to see why.

I opened the door and raised an eyebrow, blocking his entrance. "So who are you dating?"

He stepped closer and wrapped his arm around my waist, kissing me senseless.

"Good answer." I grinned, finally allowing him to enter.

"So you saw that, huh?"

"What model are you supposedly dating?" I asked nonchalantly, though I had to admit there was a bit of jealousy swarming in the pit of my stomach. But it was hidden well.

"Candayce Evans posted something on Instagram about an upcoming photoshoot we have," he said, following me into the living room.

Yeah. Full-on green-eyed monster threatened to emerge and I fought to keep her at bay. I took a deep breath and sat down, reaching for my glass of wine.

"Where's the shoot?" I asked, impressed with my impassive tone.

"PB. Next weekend," he said.

Pacific Beach! Where everyone can see you two all cozy?

It was on the tip of my tongue to shout that very thing at him, but I couldn't. It was my idea to keep this thing between us a "secret."

"You can come if you want," he said, laying my legs over his lap and pressing his lips to my neck. "I can tell them you're my PA."

"Very funny," I snorted, taking a leisurely sip of my wine.

"Why not?" he asked, not letting me off the hook.

"You can't be serious." I rolled my eyes and watched his smile disappear.

"You're not worried, are you?"

"No," I lied.

"Dani." He said my name as if he were talking to a petulant child, and didn't continue until I looked at him. "When you lie, your lips do this thing…like they're doing right now."

"Don't act like you know my quirks." I forced out a laugh.

"I just thought maybe we could go and hang out afterward…in public."

"I think I'd rather not witness some gorgeous bombshell hanging all over you," I admitted. In that one statement, I felt like I set the entire feminist movement back years. But I didn't care. I needed to be honest. "Besides, I think I have something going on."

"Yeah," he laughed. "With me. Remember? Last week I asked you if you wanted to go to Wilson's house with me."

"Shit," I muttered.

"Yep," he laughed. "You're free. So what do you say?"

"I really don't want to," I said, "but if I have to cut a bitch I'm going to blame you."

"Aren't you tired of being here or at my place all the time?" he asked.

"We've gone to my parents' and Millie's house," I said.

He pulled me up so that I was straddling him and held my face in his hands. He brought my lips to his and kissed me. My arguments faded as I surrendered to his grasp, loving the way he tasted. Tabor's hand trailed down my back, resting against my waist. When we separated, he looked into my eyes, my hands braced against his pecs, and I tried to decipher what was going through his mind.

I knew the *one* thing he was thinking about, but sex was something I had taken off the table. I needed to get to know him and the thing was, the more I learned, the more I loved. I'd know when the time was right with Tabor, and I wanted to make sure we knew what we were getting into.

"Please come with me to the shoot?" he pleaded and all I could do was nod.

***

"Call you when I get home," Tabor promised as he stepped outside.

I loved our goodnight kisses. They were filled with so much promise and I fell for him a little more every time.

"I—" It was on the tip of my tongue and I almost choked on the words that tried to escape, but I covered quickly. "I was just going to say drive safe."

After another quick peck, I watched as his form retreated to his waiting SUV.

"Shit," I muttered to myself, waving as he drove away.

I closed the door and found my phone that was charging in the kitchen. Millie had texted, and instead of answering, I dialed her number and waited for her to answer.

"I almost told him I loved him," I admitted when she finally answered.

"Really?" she asked, stunned. "Is that how you feel?"

I closed my eyes and swallowed hard. "Yes."

Millie squealed over the phone and I heard her telling Nick, who let out an *un*enthusiastic "yay."

"So why don't you tell him?" she asked.

"It's too soon, Mill. It's barely been a month," I said.

"So?"

"What do you mean, *so*? It'll freak him out."

"How do you know?" she asked.

"I just know. Hell, I'm the one who feels it and *I'm* freaked out."

"You're ridiculous." Millie snorted. "What if he feels the same way?"

"What if he doesn't?" I said aloud, realizing that that scared me more than admitting it for myself.

"Let me ask you this: do you see a future with him?"

"I think so."

"Do you want to continue spending time with someone who doesn't feel the same way? Or at least isn't moving in that direction?"

"I guess not," I answered weakly.

"Do us all a favor and think about it. Where do you see this thing going? Is Tabor the one you want to be with in the end?"

"Millie, you're talking big words here to someone who's still trying to accept that she almost said something she can barely admit to herself."

"Think about it," she said. "And then call me tomorrow when you figure it out."

"Yeah," I muttered. "Okay."

We ended the call and I was left to my own thoughts, which were screaming too many things to put in order. I knew that Tabor wanted me; I could see it in his eyes. And even though I felt like his feelings for me were growing, he hadn't admitted it to me. All I could do was assume.

I didn't feel we'd reached the point in our relationship to assess where we thought things were heading. In a couple of weeks he'd be spending his days at training camp—something I was told was rigorous. And in another month he'd be knee-deep in regular season football. I didn't want to add to his stress, not to mention my own. I was still trying to get the after-school program set up for August, and I hadn't even started getting my classroom together.

Even though Tabor was imperfectly perfect and I knew I wanted him, I had to wait. It wasn't the right time to figure all of it out. With or without him.

My phone buzzed in my hand and I felt the butterflies before I answered.

"Hey," I said.

"Hey yourself," Tabor's deep voice rumbled. "Are you okay?"

"Yeah. I'm good. You?"

"I think so," he said before adding, "I'm sorry if you felt pressured to go with me to the shoot. I don't want you doing anything you don't want to do."

My heart swelled and I wished he were there with me so I could kiss him.

"I love…" I said, before panicking, "being with you."

I heard him exhale and sound lighter when he said, "Me too."

I was smiling from ear to ear and I knew I was feeling the real thing. "So if you want me there, I'll be there."

"I want you," he said and then laughed. "There."

"Cute," I answered.

"You know, Dani, one of these days we're going to have to admit what's happening here."

"And that is?" I wanted him to admit whatever it was before me.

"That you're falling for me," he answered as if he simply knew this to be true. Honestly, it freaked me out that he said it so casually, because it completely shook me up.

"Don't confuse me with your groupies." The moment the words came out I winced, because it sounded so much crueler than the playful way I'd intended it.

"Play it that way if you want, but I think we both know it's true," he said.

"I was kidding," I said, closing my eyes and wishing I could take the words back. Tabor had never treated me like I was anything other than someone special, and I was throwing accusations at him so heartlessly.

I felt as if my insides had been sliced open without my knowledge, exposing every thought, feeling, and fear for everyone to see. Tabor knew what I felt for him, but I wasn't sure the feeling was mutual. I hoped it was. I suspected it was. But I wasn't ready to put my heart on the line without some assurance it would be returned.

"This is not a conversation I want to have over the phone," I finally said.

Before I could say anything else, I heard some noise through the phone. "I'm coming back," Tabor said, ending the call before I could argue.

CHAPTER 15

DANI

"What's going on?" I asked when I answered the door.

Tabor's hands were braced on the doorframe and his eyes trailed the length of my body, taking in my T-shirt and cotton shorts that exposed my legs. When his eyes met mine, my stomach swirled, unsure of his reason for rushing over.

"Are you okay?" I asked, breaking the silence.

"I think there's something you want to talk about," he said. "Can I come in?"

No sound came from my mouth. Somehow I'd lost my voice in that moment and all I could do was step aside. I closed the door behind him and rested my head against it, trying to quell my nerves. I took a deep breath and turned around to find him still watching me.

"Want something to drink?" I took a couple of steps, only to realize that he wasn't budging.

Tabor stood with his arms crossed over his chest, straining his shirt across his arms.

"Okay…should we go to the living room?"

"What conversation do we need to have, Dani?" Tabor sighed and looked nervous as he gauged my mood. "Are we breaking up?"

"What! Wait…what are you talking about?"

"You said you didn't want to do it over the phone, so I came back. I was hoping we could talk it out."

I closed my eyes and took a deep breath. Breaking up wasn't on my radar, and the fact that he thought that's where my head was made me feel like a jerk. I was messing the whole thing up.

I stepped around him and he followed me into the living room, sitting on the end of the couch. I took the seat farthest from him, needing the space. My wine from earlier had grown warm, but I swallowed the last of it anyway. The TV was on and still muted, offering a distraction.

"Break up," I repeated before looking at him. "Why would I want to do that?"

"I don't know, you just sounded so serious."

"I thought you knew."

"What am I supposed to know? If you don't want to break up, can you tell me what's going on?"

"I'm an idiot," I said.

"No you're not. C'mere," he said, reaching for my hand.

The living room was dark, only the TV and the kitchen light illuminating the space. I scoffed. "You come over here."

He wasted no time in bridging that gap, taking my legs across his lap as he had done earlier. His thumb was brushing over my shin while his other hand found mine.

"What's going on?" he asked.

"First off, I don't want to break up," I said.

His lips pressed to mine and I was thankful for the distraction. I ran my hand to his neck, pulling him closer to me. Tabor deepened the kiss, running his hand up my thigh. We continued kissing in the darkness and my heart thumped in my chest. I leaned up and moved, placing my legs on either side of his, knowing what I wanted.

I reached down, pulling his shirt over his head, and tossed it to the floor. His hands traveled beneath my shirt, his palms pressing against my bare skin.

My heart was pounding so hard and fast that I wondered if he felt it too. I placed my hand over his heart and kissed him one last time before pulling away. Tabor wrapped his hand over mine and I knew he was watching me as I stared where we joined on his chest.

I could hear the blood rushing and pounding in my ears, the

room feeling like a sauna.

Say it.

"We don't have to do—"

I put my other hand over his mouth and shook my head.

Say it.

He kissed the palm of my hand and I softly ran it over his jaw.

"I'm scared," I whispered, unsure if I'd said it loud enough. I stared at his lips, unable to meet his eyes.

"I'm not going to hurt you," he answered back and I shook my head.

"That's not what I'm scared of. I've been hurt and I've survived."

"Then what are you afraid of?"

"What I feel for you."

"What's that?"

"I can't say it," I said, fear lacing my voice.

"Why not?"

"Because it's been a long time."

"Say it, Dani," he pleaded.

"Why? It might ruin everything."

"Or maybe it won't."

"I've never said it to someone first," I admitted.

He knew what I wanted to say, that much was clear. Why he wanted me to say it so badly was beyond me.

"Look at me," he commanded. When my eyes met his, the light reflected in his that I'd come to know so well, I had no choice.

"I love you," I said, as if it were my last breath. I felt like my world was spinning in that instant. If I hadn't been in Tabor's arms, I probably would have passed out from the sheer weight of those three words.

Lucky for me, I *was* in his arms, and he pulled me closer, pressing his mouth to mine. My lips parted, our tongues grazing and exploring. I held his face in my hand, kissing him with every bit of love I could muster. Saying the words had freed me, allowing me to open up to him the way I wanted, and he hadn't rejected me or laughed in my face.

Abruptly, Tabor's hands gripped my shoulders, separating our lips and placing distance between us. I wasn't sure what was happening, but I was embarrassed as I began to second-guess myself.

"Hold on," he said, our shaky breaths beginning to normalize. He moved me off his lap and paced the room, placing his hands behind his head.

I couldn't help it, I felt like a fool. I'd exposed my heart, and though I didn't regret it, it hurt like hell to see his reaction. I wanted to curl into myself and hug my knees to my chest while I waited for his words, but I refused to show weakness. He walked over and sat on the coffee table in front of me.

"Dani," he said, reaching for me.

"It's okay, Tabor," I said, fighting off a wave of tears. I was thankful for the dark, and hoped he didn't see the wetness creeping its way to the surface. "It really is."

"No, it's not," he said.

"You don't have to say anything."

Please. Just stop. Walk out the door and leave me with my dignity.

He huffed a laugh and reached out for me. I wanted to slap him. How could he laugh at me?

"You don't understand," he said, entwining out fingers. "This is all wrong."

"What is?"

"This. Right now. All of it."

"Let's just call it a day and talk tomorrow," I offered, needing the space.

"Fuck," he muttered. "I fucked this all up."

"It's fine. Really," I said, mustering up all my conviction to sell it.

"Let me start over," he said, inching toward the edge of the table, closer to me. "I love you, too. And I should have said it back as soon as you said it, because I feel the same way. God, Dani. I love you so fucking hard that I think I must be crazy."

I was stunned into silence and he continued.

"I didn't want you to think I was saying it just because you said it, or to get you into bed…"

I leaned forward and silenced him with a kiss.

"I love you, Tabor," I whispered against his lips before planting another kiss on him.

My fingers grabbed hold of his shoulders, pulling him to me on the couch. His bare chest rested against mine I wanted to shed the clothing between us.

"Shirt," I muttered, hoping he'd take care of it for me. And with one fluid movement my shirt was removed, tossed somewhere on the floor along with his. My shorts offered little in the way of modesty, but I didn't care. Tabor's free hand trailed along the elastic waistband, stopping at the small of my back.

"Wait," I murmured against his lips, placing small kisses as we slowed. He shifted his weight on his elbow, almost falling off the couch, causing me to laugh. "This isn't going to work."

"I think you're right," he laughed, sitting up and pulling me with him. He kissed the tip of my nose sweetly and reached down for his discarded shirt. I scrunched my forehead and watched as he began turning the shirt right-side out. I grabbed it from his hand and tossed it to the floor where it belonged, and he looked from the floor and back to me.

"Upstairs," I said, standing up and grabbing his hand. It took him less than a second to realize what I was saying before falling in behind me. As I got to the first step, I turned and faced him, enjoying that we were at eye level.

"You're so beautiful," he said, looking into my eyes.

"Please don't break my heart," I warned.

"I'm pretty sure it goes both ways, baby."

I nodded in understanding and wrapped my arms around his neck, kissing him again. I loved the feeling of his skin beneath my hands, and I wanted more.

"Are we doing this right here?" he asked between kisses. "Because I don't care where it happens."

I moved away and darted up the stairs, disappearing into my room to the right. I stripped off my shorts, tossing them into the hallway so he could see them, leaving me in nothing but my black bra and panties. I heard his feet racing up the stairs and I stood waiting for him as he entered my room.

Tabor looked like he was about to pounce, and I smirked as his shadow loomed in the threshold. He sauntered toward me until he was up against my body. His hand ran up my back and tangled in my hair as I raised my face to his. He dropped his mouth to mine, devouring me as my fingers unbuttoned his shorts.

He was stunning to look at, but knowing his heart and that it belonged to me made him so much more amazing. I briefly closed my eyes and thanked God for bringing this man into my life, because I couldn't recall a time when I'd been happier.

I sat down on my bed and pushed myself up to the pillows, waiting for him. My entire body buzzed in anticipation of what was about to happen between us, and I was more than ready. I loved this man and though I was glad he'd said it too, somewhere deep inside, I knew he'd felt it before he said the words.

His knee pressed into the mattress, his weight shifting the bed. Slowly, like a lithe animal, he crawled onto the bed until he was positioned over me. The only things separating us were insignificant pieces of material that might as well have been cinderblocks.

"Tabor," I whispered, feeling warmth throughout my body. I reached up and stroked the side of his face, needing to touch him in some way. "I'm a virgin."

His entire body stiffened and the air shifted. "What?"

The silence settled between us and I burst into laughter.

"I'm kidding," I laughed. "That's not what I was going to say, but I couldn't pass it up."

"So not the time for jokes," he chuckled before kissing me.

"No?"

"No."

"Sorry," I murmured into his mouth. "I'll make it up to you."

"Promise?" he asked seductively.

"Promise," I whispered as his body sunk onto mine. "But Tabor..." I tugged on his boxers. "We need to take these off."

Before I registered the action, he'd taken them off and managed to remove my lace panties as his hand skimmed my thigh. Tabor's lips trailed a line of kisses up my stomach, causing it to clench in anticipation. I was about to make love to him, and for some reason I wasn't self-conscious at all. We loved each other, and that was all I needed to know. The time was right. For us.

His hand skirted along my side, causing me to squirm beneath him. As he made his way up my body, his finger ran along the edge of my bra and stopped at the strap where he slid it off. His kisses ignited a fire inside of me that I was ready to douse, though a slow burn was acceptable.

"Are you sure?" he asked once more.

I grabbed his face and put everything into that kiss, telling him, without a doubt, what it was that I wanted.

Only. Him.

CHAPTER 16

DANI

I couldn't stop messing with my hair.
Up?
Down?
Flatten it?

What will Tabor's mom like?

The thought had plagued me all day and I was nervous that I wouldn't make the cut. Of course she had to be the most amazing person on the planet. Tabor made that very clear. His mom was the sun and the moon and everything in between…though I doubted she was actually a saint.

I'd been introduced to plenty of mothers in my time.

Okay….one. But still, she had thought I was too good for her son. She told me so herself.

But Tabor was a different beast. I wondered if his mom was the protective type who thought no woman was ever good enough for her "little" boy.

When I asked Tabor to tell me something about her, the recurring theme was that she had done everything for him. Hell, the woman sounded like a superhero—a thought that was both sweet and scary as hell.

I looked at my reflection in the mirror and squared my shoulders, mustering the confidence I knew was hidden in there somewhere.

Simple. A ponytail and neutral makeup.

I knew that it didn't matter what I did—she would either like me or hate me as soon as we were introduced. Meeting a boyfriend's family had never been as important as it was that day, because by then I could admit I was completely, madly, crazy in love with Tabor. The tough part would be explaining to others that it had nothing to do with "who" he was to everyone else. It was "who" he was to me that counted.

Tabor walked into the bathroom and wrapped his arms around me from behind, joining me to stare at our reflections. He kissed the side of my neck and smiled. "You look beautiful."

My cheeks flushed at his compliment and he lightly squeezed me against him.

"Do you think your mom and sister will like me?" I asked, hating the nervousness in my voice.

He took a deep breath, his face impassive as he exhaled. "If they don't, I'm gonna have to stop seeing you."

It felt like the blood was draining from my body and I wanted to vomit. I nodded slowly, understanding what he was telling me when he laughed and turned me to face him. His hands cupped my cheeks and he placed a chaste kiss to my lips.

"They're going to love you, Dani. And even if they don't, I do. Just be you, and they'll see why I've fallen for you."

It was hard not to smile when he complimented me so sweetly. My heart was an easy thing to sway when it came to Tabor. Unfortunately, my mind wasn't as easy to convince. While I hoped what he said was true, a larger part knew how moms were about their sons.

I'd heard Millie say numerous times that no one would ever be good enough for her Colton. And he wasn't even a year old!

I wrapped my arms around his neck and looked into his eyes, searching for the truth. If he was lying, I couldn't tell, so I gave up and decided that it was possible I was worried for no reason.

"You just better hope they don't like me more," I said, adding a wink.

"God, I love you," he said, kissing me again.

"What time will they be here?"

It was the first time I'd stayed at Tabor's place since we had admitted how we felt about each other, but I felt as if I belonged. I didn't want his mom or his sister to get the wrong idea, but then again, how could they not?

"Any minute. The driver called and they're less than ten minutes away," he said before kissing me again and letting me go. "You look good."

I did a little turn and ended with a pose, showing off my fitted button-down blouse and denim shorts. I wanted to look like I hadn't tried too hard, even though it took me easily an hour to select the perfect outfit.

Tabor glanced at his phone screen and raised a brow. "We have some time."

I stepped closer to him and wrapped my arms around his neck. "You think?"

"I know," he said, kissing me between the words. Just when I was ready to give in, the doorbell rang and I stepped back.

"Quickest ten minutes I've ever heard of," I noted.

He looked at his phone again and winced. "Yeah, I guess I didn't see when the text was sent."

"Raincheck?"

He pulled me against him and kissed me, letting me know that he intended to collect.

"Let's go," he said, inclining his head in that direction.

"Okay."

We walked down the hallway hand in hand, only to see his mom and sister already standing at the entrance, waiting for us near the bottom of the stairs.

"Hey, Mom," he said, smiling widely. He dropped my hand and embraced her with such love and affection that it made *me* smile. "Hey, Abs."

They exchanged pleasantries and then his sister nudged his arm and looked at me. I ran my hands along my sides, finally settling them in my back pockets where they wouldn't flail and make me look weird.

"Oh shit." He winced and jogged over, walking me the rest of the way down. "Mom. Abbi," he started, and wrapped his arm around my waist. "This is Dani Miner."

"Hi," I said, sticking my hand out as he continued.

"My girlfriend," he said unexpectedly.

My world seemed to pause on that simple announcement. Even though I considered him my boyfriend, it wasn't something I'd said out loud because we had yet to label or discuss it. But there he was, laying it all out there for the two most important women in his world.

"It's nice to meet you, Dani," his mom said sweetly. "I'm Tabor's mom, but you can call me Marta."

"Hi, Marta, it's so nice to meet you. Tabor's said nothing but wonderful things about you both," I said, reaching out to shake Abbi and Marta's hands.

"Now I know you're lying," Abbi snorted. "Tabor never says anything good about me."

She playfully hit at his stomach and he wrapped her into a single-arm hug.

"Let's go sit down," he said, dragging Abbi into the living room.

I started to follow when Marta reached out and touched my arm loosely, holding me back.

"Let's just give them a second to catch up." She smiled sweetly. "I've heard a lot about you."

"Ah, Tabor bragged about saving the damsel in distress," I joked, but went silent when she shook her head.

"No. He told me about the strong-willed woman who had no clue who he was."

"Really?

"Yeah."

"He's a great guy," I complimented.

"He is," she agreed. She cocked her head to the side and crossed her arms. "Did you really not know who he was?"

Her tone wasn't accusatory, but I could tell that it was something she found hard to believe.

"Mrs. Hunter…" I paused and shook my head. "My sister had to tell me that Tabor and JT Hunter were the same person. That's how oblivious I am to all things football."

She gently wrapped an arm about my shoulder and squeezed. "I'm glad. He's had a run of women chasing after him on name alone, so I'm afraid my son has been more than a little gun-shy when it comes to dating."

"I can imagine," I said. "You must be so proud of him."

"I am." She smiled.

"Can I ask you something?"

"Sure."

"Where did you get the name Tabor?"

"Funny story, actually. I met my husband at a concert when I was eighteen. I can't tell you the names of any of the bands that played, but I can tell you exactly what Paul was wearing when I first spotted him. We went on a few dates and he said that it was his dream to play in a band someday."

"Was he a musician?" I asked.

"No," Marta said, laughing softly. "He couldn't carry a tune to save his life and tried to play just about every instrument. Never had the gift. So when we found out that we were pregnant, he said if he had a son, he hoped he'd grow up to be a rock star so he could live out his dreams through his boy."

"That's sweet," I said.

"Yeah, except when it came time to choose a name, we agreed on Jordan right away, but the middle name was a constant battle. He said he'd heard the name Tabor somewhere and that it meant drummer. The man practically begged me to allow it."

"And you gave in," I observed, smiling at Tabor as he talked with Abbi.

"Only after making a list of my own demands—like nightly foot massages for a year, and I would get to select all future baby names."

"Nice."

"Yeah, except we later heard that Tabor also meant *loser*," she laughed. "His sister had a field day when she found that one out."

Abbi heard that last part because she started laughing as Tabor put his head down in defeat, shaking his head.

"Thanks, Mom," he said.

"She asked me a question, what was I supposed to say?"

"You could have just left it at what Dad thought the name meant," he huffed. He was outnumbered and he knew it, though it appeared the teasing was par for the course with the Hunters.

"Where's the fun in that?" Abbi asked, winking at me and laughing.

I excused myself to give them some time to visit and allow me to get some air into my lungs. It felt as if I'd been holding my breath, waiting for them to be tacky or rude. But they were far from either of those. Abbi seemed like someone I would have been friends with, regardless of meeting Tabor. And Marta was one of those ladies who was genuinely nice all the way to her core, and it was pretty amazing.

***

"So is it serious?" I heard Abbi ask as I made my way back to the living room.

I shouldn't have stopped, but I knew they were talking about me and my curiosity got the best of me.

"I think so," he answered and I smiled. "But there is this *one* thing."

A shock ran up my spine and I cocked my head to the side to get a better listen. I knew I'd regret hearing whatever he was about to say, but I just couldn't seem to walk away.

"What's that?" Abbi asked.

"She doesn't like football," he said, growing silent.

"Yeah, so what's the big deal?" she asked.

I leaned my back against the wall and found myself disappointed. I knew the sport was a huge part of his life, but knowing it was a tick against me hurt. I took a deep breath and prepared myself to enter the living room, but when I turned, Tabor was standing right in front me with that all-knowing smirk.

"I saw your shadow," he said, raising an eyebrow. He tilted his head toward the living room and I followed to see Abbi chuckling as she patted the seat next to her.

"I like you," she said. "Besides, you have no idea how weird this one got over you."

"Abbi," he said, trying to remain straight-faced. "I'll disown you."

"What are you talking about?" I asked, angling my body to face her.

"He was all awkward and stuff. And then he said that he introduced himself as Tabor and I died laughing," she said. "Loser."

"There went the expensive flowers you wanted for your wedding," Tabor teased.

Abbi narrowed her eyes, clearly not concerned by the threat, and nudged my arm. "And then he went all girl on me. '*When should I call her?*' I don't think I've ever been so embarrassed to be his sister, and trust me, he's done some crazy shit."

"That's it, wedding's canceled," he laughed, his eyes crinkling at the corners. "You suck."

"Hey, you're giving her a hard time, I figure it's only fair to level the playing field," Abbi defended. Then she turned back to me and sarcastically added, "A field is what Tabor plays football on."

I rolled my eyes and laughed. "I *know* what football is, I just don't watch it."

"If it wasn't for this one, I wouldn't watch either," she said, nodding her head at Tabor.

"Does your family like football?" Marta asked.

"They do. In fact, I'm convinced I was switched at birth because that's just one of the things I don't have in common with them," I joked.

"Yeah, but she does have their sense of humor," Tabor admitted. "Good people."

I smiled and nodded, agreeing.

***

"It was so nice meeting you both," I gushed as I grabbed my purse and walked to the front door.

Marta hugged me to her and squeezed gently. "Take care of my boy, okay?"

"Yes ma'am," I said, returning the hug.

"But don't kiss his ass," Abbi said good-naturedly.

"I'll keep that in mind," I said. "I hope I get to see you both before you leave."

"I'm sure we will," Marta said. "Be safe."

Tabor threaded his fingers with mine as we walked to the front door. I hated to leave him, but I wanted to give him space. When we stepped onto the front porch, he looked down at me and lifted my chin so we were looking at each other.

"Told you they'd love you," he said.

"They're really great, Tabor."

"You know you don't have to leave." He pulled my body against his, relaxing into me. "I want you to stay."

"I'd love to. But you need to be with your family."

"I *need* to be with you," he shot back.

"Go inside. Call me later."

"Yeah," he muttered and kissed my cheek. "Okay."

He walked me out to my car and opened the door but didn't shut it. Instead, he draped his arm over it and gazed down at me.

"Text me when you get home?"

I nodded and turned the key in the ignition after he shut the door. He squatted next to the door and tapped on the window so I rolled it down.

"Yeah?"

He wagged his finger, beckoning me closer, so I did as requested and willingly accepted his final kiss of the night. He ran his knuckles along my jaw and his lips quirked into a smile.

"Goodnight," he said.

"G'night," I answered, watching as he started walking away.

I threw the car into reverse but when he called my name I stopped.

"I love you," he said with a smile. My heartbeat increased every time I heard those words come out of his mouth.

"I love you back."

CHAPTER 17

DANI

I didn't plan on going back to Tabor's house the next day, but he insisted that his mom and sister wanted me around. Marta and Abbi proved to be as charming and entertaining as Tabor. Their closeness wasn't contrived or superficial; it was real and sweet. I felt at ease with all three of them because they were so similar to my own family. I found myself joining in on the banter the more comfortable I became.

When I asked Abbi about her fiancé Marshall and how they met, she looked at Tabor and scoffed. "Didn't tell Dani about the blind date from hell, huh?"

"He failed to mention that," I remarked. "Do tell."

Abbi scooted forward as if she was letting me in on a big secret. "It was the blind date from hell," she whispered before bursting into laughter.

Tabor laughed and I looked between the two of them, waiting for the punch line, but it became clear that there wasn't one.

"Abbi was set up by Tabor's old girlfriend," Marta explained, much to my horror. I knew there were others, but I didn't want to *know* about them. "Tabor and Jenny were on and off for years during college, and when he was drafted—they were off. But when she heard Tabor was coming home for the weekend she

133

'accidentally' ran into Abbi."

"Yeah, on purpose," Abbi interjected. "She did the old 'whoops, I didn't see you there' when I was at the coffee shop. Chick nearly made me spill hot coffee on myself."

"So what happened?"

"Jenny happened," Tabor pointed out. "She was always good at getting people to talk, and she'd pick the bits of info that would benefit her."

"Yeah, like when I mentioned I was single, I swear, her ears perked up like a rabid dog. She was practically drooling at that bit of information," Abbi laughed. "She suddenly remembered this friend of hers that just got out of a relationship and he was ready to get back out there."

"But there was a stipulation," Marta said.

"And that was?"

"Dear, sweet Jenny was worried about this friend Max and didn't want to abandon him."

"And you went out with him why?" The words flew out of my mouth before I could stop them and I slapped my hand over it, completely mortified.

"That's what I asked when Abbi called me," Tabor said, patting my leg. "But she insisted that Jenny was up to something and she wanted to catch her in a lie. So she agreed to the date."

"Yeah, and she was uncomfortable about being the third wheel, so she asked if I thought Tabor would join—just as friends," Abbi mocked, using air quotes.

"So what happened?" The tale was entertaining, but I liked the glimpse into the sibling dynamic they shared.

"Abs told me about her theory, so I went for the show. When we walked up, Jenny was in deep conversation with the friend. She saw me and started smiling and waving at us," he said with a smirk.

"Tabor said hello and Jenny stood up, expecting a hug or something. The look on her face when he just sat down was priceless. I was waiting for her to introduce me, and she was so lost in her own head that she waved at the guy next to her— 'Marshall, this is Abbi.' And the moment the words came out her eyes shot open. 'Marshall Maxwell. I call him Max. Or Marshall.' She was caught in her lie, but she just. Kept. Going," Abbi said as she laughed.

"Marshall actually looked pretty entertained too, because he sat back in his chair sipping his coffee as the crazy Jenny show unfolded," Tabor said.

Marta was shaking her head and chuckling at the story while I looked on, waiting to see how it played out.

"So Tabor looks at Marshall and points at him. 'So how do you know Jenny?' And Marshall just shook his head. 'Just met her five minutes before you two walked in. She was in the middle of begging me to play along with her game.' The look on Jenny's face was perfect," Abbi said through her laughter.

"Turns out, Jenny had been running around telling people that we were still dating and when she found out I was coming home for a visit, she had to do something to make it all believable," Tabor said. "That was the last time I saw her."

"She ran out of there so fast," Abbi said.

"And Marshall?" I asked. He was, after all, the reason for the story.

"I walked over to introduce Tabor and myself and apologize for Jenny and her crap. He was adorably sweet and barely paid any attention to Tabor. And a big selling point, he didn't know who Tabor was." She smiled shyly before narrowing her eyes, a playful gleam in them. "I think you and Marshall have something in common."

"So I left the two lovebirds alone and the rest is history," Tabor finished.

"Not exactly," Abbi interjected. "Because about a week later, Jenny showed up to the same coffee shop and tried to get Marshall to go out with her. I guess it was some sort of payback, but he turned her down and said he was seeing me. Needless to say, she was *not* happy. And word got around what she tried to pull."

"Wow, that's pretty bad," I huffed when the story was done. "When was the last time you saw her?" I asked Marta and Abbi.

"I see her every once in a while at the grocery store, but she practically runs in the other direction," Marta said.

The rest of the evening's conversations were full of stories about Tabor as a kid and how much he and Abbi fought growing up. They were so easy to talk to and made me feel like one of them. It must have been a Hunter family trait. Despite my efforts to give them alone time, they insisted that I go to dinner.

When dinner was over, they suggested we go back to Tabor's for dessert and a movie.

And when the movie ended, they demanded that I stay the night because it was late and staying at his place would be safer.

"Goodnight, you two," Abbi teased. "Just keep in down, will ya? Some of us have a long plane ride tomorrow."

My cheeks burned and if I'd known Abbi a little better, I might have pushed her or come back with something witty. But my mouth was frozen shut and I wanted to die.

"Ignore her," Marta cooed, wrapping me in a warm embrace.

"I have a sister...I know how it goes," I confessed.

"Thank you for loving my boy," she whispered in my ear.

She released me from her hold and gave me a knowing wink, but all I could do was nod lamely.

Walking into Tabor's room felt weird with his family in the house. Nothing was going to happen, but it still felt inappropriate. Tabor tossed me a T-shirt and I scurried off to the bathroom to change my clothes. I pulled the shirt on and it swallowed me up. Of course it did, considering Tabor's size. I laughed and pulled my hair into a ponytail so I could wash my face, and when I looked down I spotted a brand new toothbrush on the side of the sink.

I peeked my head out of the door and saw him reclined on his bed, flipping the channels on his TV.

"Is this for me?" I asked, waving the package in the air.

"Sure is," he said without bothering to see what I was talking about.

I loved that he did this little thing, because it meant so much. Sure, it was just a toothbrush, but it also showed that he cared and he wanted me to be comfortable in his place. And I was.

As I finished getting ready for bed I stared at my reflection, wondering where the time had gone. I'd met Tabor over a month ago, but I felt like I'd known him forever. Despite my comfort with him and his family, I was not so at ease with the sleeping situation. He had undressed into nothing more than boxers and was still channel surfing.

Sleeping at his place the other night had easily been the best sleep I'd ever had. I wasn't sure if it was him or the bed that lulled me into my rest, but I was willing try over and over again until I figured it out.

I turned off the lights and joined Tabor. He inched closer to me, until we were huddled together in the middle of his king-sized bed. My back rested against his chest, the warmth of his skin offering me contentment.

"What are you thinking?" he whispered in my ear.

"Your mom and Abbi are great."

He nuzzled his face into my hair and began kissing my neck, sending chills all the way to my toes. His hand was splayed over my stomach, holding me against him, and my eyes began to flutter closed but I jolted upright.

"What's wrong?" he asked, sitting up next to me.

Tabor's hot breath was tickling my shoulder before he started kissing a trail that had no rhyme or reason. I shook my head, silently telling him to stop, but I didn't really want him to.

"I thought you liked that," he murmured against my ear before kissing my jaw.

"I do," I answered breathlessly. "But your mom…and Abbi…we can't."

I laid back and Tabor leaned over, partially covering me with his body. My hands roved over his body as he began to kiss me. His hand was caressing the side of my face and it was absolutely perfect.

"Mercy," I conceded against his mouth and his soft snicker was my reward before he deepened the kiss.

***

I woke up cradled in Tabor's arms as he slept. He was snoring lightly, his warmth radiating off his body. I tried to free myself so I could get dressed, but he only held me tighter.

"I need to get up," I said, turning to face him.

"No," he mumbled. "Sleep."

"Your mom and sister are leaving in a little bit and *you* have to get ready to go to your friend's house," I said.

"*We* have to get ready," he reminded me, probably knowing that I really hadn't forgotten.

"Okay, so now you really have to let me get up."

I kissed his neck and pushed away so I could move. I threw some water on my face and tried to wipe away the smudged liner and mascara that had escaped their boundaries in my sleep. My clothes were still folded neatly on the countertop and I made quick time of getting them on.

When I emerged from the bathroom I found Tabor sitting on the edge of his bed, stretching and yawning. I averted my eyes because it was like looking into the sun. That and I knew he'd give me a hard time if he caught me checking him out.

"Are you leaving?" he asked, his brows pinched together.

"No, just heading to the kitchen." I smiled. "Join me when you're ready."

"What are you up to?"

"Nothing," I said, adding a wink.

I closed the door quietly behind me, but screamed when I turned around. Abbi was coming from the hall bathroom and had her arms crossed over her chest.

Tabor's steps could be heard from the other side of the door, and when he opened it he looked between Abbi and me, trying to figure out what was going on.

"Sleep good?" Abbi asked and then cringed. "No. Never mind. Forget I asked."

I laughed and looked at Tabor, who was trying not to give her any more ammunition.

"Are you leaving?" she asked, looking me over, ignoring the reason I'd given her.

"Nah, just getting something to drink."

"I'll be there in a few," Tabor said, kissing the tip of my nose before closing his bedroom door.

"You do realize he's completely fallen for you, right?" Abbi said, dropping the volume of her voice to just over a whisper. "I've never seen my brother as happy or at ease with anyone as he is with you."

"Really?" I asked. Because I felt the same way, and it made my heart soar hearing her words.

"Really."

Fifteen minutes later, Marta joined me in the kitchen where I was frying a package of bacon and scrambling eggs. Tabor's fridge was stocked with enough food to feed an army, but watching the way he ate, the army consisted of one—Tabor.

"Dani," she said, standing next to me at the stovetop.

I looked at her and smiled, encouraging her to continue.

"I'm glad the two of you found each other. Tabor's wanted to find someone, but he's never been able to open up because it's too hard. He's been hurt a lot."

I continued stirring the eggs, though I was only going through the motions. I turned the heat down and gave her the attention she deserved, considering she was opening up about her son, the man I loved.

Marta took my hands in hers and looked directly into my eyes. "Be patient with him. He can be stubborn when he thinks he's right, and even worse when he knows he's wrong. But the way he talks about you, I know he's more serious than you realize."

Tabor entered the room and his face-splitting grin was infectious.

"Mom, you cooked for me?"

"That would be the work of your girlfriend." She squeezed my hand and let go before walking over to give her son a hug.

He wrapped his arms around me from behind while I finished getting things together, and kissed my cheek.

"I wanted to make sure everyone ate before you take them to the airport."

"T had to get a driver again," Abbi said, walking into the room and grabbing a piece of bacon.

"You're not taking them?"

"I have to get some things done before we go to Wilson's place."

The Hunters were gathered in the kitchen, filling their plates and talking in nonstop chatter. I wasn't hungry because I had the next hurdle coming up—meeting the friends.

I walked over to Tabor, wrapped my arms around his waist, and looked up at him. "I'll see you in a little bit."

"Okay, babe, I'll walk you out."

Marta pulled me into a hug and squeezed me gently. "It was so wonderful meeting you, Dani."

"You too, Mrs. Hunter."

"Marta. Please." She smiled sweetly. "And I look forward to seeing you again."

Abbi walked over and wrapped an arm around my shoulder. "See you later, *babe*."

We started laughing and she tugged me close for a beat before letting me go.

Tabor escorted me to the front door and kissed me goodbye. He watched until I was in my car and the engine was started before closing the door.

"I'm going to marry that man," I said aloud and snapped my mouth shut.

Talk about putting the cart before the horse.

CHAPTER 18

DANI

"Your mom and Abbi get to the airport okay?" I asked as he walked into my condo.

"Yes, and they asked me to give you this," he said, pulling me into his arms and pressing his lips to mine in a heated kiss.

When we parted I cocked my head to the side and bit my lip. "Your mom and your sister wanted you to give me a kiss?"

"No, I added that," he confessed.

Tabor walked into the living room and sat down on the couch while I grabbed two water bottles from the kitchen.

"What time do we need to leave to get to Wilson's house?"

"You remembered his name? I only mentioned it once," Tabor stated, impressed.

"I'm a teacher," I said. "It's in my DNA."

Tabor took the water bottles from my hands and pulled me onto his lap.

"What you thinking about?" I asked him, wishing I could read his thoughts.

"My mom and Abbi really liked you," he said. "I don't think they've ever taken to someone like they did you."

"I'm glad, because I like them, too."

He was lost in thought, so I lifted his face to look at me,

pressing a chaste kiss to his lips.

"Are you okay?"

"Dani, I've told you how I feel, but this is all so new to me," he said quietly, and I felt the pang of rejection around the corner. I tried to slip off his lap to give me some sort of reprieve, but his hands tightened, holding me in place.

"I understand," I lied. "Really."

Tabor shook his head, uncompromising as he placed his hand to my neck. "I don't think you do. Last night, when Mom and Abbi brought up Jenny, I hadn't thought about her in a long time."

"Are you really talking to me about your ex-girlfriend?" I asked, masking my jealousy…or maybe anger.

"Let me explain," he said and I nodded. He looked adoringly into my eyes before sliding me off his lap and standing up while he paced the living room.

"With Jenny, she saw me in dollar signs and future deals. We met my freshman year and Mom wasn't lying when she said it was an on-and-off relationship. I loved her, I did. I guess that's why I was always willing to give it another shot."

I winced at his admission, though I wasn't angry. I had loved Philip—before he became a monster. Tabor must have seen my reaction because he was on his knees in front of me with his palms against my thighs.

"Keep going," I said, meeting his eyes and giving him a coaxing smile.

"It was always drama and tantrums, but I tried so hard to be what she wanted. I was never going to be good enough. Then I got signed to the Quakes and she showed up out of nowhere, telling me how much she missed me and loved me. She fucked with my head so many times that I wasn't sure if she was the crazy one or if I was."

"Did you give her another chance?"

"I was going to," he admitted. "For some reason I felt *I* owed *her*. Can you believe that? She's the one who bailed on me, but she made me feel like I did something wrong."

"But you didn't."

"I didn't. Because of my mom. She told me that I would get the love that I deserved. And if I stayed with Jenny, I would be getting the love I settled for. And I didn't want to settle."

He looked so boyish and innocent, a far cry from the gladiator people in the city were used to seeing. I felt special that I had a piece of him that others would never know. Tabor was sweet, attentive, gentle, and selfless—all things I'd come to love about him.

"It was almost six months before I told Jenny I loved her, and even then I only said it because I was supposed to. And with you, it's easy. It's almost too easy. Is this how it's supposed to be?" he asked. "I love you, Dani, unlike anyone I've loved before, and that scares me more than anything, more than getting hurt on the field, because you have the power to break me."

"The feeling is mutual, Tabor," I admitted nervously. "I know, when my story is written, you are my happily ever after. How's that for scary?"

"Well, I don't I want a future without you," he answered. I felt as if the air was leaving my lungs. I half expected him to bolt when I told him what I was feeling, but he was in the same boat. That tidbit might have been most terrifying of all. I was envisioning forevers with Tabor after just over a month of being together—that couldn't be normal.

"So where does this leave us?" I asked, leaning forward so I was inches away.

"Here. Now. Together. Does that work for you?" he asked.

"It does," I said, closing my eyes as my stomach flipped. "I just want you. I don't need all the extras, Tabor. Just you."

***

"We're going to be late," I said, frazzled as I adjusted my shirt and fixed my hair.

"Worth it," he said, putting on his shoes.

"Do we need to bring anything to Wilson's?"

"Well, I'm bringing you...so you can bring whatever you want," he teased, brushing my hair aside and kissing my neck.

I swatted his hand away playfully and turned to face him.

"You wanna go again?" he challenged, but I shook my head.

"We need to go. There's fashionably late and then there's just rude," I informed him. "Let's go."

We pulled up to a house that was something I would have expected to see on the *Real Housewives of Fill-in-the-Blank*. Cars that cost more than my condo were lined in the driveway and I felt ill-prepared.

I took for granted how down to earth Tabor was, and didn't consider that his teammates might not be so. Sensing my apprehension, Tabor gripped my hand a little tighter and kissed my temple.

"You look beautiful," he complimented, eyeing me.

My mind instantly flitted to our earlier impromptu make-out session and when my eyes met his, I knew he was thinking the same thing.

"JT," a massively built and attractive man called out from the front door. "Get your ass in here. And bring your lady."

"Wilson?" I asked, nodding at the man.

"Yep."

"Damn," I whispered to Tabor, who leaned in to hear me. "He looks like Idris Elba."

"Who?" he asked, but we were too close for me to repeat the name.

"J…T!" he called out as we walked up the steps. "'Bout damn time."

"Sorry," I said, straight-faced. "It was his fault. He tried on like a dozen outfits before we got here."

"I like her," he said, eyeing Tabor and moving toward me. "You must be the Dani I've heard so much about. I thought you either didn't really exist, or you were a dude."

"I exist," I laughed, "and I am, in fact, a woman."

"So I see." He smiled. "C'mon in and meet everyone. Might as well get it over with."

"That sounds totally intimidating," I remarked with a smile.

Tabor gave me a wink and dropped his hand to the small of my back as he trailed me inside. The warmth of his hand disappeared quickly as he began greeting everyone who congregated in the enormous kitchen.

I thought Tabor's kitchen was big, this one looked like it belonged in a five-star restaurant.

"Everyone, *this* is Dani, JT's girl," Wilson announced.

I laughed at the people and their comments, unsure who was

saying what.

"She exists?"

"Damn, J, how'd you land her?"

"Tell us what you see in him."

Tabor walked over and wrapped his arm at my waist. "You're gonna scare her off."

"She needs to know what she's getting into," a woman's voice said as she walked over to me.

She was stunning.

Her dark hair was pulled back with a headband and her curly ringlets bobbed easily with her steps. Her skin was a creamy cocoa, but it was her light brown eyes that drew attention to her face.

"These guys are ridiculous. You should come outside with me so I can save you the headache." She smiled before giving Tabor a hug and leading me outside.

There were five other women outside by the pool, drinking wine and laughing. It made me miss the times I spent with my roommates, and I made a mental note to call them later.

"Steph, Tawnie, Ericka, and Lisa," she pointed as she said their names, "this is Dani, JT's girlfriend."

"Hi." I waved lamely and looked back at the hostess. "I'm sorry, I didn't catch your name."

The other ladies laughed and I felt foolish, but the woman smiled. "I heard that you're not a football fan…I figured that was a joke, but you're serious."

"Afraid so."

"I'm Deloris Wilson, but everyone calls me Dee," she said, shaking my hand.

Her name echoed in my head for a moment when it dawned on me.

"Dee Wilson, former model and spokesperson for Elemental?" I asked, closing my eyes when I realized I was right. She was one of the top models who'd decided to retire and focus on her family when she got married.

"It's okay, honey. I like that you're new to this world—makes it a little more interesting around here," she teased. "So tell us about you. JT said that you're a teacher?"

"Yeah, I teach history at River Valley."

"Tough school," she said. "How do you like it there?"

"It's really not as bad as everyone makes it out to be," I said, hoping I didn't come off as too defensive. "We have some amazing kids and great teachers. Unfortunately, our campus has become the last chance school for a lot of these kids. But what people don't realize is that our graduation rate has increased over the years, with more of our students going on to finish college."

Dee's eyes were wide and she looked impressed with my information. The other women kept their eyes on Dee, who I assumed was their leader, of sorts. They were waiting for her reaction, and I realized they were little more than lemmings.

"But you don't love your job or anything," she said with a wink and a smile.

I returned the smile and shook my head. "I really do love what I do. My after-school program has been my biggest passion."

"Until JT," she interjected and I laughed.

"Until Ta…JT," I agreed.

"Are you going to the shoot with him tomorrow?"

"He asked me to, but I didn't plan on it."

She offered me a glass of wine and invited me to sit among the other women. Dee didn't say anything, but I could see she was thinking. Steph, Tawnie, Ericka, and Lisa were talking about some new boutique that had opened up, but I couldn't muster the interest to engage in the conversation.

Fortunately, Dee turned to me and began talking.

"Look, Dani, you seem really sweet and I can see JT is happy with you."

"Thanks," I remarked, leery of accepting the compliment. "But?"

"You need to go to that shoot. You are dating *the* star player of the Quakes—and if you tell my husband I said that, I will lie—but you can't just let him wander free. There are women climbing over themselves, probably sacrificing babies, for a chance with JT."

I began laughing, but she gave me a narrowed glance and I realized that she was being honest.

"Wilson and JT joined the team together, so I've known him a while. I've seen how desperate these women are to get a piece of him. It's crazy."

"But we really haven't told people that we're together—my decision, not his—so my being there wouldn't really serve a purpose anyway."

"Trust me when I tell you, you *want* to be there. If for no other reason than to see for yourself what comes his way when he's out there."

I took a big sip of my wine and tried to hide the panic and fear that I was certain she could see in my eyes. This was what I'd been afraid of all along. How was I supposed to compete with these women who threw themselves at Tabor?

Dee placed her hand over mine and patted it gently. When I looked at her, she was giving me a defeated smile, and I knew that it was something she knew all too well.

"This is the life we are exposed to, Dani. If you want to be with these men, it goes with the territory. But JT is worth the trouble. He's one of the good ones," she said.

I looked over my shoulder and saw him inside talking with his buddies. Tabor's smile was wide when he saw me and lifted his head to check on me, and I simply waved.

"Yeah, he is," I agreed when I looked at Dee. "Thanks for the heads-up."

"We look out for our own," she said. "And if JT says you're good people, that's enough for us."

"How do you do it?" I asked. "The whole…sports thing and being apart?"

"You get used to it. You talk every day, and if you're able, you go to the away games. Training camp starts this week and it's going to be madness."

"How long does it last?"

"About a month. A month of them running their asses off, working out, and then calling you and complaining," she laughed.

"Ever since we started dating, I've gotten used to seeing him almost every day."

"It's not so bad…you'll see," she said evenly.

I nodded, but inside it was nerve-wracking.

We spent about four hours with his friends, and they were great. Wilson and Dee were adorable together and made me laugh so much. The other women turned out to be very down to earth, unlike my initial impression. The entire weekend had been spent with Tabor's friends and family, and I felt like I was exactly where I belonged.

By the time we got back to my place, I was exhausted. Tabor unlocked the door with the key I gave him and I started to walk up to my room when he reached for my hand and turned me to face him.

"I didn't think it was possible."

"What's that?" I asked, wrapping my arms around his neck.

He kissed me and then stared into my eyes. "That I could love you more than I already did."

I pushed onto my toes and kissed him back, because it was the only thing I could think to do. I fell for him more every time we were together, and knowing he felt the same was the perfect end to a perfect day.

CHAPTER 19

TABOR

"How do these things work?" Dani asked as she turned the page in the magazine she was reading.

"How does what work?"

"The shoot. Do they put makeup on you? What is it you're advertising?"

"This is for a menswear company. I've only done shoes and sports drinks, so this one's new to me."

When we had left Wilson's house, I'd asked Dani to reconsider going to the photo shoot with me and I was happy when she consented. I was a football player, not a model, so I always felt stupid doing those things. The first photographer I'd worked with had kept trying to get me to give him a certain smile when I sipped the god-awful drink I was endorsing. Not only did it taste like shit, I was forced to pretend I liked it. When he showed me the proofs, it was a little embarrassing to see the pained look on my face. Luckily, he was able to make one of them work and I vowed never to sign on to endorse something I didn't actually like.

A few months ago, my agent was contacted by Radical Generation to model their line of casual and dress wear. After I was signed by the team, my mom and Abbi took me shopping so I'd look the part. My sister heard of Radical Generation because it had become popular on college campuses. The owner, Damian, started the company from his home in Chicago, and within a year it exploded into stores across the country.

"Is this it?" Dani asked as I pulled into a parking lot. It was a nondescript brick building with several cars in front of it.

"Probably," I said, turning off the engine. "Let's go find out."

She set the magazine aside and stepped out of the car. Dani had insisted on taking her car when I told her the majority of the shoot would take place on the beach. She said that her Bel Air loved the beach.

We grabbed our things from the trunk and walked into the office, which looked nothing like I expected.

Stained concrete floors were set against red brick walls with contemporary lights hanging over the front desk. A woman wearing her hair in a high ponytail greeted us and said that Damian would be with us soon. Dani walked to the waiting area and I sat down next to her as she took it all in.

"This place is pretty cool," she said, still looking around.

"I've never been here before," I admitted. "My agent did the talking with the owner, so it's a first for me, too."

"Are you nervous?" she asked.

I scoffed and shook my head. "Yes."

Dani's laugh made me smile and I was glad that she had agreed to accompany me. My hope was that she'd see how the things go and be at ease with them in the future if they came up.

"JT," a short, thin man with blond hair said as he walked toward me. "Damian Salinger, nice to meet you."

"You, too," I said, shaking his hand. He looked at Dani and I noticed his smile grow. "This is my…"

"Assistant. Danielle," she interrupted, shaking his hand.

"I didn't realize you were bringing an assistant. Nice to meet you, Danielle," he said, holding her hand longer than I liked.

"So what's the plan?" I interjected, breaking the connection for them.

"Martin should be here soon, and then we'll get you into makeup while I go over the set with the director," Damian said.

"I thought this was taking place on the beach," Dani said.

"It will, Danielle. But we have some things to take care of before we get started," he said. "Would you like to see what the models will be wearing today?"

I started to object because she was there for me—*with* me. She had no idea how much I hated these things, but before I could say anything, she spoke up.

"Actually, I'm working," she said, stepping closer to me.

Damian opened his mouth to speak, but the front door opened and a tall heavy-set man in all black stepped through with two petite women following behind. He walked over to Damian, shaking his hand, and exchanged pleasantries while Dani and I looked on. She turned to me and raised a brow, questioning who it was, and I shrugged. Of course I assumed it was the photographer, but I couldn't be sure.

"JT, why don't you go with Martin so he can tell you what we're looking for, and I'll show Danielle around."

"I…" Dani said.

"Don't worry, your boss can give you a few minutes alone. He's got some things to take care of," Damian said.

I hated him.

He had his hand on my girlfriend's back and I wanted to tackle him like the opponent he was.

***

DANI

I squirmed slightly so his hand fell away from my body. This Damian guy seemed to think that personal boundaries didn't apply to him, and it made me despise him instantly. When I glanced over my shoulder, I saw Tabor looking murderous and I wished I could ease his nerves.

"So tell me, Danielle, how did you meet your boss?" Damian asked as he led me toward a narrow corridor.

"Lucky coincidence," I said, not wanting to share the details of how we met.

"Well, I'm always looking for a good *assistant*." He smirked, causing my stomach to churn. "If it doesn't work out with Hunter, give me a call."

"Thanks," I said cautiously. This guy was sending my creep-o-meter off the charts, and I was beyond grateful when the receptionist found us and said that Martin needed to speak with Damian.

"We'll be right there," Damian said, dismissing her and leaving us alone once again before turning to me. "Are you free tonight?"

"I'm afraid not, Mr. Salinger," I said, pleased with myself that I didn't apologize. "I'm actually seeing someone."

"That's too bad," he said as he looked me up and down.

I cringed under his obvious perusal, and if he noticed, he didn't seem to care.

Damian began walking to the front and I shivered openly, as if I had bugs crawling on me. He was so gross and I wondered how many others he made to feel like they were in need of a scalding shower.

"That was cute," Tabor smirked when I turned around.

"What?" I asked, laughing.

"That little dance you just did. Do it again," he teased as he walked closer.

I wrapped my arms around him and rested my head against his chest, listening to his heart beating beneath his shirt. His hand rubbed soothingly up and down my back and I felt my body relax. When I stepped away, he was looking down at me adoringly.

"Assistant, huh?" he asked.

"I panicked...I didn't know what to say."

"I'm just giving you a hard time." He kissed my forehead and put his hand on my back. "Let's go see what's going on."

***

TABOR

"JT," Damian said as we rounded the corner. "Just in time. I'd like for you to meet Candayce Evans, your co-star for the day."

Dani's mouth fell open, but she snapped her jaw shut and smiled. I took a step forward and introduced myself to the woman I'd seen on countless magazine covers. She was beautiful, and the way she carried herself, she knew it.

"Candayce, it's nice to meet you. This is my assistant, Danielle," I said, choking on the title.

"Hi Danielle," Candayce said, but didn't look at Dani when addressing her. "So JT, are you ready for this?"

"As ready as I'll ever be," I said, and it was the truth. I didn't like people fussing over me and this was in the top five of what I hated about my status.

"I'll go easy on you," she cooed, and I noticed Dani's fist clench and release.

"I'm sure I'll be fine." I smiled.

"Candayce, why don't I show you to makeup," Damian said, stepping in front of me, no doubt wanting her attention for himself. He could have it, for all I cared; as long as his focus was off Dani, that's all that mattered to me.

"Shall we?" Candayce asked me over her shoulder.

I looked at Dani, who had a fake smile plastered on her face, and cleared my throat.

"I'll be fine," she said, looking up at me, giving me the smile I knew to be just for me. "See you in a few?"

"Okay," I said, reluctant to follow.

Candayce sat in a chair like the professional she was and relaxed as the people began working on her hair and makeup. We sat in silence as the experts worked and I was thankful for their distraction. My senses were on alert for anything Dani-related, and I wished that she was by my side.

I wasn't sure how much time had passed, but I heard some shuffling and hushed whispers, and when I looked over, Candayce was gone.

"Everything okay?" I asked.

"It's fine," Martin said dismissively. "Just relax and let us take care of everything else."

***

DANI

I was flipping through a magazine when the commotion started. First it was the woman I had seen earlier standing next to Candayce talking urgently on her phone. She jumped out of her seat and ran to the back, and moments later when she returned, Candayce was following behind her and her red eyes and nose gave away her distress.

I had no idea what was going on, but the way everyone was running around frantically, it wasn't good for the shoot.

"What in the hell are we gonna do now?" Damian demanded of the photographer.

"Her mother is in the hospital, she needed to go. But in the meantime we can always just shoot Hunter and then add Candayce in later," Martin said calmly. "I do it all the time."

"No. Fix this. Now."

"What am I supposed to do, just pick someone up off the street? I'd probably be arrested for solicitation and I don't even date women," he argued and I laughed.

"What?" Damian scolded but softened when he realized I was the one laughing.

"I'm sorry," I said, looking at Martin, who smiled back. "That was funny."

"Danielle, now is not the time for laughing. I have a major campaign I'm about to spend a lot of money on, and now I have no model to pair with your boss."

"What about her?" Martin asked.

I looked around and realized he was talking about me. Damian sized me up and down again, but that time I didn't feel as disgusted.

"How tall are you?" Damian demanded.

"What? Why?" I asked defensively.

"How tall?"

"Five seven," I answered.

Damian turned to Martin, who nodded, some unspoken discussion between them.

"Danielle, I need you to fill in for Candayce. Can you do that?"

"Mr. Salinger, I'm a teach—assistant," I answered as explanation. "Thank you, but no."

"Danielle," Martin said, drawing my attention to him. "If we don't get this done today, we have to push the entire shoot back and there's a strong likelihood that your boss will be unavailable. Would you please help us?"

I was uncomfortable with the request, but I could tell he was being sincere.

Deny the request and leave Tabor without the endorsement he seems excited about?

Accept the request and help out your boyfriend?

"Danielle, we really need answer," Damian said, less forcefully than before. "It would mean a lot."

"Okay…I'll do it."

Damian's smile was victorious and Martin clasped his hands together and looked up to the ceiling before grabbing my hand and dragging me to the back.

Tabor was still in the chair when he saw my reflection in the mirror. Before he could speak, Martin introduced me.

"JT, I'd like for you to meet your partner for the day, Danielle."

Tabor's smile crept slowly onto his face as I took a seat in the chair next to him. A woman walked over and began brushing and styling my hair while I sat helpless.

"This is going to be fun." Tabor smirked.

***

TABOR

We were driven to a remote part of the beach the set director had located, near an old pier. Dani was modeling the first of five outfits she needed to wear. Damian had Gertie, one of his designers, come with us to make any last-minute adjustments to the wardrobe because everything had been made to fit Candayce's taller stature.

"Okay, so here's how this is going to go," Martin said, moving me against one of the pilings. "JT, you lean against this and Danielle, I'm going to have you stand against him with your hand on his chest."

He positioned me and moved me around as if I were a mannequin and did the same to Dani. Once we were in position, one of Martin's assistants walked over and moved Dani's hair out of her face before stepping away.

The two of us stood there and I looked down at her. She looked beautiful. But Dani was always beautiful to me, even when her hair was undone and she was wearing messy clothes. Martin stepped behind the camera and told us that he was going to take some test shots and then we'd be set.

Since we had a moment to ourselves, I placed my hand on Dani's hip and looked into her eyes. She looked uncomfortable with the attention being given her, but I loved that she was with me.

"You look beautiful," I said, smiling down at her.

She tilted her chin up and smiled shyly, shaking her head. "I look like myself...only a little too fake."

"It's all for the camera," I said. "I think they should've left you as you were, but you're always sexy to me."

Dani playfully hit my chest and dropped her forehead against her hand with a forced laugh. I cleared my throat and she looked up at me again. She crossed her eyes and stuck out her tongue and I huffed a laugh.

"See? Still sexy," I said. "It sucks that I have to leave this weekend, for camp."

"Are you gonna miss me?" she fished and I laughed.

"Question is, are you going to miss me?"

When her mouth opened to speak, she was cut off by Martin walking up again.

"Okay, let's get you two into another outfit," he said.

"But we didn't pose yet," Dani said.

"I got what I needed while you two were waiting. Very natural," he said. "You two have great chemistry."

"Thanks," I said.

***

DANI

"One second while I pin the dress back here," Gertie said as she pulled and tugged.

We were standing inside of a pop-up tent so I could dress and undress easily. Gertie commented that she liked working with real women, and hated stick figures. She flinched when the words came out, but I thanked her because I considered it a compliment.

"Okay, we're all set. Let's get you out there to that gorgeous partner of yours." She smiled.

We walked out and I saw Tabor sitting on a blanket next to

the shoreline. Martin and his assistant were in the middle of posing him when he spotted us.

"You look stunning," Damian said as I walked past. But I ignored him because my eyes were glued to my boyfriend, who was watching me with hungry eyes.

"Danielle, I want you to sit down as close as you can to JT and put your legs over his lap. It's going to feel awkward to be so close, but this is the shot I need," Martin instructed and I complied as I took my place.

Tabor reached down and fixed my skirt that crept up as I got into position, intentionally grazing my thigh. I looked at him and narrowed my eyes playfully and he shrugged, challenging me with a raised brow.

"Okay you two. JT, I want you to run your hand through her hair and Danielle, I want you to grab ahold of that hand like you want it to stop but are torn.

"That's easy," I muttered so Tabor would hear.

He lifted his hand and slowly touched my jaw as he moved his hand to my hair. I tried not to laugh, because acting wasn't something I was accustomed to.

"This is so weird," I laughed.

"Shh," Tabor said. "Close your eyes and pretend it's just the two of us at my place."

I took a deep breath and did as he said, allowing his touch to ignite every one of my nerves. My breathing became heavy while Tabor's voice lulled me.

"I love you so much, Dani," he whispered.

I opened my eyes and stared into his, falling for him even more than I thought possible. Leaving all my apprehension and fears in the sand below, I leaned forward and kissed him, ignoring the camera, the people, and the concerns of others finding out. I loved this man, and he was putting it out there for me.

When we separated, he rested his forehead to mine and I closed my eyes, reveling in our shared moment, but forced them open when I heard someone clear their throat. I looked over to see Damian moving his phone from his ear while Martin stood next to him smiling so wide that I was certain I had seen his molars.

"So, that was interesting," Martin offered with a chuckle. "Is there something we should know?"

I looked at Tabor, who smiled and shrugged, leaving it to me to decide.

"We're dating?" I answered as if it were a question.

"Looks like more to me," Martin teased as Damian crossed his arms over his chest.

"Observant man," Tabor said.

"All right, you two, now let's try it the way I said," Martin instructed with a wink.

"We've got a job to do, babe. Try to control yourself," Tabor mocked.

"I promise nothing."

CHAPTER 20

DANI

"So I guess you decided to make it official," Grace said when I answered my phone.

"What are you talking about?"

"That site Fangurl Sports Gossip just showed leaked images from Tabor's shoot yesterday. Since when do you moonlight as a model?" she teased. "You looked amazing, by the way."

"I stepped in to help, that's all. One-time gig, I assure you," I said as I opened up a search on my computer.

I typed in Tabor's name and under *recent news* were several images from the shoot. Someone had captured a shot of him mid-change and shirtless—he looked hot. These weren't the images that Martin took; they were too far away and pixelated. Another caught my eye, and it was me sitting on the beach in his arms. I smiled, remembering the moment I had given in and decided I didn't care who knew about us.

"So?" Grace asked.

"I didn't see anyone else out there," I admitted. "But yeah, I guess it's publicly official."

"Good for you," she said proudly. "'Bout time."

I muttered a thank you, distracted when I opened the link that Grace had told me about.

Hunter's Latest Prey

Bad news, ladies of San Diego: looks like JT Hunter may be off the market, at least for a little while. It's been rumored for some time that he's been seeing someone, though we've been unable to confirm the story. Until now. From the images below, looks like things are hot and heavy. She's one lucky lady.

But don't worry, he probably won't be taken for long. If you recall, he was involved with starlet Natasha Dion several months back, but that ended amid rumors of cheating. So don't count Mr. Hunter out just yet, because you never know.

As for his current leading lady, sources confirm that he's been quietly dating a schoolteacher named Danielle. We can't help but wonder what she's teaching him. And why they're so determined to keep it secret. Stay tuned as the story develops.

"Gracie," I mumbled. "This article makes me look pathetic, and Tabor like he's a jerk."

"Fangurl is in the business of generating gossip, Dan. You need to let it go," she warned.

"This is what I was nervous about all along. I hate the idea of people making up shit about me. They don't know me."

"That's right, but Tabor does. So who gives a crap what they say?"

"Easy for you to say—it's not your name they're putting out there."

"At least they didn't put your last name," she consoled. "And what's with the Danielle thing?"

"Fucking Damian," I said flatly. "That bastard is the one who sold the story."

"Who's Damian?"

"The owner of the company we were modeling for. He was hitting on me and asked me out, but I told him I was seeing someone—I just didn't say who. But he was right there when I kissed Tabor."

"Someone sounds jealous," she teased.

"Are those stories about Tabor and the ex true?" I asked. Grace had been his fan long before I ever met him.

"I have no idea. I remember seeing some things about them

dating, but other sites claimed they were just friends. You should ask him."

"Yeah, I will. I need to go. We're going out to dinner tonight—first time since our date."

"Where to this time?"

"I'm not sure, but I guess I should be prepared for anything."

***

"Are you ready for this?" Tabor asked as we climbed out of his SUV.

"As I'll ever be," I admitted, nervousness flooding my core.

We walked into Moonbeams, a small restaurant that I'd wanted to take Tabor to for a while. Since everything was out in the open, I figured it was as good a time as any.

Kayla, the owner, was at the hostess stand when we walked in, and her eyes grew wide at the sight of Tabor. She was unable to tear her eyes away until I cleared my throat.

"Kayla?"

"Hm?"

"Kayla," I snapped, laughing as she finally turned to me.

"It *was* you in that picture," she said excitedly. "I knew it!"

"Guilty," I admitted. "Ta—JT, this is Kayla. Kayla this…"

"JT Hunter. Holy crap. JT Hunter is in *my* restaurant?"

"I've been bragging about this place for a while, and well, since the cat's out of the bag, figured this is the best place for our inaugural public date."

"Come on, I'll get you my best table," she gushed, hurrying over to a corner table.

"She says every table is her best," I said jokingly.

Kayla looked over her shoulder and smirked, wagging a finger at me. "Don't give my secrets away."

Tabor chuckled and thanked her as we sat down with menus in hand. He looked around and took in the eclectic decor and odd table/chair combinations. There was no method to her madness. Kayla had opened the place with her husband because it was her dream, and she'd managed to be successful. I became friends with her when, during my third visit, I'd talked her ear off about my kids at school.

"What's good here?" he asked.

"Everything," I said honestly. "I've never eaten anything I didn't like. But my favorite is the pot roast."

"In the summer?" he asked, seemingly shocked.

"It's that good." I nodded, my mouth watering at the suggestion, and I knew what I was getting.

Kayla came back with two glasses of water and looked from me to Tabor and back. She didn't walk away, and looked like she wanted to say something.

"How's everything going?" I asked. "Sorry I haven't been in lately."

"Yeah, I guess you've been busy," she laughed sweetly. "Things are great."

"This is a cool place you have," Tabor said, and I watched as her eyes glazed over and a sappy smile appeared.

"Thanks, Mr. Hunter," she said with a giggle.

"JT," he said. "Dani tells me the pot roast is her favorite, so I'm gonna give it a try."

"Two, please," I said.

"Coming right up," she said before disappearing.

When she was gone, Tabor reached over, took my hand in his, and rubbed his thumb over the back of mine.

"Gracie called me today. Told me about that gossip site outing us," I admitted.

Tabor exhaled loudly and leaned back in his chair, still holding onto my hand. He looked disappointed with my words, but I also had to ask. I needed to know the answers that were plaguing my mind.

"So is any of it true?" I asked him.

"I'm dating you," he said, dodging the question.

"What about the part about you dating Natasha?"

He sucked in a breath and shook his head. "Long story."

"I'm not going anywhere."

He huffed and looked uncomfortable, as if my question was too intrusive. But we were together, and if we wanted a chance to make this work, in private or public, we needed to communicate.

Tabor finally looked me in the eyes and nodded. "Yeah, we were dating. It wasn't serious—mostly going out when she was in town between shoots."

"What happened?"

"You read the article," he answered defensively. "Apparently I cheated."

"Did you?" I asked, but hated myself for it.

"When I'm with someone, I am exclusive, Dani. So no, I didn't cheat."

"Did she?"

"Among other things," he said sadly.

"I'm sorry, I'm not trying to make you feel uncomfortable," I said, embarrassed with my need to know right then and there.

He leaned forward in his seat and dropped his head to look into my eyes, a small smile playing on his lips. My pulse increased as he gave me so much in that look.

"Dani, I love you, and I'll tell you anything you want to know. I know that this is what I wanted, to tell the world that you're mine, but now that the bubble's been burst, a lot of things are going to come out."

"Like what?" I asked nervously.

"Women, stories, rumors. Lies. Some have truth mixed in, but I hate that when you hear them, you might look at me differently."

I squeezed his hand and forced a smile. "I trust you. I'm just trying to keep myself from any surprises that may pop up."

"I understand, and like I said, I'll tell you anything."

"So why did it end with you and Natasha?"

"She invited a bunch of her co-stars to my place while I was away for a game. She threw one hell of a party that was caught on my surveillance."

"Did she not clean up or something?"

"No, she cleaned up just fine. But I have a bit of a problem with someone I'm dating shacking up with some dude in *my* bed and bringing drugs into my place."

"Damn," I muttered.

"When we broke up, she begged me to keep quiet about everything and I had no intention of making a big public announcement about anything. I like to keep my private life...private. But the next thing I knew, my name was splashed all over that site claiming that Natasha was brokenhearted because she'd caught *me* with someone else."

"Did you confront her about it?"

"I did. Told her I had the video that showed her with some guy. But she said it could ruin her career and I just gave up and told her I never wanted to hear from her again."

I was quiet for a moment as I considered his story and couldn't help but laugh before explaining.

"I thought sex tapes are all the rage out there in Tinseltown. Wouldn't that have just skyrocketed her career?"

"I said the same thing," he laughed. "I think it had more to do with her parents finding out."

Kayla brought out our food and stood by quietly with something in her hand. Tabor glanced at me and I nodded my head toward Kayla, and he gave her his attention.

"Could I get your autograph?" she asked timidly.

"Yeah, no problem." He smiled, taking the pen and paper from her.

She walked away, smiling and bouncing off toward the kitchen, leaving us to eat in silence.

I was about to take a bite of food when I noticed several pairs of eyes watching us. I tried to ignore them, but it was so weird and uncomfortable.

"Just keep talking to me," Tabor said, acknowledging what I was seeing.

"I don't know how you do it," I muttered. "It's so rude."

"You get used to it after a while," he admitted, a hint of sadness in his voice.

***

"Dinner was fantastic, Kayla," Tabor gushed as he paid our bill. She flushed at his compliment and thanked us for coming in.

"See you soon, Dani?" she asked, and I knew she wanted details.

"Will do," I said giving her a quick hug before walking to the door.

Outside there was a crowd of people and I knew this was a repeat of our first date. Tabor would be signing things and chatting with people, but it was something I needed to get used to. It was part of his life.

"Ready?" he asked.

I slipped my hand into his and squeezed before we stepped out to a throng of people calling out his name.

"Just stay next to me," he instructed, and I willingly complied.

"JT! JT! Can you sign my ball?" a little kid asked. He was tiny and being pushed by a grown man behind him with a massive camera.

"Hey buddy," Tabor said to the cameraman, "can you watch out for this little guy?"

He took the ball and marker from the kid and began asking him about school and if he was ready for it to start.

"I hate school," the kid said defensively.

"Don't say that too loud." Tabor glanced over his shoulder at me. "My girlfriend is a teacher and that might hurt her feelings."

The kid looked around Tabor and saw me, so I waved and smiled.

"She's pretty," he said sweetly.

Tabor was still talking when someone shouted, "Danielle! Where do you teach?"

I shook my head, unwilling to provide that information.

"Aw, c'mon, you know we'll find out anyway. Might as well tell us."

"JT, can I take a picture with you?" a stocky woman asked.

"Yeah." He smiled, wrapping his arm around her and smiling as she took a selfie. She handed him a magazine that sported his image and he took the marker she offered. "What's your name, sweetie?"

"Mercedes," she said excitedly. "Thank you, JT!"

She threw her arms around his waist and squeezed tightly and I laughed. He returned the gesture and I swear she almost fainted.

"JT, are you ready for training camp?" someone called out and Tabor shook his head.

"As ready as ever," he laughed.

After another fifteen minutes of people calling his name and asking him to sign things, he waved at them and said we needed to get somewhere.

As we walked to his waiting SUV, the same obnoxious

photographer followed us, but stopped when Tabor turned around.

"Can I help you?" Tabor asked sternly, and it was clear that help was not what he was interested in offering.

"Danielle, how comfortable are you dating a cheater?"

Tabor's body tensed I stepped back, pushing my back against his chest, giving his hand a squeeze.

"I think the better question is, how comfortable are you being an intrusive, rude, unimportant asshole?" I asked calmly before turning my back and pulling Tabor behind me.

He began opening the door when we heard the guy mutter "*bitch*" under his breath and Tabor stopped moving.

"Let it go," I urged. "He's not worth it."

"That's bullshit," he said gruffly.

"But it's our new reality. Right?"

He nodded and closed the door behind me, and stalked over to the guy, who looked like he was wanted to run away. Tabor raised his hands up in surrender and the man stood still. I opened my door to get out and heard Tabor's voice.

"That wasn't cool man. I know you have a job to do, but I love that woman, and she doesn't deserve that shit. The only reason I'm not beating your ass is because she told me not to. How would you feel if someone insulted your wife or girlfriend?"

"I got it," the man said apologetically.

There was a short conversation that took place with hushed tones, and I wished I knew what was said. I watched as Tabor shook his hand and walked back to the car with a boyish grin on his face. I closed my door and saw the guy disappear into the darkness as Tabor climbed into the driver's seat.

"Impressive," I complimented.

"Our new reality, right?" he said, repeating my sentiment.

"Yep."

CHAPTER 21

DANI

Watching Tabor pack his stuff for training camp was tough. He would be gone for two weeks. Granted, it was only at a hotel downtown, but I wouldn't have as much access as I was used to. I knew that it would be a new experience and Tabor was worth it. My heart grew heavy watching as he prepared to leave me, but I was thankful I had work to occupy my time and hopefully distract me.

"You all set for tomorrow?" I asked as Tabor put the last of his clothes in his duffle bag, shaking me out of my depressing thoughts.

"No. Because you won't be with me," he said honestly.

I was lying across his bed on my side, resting my head on my arm. I knew he'd be close and I could call at night, but then he'd also have some preseason games that would interfere. I had gotten used to calling and having him answer almost every time.

"Where's your first game?"

"Here." He smiled and crawled over me on the bed, dropping his lips to mine and kissing the corner. "Are you going to be there?"

"Do you want me there?" I asked against his mouth before kissing him.

167

"Maybe." He smiled as he slowly moved away.

"Well, maybe I'll be there," I answered coyly.

"Good."

"How many games do you play?"

"Four. Two home, two away. One in New York and one in Tennessee."

"I wish you didn't have to go," I said, picking at an invisible piece of lint on his comforter. It was the most honest thing I could say, and I needed to tell him that.

"I know. Me too," he said. "But we'll be fine, right?"

"I suppose," I said with a shrug. "But what if while you're gone, some tall, dark, and handsome stranger appears and tries to sweep me off my feet?" I asked innocently.

"Then you tell him that your tall, pale, and scary boyfriend will beat his ass," he answered over his shoulder with a laugh.

"Aw. Would you do that?" I asked, batting my eyelashes and smiling.

"For you, I'd do just about anything."

"Really?" I asked excitedly, sitting up and tucking my feet beneath me. "Like what?"

"I'd go to a chick flick," he conceded, as if it was the biggest sacrifice in the history of sacrifices, and I laughed.

"And what else?"

"I could hold your purse while you shop?"

"I hate shopping," I retorted. "What else do ya got?"

I loved our playfulness; it made me smile, and I felt like it was something we'd done forever.

Tabor walked over to me and reached for my hand, guiding me to my knees. I inched to the edge of the bed and he wrapped his arms around my waist, mine going around his neck.

He kissed me once. "I would..."

Another kiss. "...go to the..."

And another still. "...store and buy feminine products."

He dipped his head to kiss me again and I covered his mouth, his breath hot against my palm, and I was laughing. I shook my head, unable to say anything, and I felt his smile grow beneath my hand.

"You'd do *that*?"

"Baby, that stuff doesn't matter to me," he answered.

"And you really have to leave tomorrow?" I asked, still wrapped in his arms.

"Unfortunately," he said, looking deep into my eyes, giving me so much with one action.

I wanted to stay wrapped in his arms forever. Instead, I opted to enjoy the short time we had left and rested my head against his chest. The steady rise and fall as he breathed forced my eyes shut as I cataloged it to memory. Being without those arms, those lips, those eyes…that body, was something I wasn't prepared for.

Tabor had everything packed and he was waiting downstairs. We'd already had dinner, and I was staying at his place because I wouldn't see him for a while. There wasn't much left to do, but I knew we'd find something.

"We still have tonight," he finally said, holding me tighter.

"Tonight," I repeated.

***

The next morning we left his place together, going our separate directions, and I ended up at Millie's front door, a pathetic excuse for the woman I had been before Tabor.

"Suck it up, Dani," I told myself as I looked at my reflection in the rearview mirror and swiped the tears from my eyes. "It's not like he's gone for good."

I tried to hide the red nose and glassy eyes, but I knew it was no use: Millie would see it all, even if a single tear was never shed. I stepped out of my car and closed the door behind me, but before I got a chance to knock, the wooden door flung open and Millie stood at the threshold with Colton propped on her hip.

"Dani! Where the hell have you been?" she asked.

I was quiet, trying to stop the tears, and then it happened. I sniffled. That was all it took.

"Are you…crying?" she gasped. "Dani, you never cry. Did you and Tabor break up?"

I shook my head and realized from the panicked look on her face that she was scared.

"No," I sniffled and huffed. "He left for training camp this morning."

"Damn, you've got it bad," she noted. "Come in and play with your godson."

I reached out my arms and Colton willingly came to me, dirty diaper and all. I wrinkled my nose and made a face as I tried to hand him back to his mom, but he had a death grip on my hair.

"He's got a dirty diaper, Mills," I said, but when I looked up she was halfway to the kitchen.

"You know where the diapers are," she called out. "I'll get you some coffee."

I looked at the baby and snorted. "Coffee in exchange for your nasty diaper hardly seems fair."

Colton was making faces and babbling with his hand in his mouth. I was almost tempted to leave him be, considering he seemed content in his mess, but I knew it would be only a matter of time until he was in full tantrum mode. When he was cleaned and changed, I brought him downstairs to join his mommy in the kitchen.

"So tell me all about it," she said, handing me a mug and a huge chunk of chocolate cake.

"Did you make this?" I asked. Millie wasn't typically the baker, but stranger things had happened.

"I did," she beamed proudly.

I raised a brow and pushed it toward her. "You taste it first."

She pressed her hand to her chest and pretended to be offended and then shrugged. "Fair enough."

Her fork was loaded with a huge chunk. She shoved it into her mouth and chewed, closing her eyes as she enjoyed it. When I was sure she wasn't lying, I took the fork in hand and did the same. It was, quite possibly, the best cake I'd ever had. Millie took Colton from my arms and placed him in the highchair, and put some Cheerios on it before sitting down next to me. She'd taken care of everything and she was ready to focus on me.

"Okay, so spill," she said, leaving no room for argument.

"Is this really going to work out?"

"What's that?"

"Tabor and me? I mean, he's got preseason now, and sure, he'll be home in a couple of weeks and then what? He's got practice and games and everything else. We're just getting started."

"It's a few months, Dani," she said, reaching for my hand.

"That's nothing."

"I get that this is his career and he loves the game. I want him to be happy. But a part of me wants to be incredibly selfish and have him all to myself."

"Dan—"

"I know it's unreasonable, and that's not what I *really* want. I'm just sad and mopey because I miss him already."

"It's not like you won't see him. He'll still be around all the time, and something tells me that his free time will be spent with you."

I looked at Millie and smiled because I knew she was right. Tabor would spend as much time with me as he could because he loved me. He was as miserable about the situation as I was, and oddly, that made me feel better.

***

I had no idea what I was in for or what "camp" entailed, but I quickly learned. Tabor called every night before he went to sleep, and every night I heard about the grueling practices and drills. We barely spoke for fifteen minutes because he was too tired and had to get up early the next morning. And I tried not to sound too disappointed when the call ended.

My first experience as a football player's girlfriend came a week after camp started, during the opening preseason game. To say it was a strange experience would be an understatement considering that people in the stands seemed to know me. Not necessarily my name, but sitting in the stands with Marta, who flew in to be there for Tabor, there were whispers of "that's his girlfriend."

Mid-way through the game, I watched in horror as he made a tackle, only to be hit by another player. He stayed down for a bit before climbing to his feet and getting back to the game. Marta wrapped her arm around me and told me what was going on while trying to calm my nerves.

Everyone was right: I hated football.

"He's fine," Marta said in her soothing tone. "See, he's already back up."

"I don't know how he does it," I said.

"He's been doing it for so long, he just knows," she said.

"But what if he gets seriously hurt?" I questioned, but instantly regretted the worry I saw on her face.

"*If* that happens, you go to Larkins General Hospital and meet him there. Just say you're there for Tabor and you're his sister or something so they let you see him."

"Gross," I said, making a gagging noise.

"If you want to see him, you'll lie through your teeth. And if that doesn't work, just find Wilson."

I refocused on the game, but watching the person I loved going head to head against men of equal or greater size terrified me. It was a lesson in etiquette sitting next to Marta, who kept her chin up and cheered on her son. Without a word, she showed me how I needed to carry myself, though it would take some practice. But spotting photographers with their zoom lenses as they tried to catch us together made it hard to adjust to the spotlight I was thrust in.

And of course there was always Fangurl, with the biting news stories related to Tabor and me. After the first game, she came out with a clever story.

Teacher Shows Hunter How It's Done

We've learned a little more about JT Hunter's latest fling. We've heard from multiple sources that Hunter isn't the only man in her life. While we don't yet have the details, teacher, Danielle Miner is rumored to also be seeing a high-profile CEO. But don't feel bad for him, because it appears she and the football hunk have an open relationship. Mr. Hunter, if you're reading this, call me. I'm game.

Guess it goes to show, men like JT Hunter like open-minded women.

Fling? I was considered a fling? My sister had to talk me down when I called her screaming about the blatant lies this person was spewing. Everything about that article made me look like a tramp and I hated it.

"Hey babe," Tabor's low voice soothed through the phone.

"Hey," I answered.

I spoke to him when he got a break in the middle of the day, but it wasn't enough. It was never enough.

Without Tabor, my condo was quiet, my hands were lonely, and I missed him like crazy.

"What's wrong?" he asked, the concern etched in his tone.

"I'm fine," I lied. "Just missing you."

"I miss you," he responded before continuing. "If I flew you out here, would you come?"

"It's only a few days, right?"

"Yeah," he said, and I felt bad for his obvious disappointment. "But I wouldn't mind training so much if you were here."

My heart swelled and I wished he were in front of me so I could climb into his arms and never leave. It was disturbing how quickly I'd come to depend on his presence in in my life.

"I wouldn't mind either," I admitted.

"So come out here."

"I really can't...but you know, it's hardest at night when I have time to think. During the day, I'm busy enough that I'm not obsessing," I told him.

"I know what you mean. But I'll be home soon," he said, giving me some perspective.

"Soon."

By week two, I was a seasoned pro. Or at the very least, good at pretending. His second game was away and I watched it with my parents, cringing with every crushing blow and tackle—it didn't matter who was on the receiving end of it.

After two weeks of Tabor gone with no visits, I was excited when that game ended because it marked the end of hotel stays. But I got an early surprise when obnoxious sports commentator Kip Stanley caught him as he was leaving the field to interview him after the game.

"JT, the Quakes managed to pull out a win today, but there were a lot of mistakes. What do you think the team needs to do before the game against the Hustlers?"

"You know, we're still working on it and we have a great coaching staff who's figuring it all out, so we just need to listen

and see what they come up with," he said while the short man man nodded.

"The defense was pretty good out there, but it looked like you had to rein in a few of your teammates," short, obnoxious Kip noted.

"These guys are my brothers. We're good."

"We heard that your girlfriend Danielle wasn't able to make it tonight. Do you think that affected your concentration?"

"Absolutely not. She's working and I know she'd be here if she could," he said with a smile before looking right into the camera. "I'll see you later tonight, baby. I love you."

Dad looked at me and laughed, nudging my knee with his. "He'll see you soon, baby," he cooed.

"Shut up, Dad," I laughed and flushed with embarrassment.

Tabor would be home soon. The game was over, and even though training camp wasn't, he was at least able to return to his home. I'd finally get to spend a little more time with him. There were still daily practices and long days, but at least he'd have the chance to come to my place or I could go to his. The only thing that mattered to me was being able to see his face...and *not* see it on a television screen.

I left Mom and Dad's and decided to wait at home for Tabor's call – only the silence was excruciating and made the time seem to pass too slowly. I'd cleaned my kitchen, folded some laundry, and organized my pantry, all in an effort to keep me busy. My phone rang and I jumped up to answer it, almost dropping the device in the process.

"Hello?" I asked, without looked at the caller ID.

"You okay?" Grace asked. "What time does he get in?"

"Anytime now, I think. He's supposed to call. Hopefully it won't be too late, because I'm dying to see him."

"Have you gotten everything set up for your classroom?"

"Almost. I was there every day last week, but between my class and getting the program ready, I'm spread so thin."

"I'll bet your boss is pretty happy you were able to get the funding to come through," she said. She was proud of what I'd done for the students.

"Actually, I haven't seen Mr. Lopez. I've heard chatter that he might be getting a promotion, so maybe that's why he hasn't been around."

There was a knock at the door and I walked over to peek through the window. I sucked in a rush of air, seeing Tabor's towering figure looming in front of me.

"Gracie, I gotta go," I said absently, hanging up the phone before she could ask any questions.

When I opened the door, Tabor dropped his duffle bag to the ground and I leapt into his arms, holding him as if I hadn't seen him in years. Two weeks wasn't long for many, but to me, in a very new relationship with someone I adored, two weeks had been an eternity.

His arms wrapped around me, holding me close as he buried his face in my neck, breathing me in. I don't know how long we stood outside, without speaking, but it was perfection.

"I missed you so much," I admitted.

He set me on my feet and looked down at me.

"What are you doing here? I thought you were going to call me when you got home."

"Got my car and drove straight here. I didn't want to wait to see you."

I stepped aside and he grabbed his things, walking in behind me. He looked absolutely worn out, so I took the heavy bag from his hand and dropped it on the floor, leading him upstairs to my room. Tabor sat on the edge of my bed and watched as I scurried around, straightening up the clothes tossed on the floor.

"Leave it. Come here," he instructed with his arms outstretched. He enveloped me and lay back, pulling me on top of him. I laughed when he groaned, exhausted from his weeks of practice and torture.

"Are you tired?" I asked, snuggling against his chest. "Because I could so sleep right now."

"I'm exhausted," he admitted.

He sat up and brought me along with him, his arm still wrapped around my waist. He had to look up to see my face and I liked the angle; he was beautiful.

"I missed you too," he said, responding to my earlier admission, and then he kissed me softly. "Let's go to bed."

"Sounds good to me," I answered. "I'll be right back, I need to turn off everything downstairs."

I disappeared down the steps and made my rounds to make sure the condo was locked up. I returned to see the shirtless back of Tabor as he pulled the covers back on my bed. But when he turned around, I gasped as I caught sight of a purpling bruise near his ribs. I rushed over and examined it closer, dread filling me.

"It looks worse than it feels," he said quietly. "Doc checked it out already and says it'll be fine."

I stood upright and looked into his eyes, trying to hide my fear, but I knew it was there for him to see. Tabor wrapped his arms around me and my hands gripped his bare back.

"Dani?" He moved his hands to my arms and moved me so he could see my face. "I promise, I'm okay. I wouldn't lie to you."

"Okay," I conceded. I wasn't a doctor—who was I to argue? But I was the girlfriend, and I needed him to be whole.

"But I could use some aspirin, I have a bit of a headache," he admitted.

"Did the doc check that out too?" I asked. "You took some big hits tonight."

"Nah, I'm probably just dehydrated, that's all," he answered dismissively.

"Are you sure?"

"I just need aspirin, water, and you…and I'll be fine," he said with a smile.

The medicine was in my bathroom and I closed the door behind me so he didn't see the fear I was trying too hard to hide. I took a few deep breaths and glanced at my reflection in the mirror. To myself I appeared more haggard than I'd seen in a while, and I couldn't help but wonder if those new lines on my face were of the *worry* variety.

"He's fine," I whispered to myself.

I grabbed the pill bottle and filled a cup with water from the tap and exhaled.

"He's been doing this for a long time," I reminded myself as I opened the door and found Tabor in my bed.

"Did you say something?" he asked when I handed him the cup and medicine.

"No," I lied, as I turned out the lights and climbed into bed. I snuggled against him and pressed my ear to his chest so I could listen to his heartbeat. The sound lulled me into a peaceful rest and it was there that I let my fears dissipate.

At least for the night.

CHAPTER 22

DANI

"Ms. Miner," Mr. Lopez called out as I was walking toward my classroom, a loaded box in my arms. "I need to see you in my office."

"Okay, just let me drop this off in my room," I answered absently.

"No. We need to talk now. Just set it on the front desk."

I stood immobile, trying to wrap my mind around his words. I felt like I was in trouble, but I sat my things down and followed him into his office.

"Close the door, please," he said, taking his seat and waiting for me to join.

"Is everything okay?" I asked.

"I'm afraid not," he started slowly. "I'm not sure if you've heard the news, but I've been promoted to the high school, effective immediately."

"Congratulations. That's wonderful news for them—of course I hate to see you go," I admitted, and it was the truth. He'd been a strong ally for all the teachers, always going to bat for us when he was needed.

"There's more," he said. He clicked the keys on his computer and cleared his throat. "I've been asked to handle a certain situation before I leave."

"What *situation* would that be?"

He turned the screen to face me and I saw pictures of Tabor, similar to the ones I had seen with Grace. But these were ones I hadn't seen of the two of us before. Private alone time with my boyfriend had been posted for public consumption.

Upon further examination, they were taken using a long lens, something I knew because of Grace's love of photography. It was extremely intrusive and made me want to cover myself as if I had reason to hide. There was nothing inappropriate, but it was still alarming.

Personal moments between the two of us were captured and plastered on the Internet for curious and nosy people to view and comment on. It was easy to forget that I didn't have the same luxuries afforded to other couples, because I was with JT Hunter and *he* belonged to the city. Our sweet hugs and innocent kisses were made to look tawdry and scathing—but we had assumed we were alone.

"I'm not following," I finally said. "It's not exactly news that I'm dating JT."

"I know, but there's more," he said.

"More?"

Mr. Lopez nodded and looked away, dejected—maybe even apologetic—as he turned his screen around and tapped his fingers on the keys again. Slowly, he moved it so I could have the same view, and I was humiliated.

No one knew of my stand-in for the real model for the Radical Generation photo shoot. Well, at least until my sister found out. I figured that Damian would see the proofs and demand a reshoot, possibly find someone else to endorse the clothing line. I never expected the images to see the light of day. Yet there they were splashed across the Fangurl Sports Gossip homepage.

The images were beautiful, capturing sweet moments between Tabor and me from the session. They were not inappropriate in nature, but it was the first time I'd seen them.

"Now you see what's going on," Mr. Lopez said.

"I really don't. Mr. Lopez, what are you saying?"

Without saying a word, he pointed to the screen and I realized there was a write-up along with it.

Hunter or the Hunted

Looks like JT Hunter and his girlfriend were seen making a splash on the beach prior to training camp. Hunter was on location shooting an ad for Radical Generation Clothing and was set to pose alongside Candayce Evans. Sources claim that Ms. Evans and Mr. Hunter's heated chemistry was enough to make his new girlfriend see green.

Another source was quoted as saying that Ms. Miner was seen cozying up to the Radical Generation clothing designer and owner, Damian Salinger, when Hunter wasn't around.

We can only imagine how stunning the shoot would have been with Hunter and Evans as the subject, but one can dream. Apparently, after seeing the vibes between the two, Miner made sure the pair was unable to work together.

According to Ms. Evans, Hunter's girlfriend threw a tantrum and accused the popular model of flirting with her boyfriend, making a scene. Danielle Miner, a teacher at River Valley Junior High, demanded that Mr. Hunter walk from the job or find another solution. It was then that Ms. Evans, ever the professional, graciously backed out.

Sounds like Ms. Miner needs a wakeup call. Men don't like possessive, demanding, needy women. We reached out to Ms. Miner, but she was unavailable for comment.

Leads one to wonder if the mild-mannered schoolteacher is nothing more than a gold digger. Stay tuned for more.

My knees trembled and I covered my mouth. I was never contacted in any way for confirmation of the story, and I wanted to scream. Finally looking over to the man I considered not only my boss but my mentor, I shook my head.

"This isn't true. None of it is," I defended weakly.

"I believe you," he said sadly, but clasped his hands together solemnly. "But it's not enough."

"What does that mean?"

"The administration got wind of the story, and though they can't force anything, they have asked that you take a temporary leave of absence—paid, of course."

"But if I didn't do anything wrong, why do I need to hide?"

"Truth is, we've been getting a lot of phone calls since your relationship with JT Hunter came to light, but after this latest story, it's putting you in a bad light. Since the story mentions our school, we can no longer bury our heads in the sand."

"I've been coming in for weeks setting up my class, organizing everything for the after-school program, and no one has said anything to me about people calling the school."

"It wasn't an issue until today," he admitted. "I was handling it and instructed the office staff not to answer any questions. Everyone here has great respect for you and knows the story isn't true. Unfortunately, perception is reality."

"So I'm fired?"

I'd given my blood, sweat, and tears to that school. I wasn't a teacher because it was an easy job or for the summers off—I did it because I *loved* my students. How were they able to toss me aside like trash over one damn story…a story that was absolute bullshit?

"Not fired," he corrected. "We just need you to take a break. Go on vacation. Spend some time with family. This will blow over in a few weeks."

"Weeks? What, and then I can come back? What about my students? What about River's Kids?" I asked the questions in rapid succession.

"We're working on finding someone to carry it in the interim. I know this is difficult to hear, Dani, but it's only temporary."

"When does this happen?"

Mr. Lopez remained quiet, unable to look at me, and I knew.

"Immediately," I muttered. I stood up and ran my palms along the sides of my jeans and righted my posture. "Thank you, Mr. Lopez. I appreciate you seeing me and I wish you good luck in your new job."

Before he could say anything, or before I would break down, I left his office, ignoring the box I had set on the front desk. Millie was walking toward me, and I didn't stop on my quest to get outside into the safety and solitude of my car.

"Dani," she called out, but I threw my hand up, waving, unable to speak.

***

Millie called numerous times between the time I got in my car and when I got home. I hadn't answered a single one. Grace called and left a message, but I didn't bother listening to it. In my case, misery loved solitude.

And then there was the call from Tabor that I declined as soon as it rang.

It wasn't his fault. He didn't do anything wrong, but I was angry and hurt and humiliated.

It was only one o'clock when I got home, but I had nothing better to do so I opened a bottle of wine and poured myself a glassful. I was afraid to turn on the television, unsure what I'd see, so I plugged in my iPod and let the music play at an unreasonable decibel.

Before I knew where the time had gone, I'd finished the entire bottle and it was only three, so I did what any depressed, angry woman would do…I opened another bottle.

"Dani," a muffled voice said as my body rocked gently from side to side. "Wake up."

My lids began to open slowly, feeling like sandpaper against my eyes, but I kept them closed, feeling a slight relief. My head pounded from the loud music, so I grabbed a pillow to cover my ears in an attempt to drown it out.

"Dani, wake up."

When I finally found the source of the movement, I jolted upright and moved backward, staring at Tabor kneeling in front of me, his concern etched on his face.

"I've been calling you all day," he said.

I closed my eyes and recalled the earlier conversation with my boss and grew both angry and sad. There I was, the man I loved worrying about me, and all I could see was what the relationship was costing me.

"Bad day," I said, not caring to elaborate. "I'm sorry I worried you."

"Are you okay?" His hand rested on top of my shoulder, his eyes full of concern.

"What time is it?" I responded, ignoring his question.

"Nine," he answered.

Nine?

I sat up and cradled my head in my hands as my arms rested on my knees. Recalling the disastrous day, I shook my head and I could feel a wave of defeat overcoming me. *Again.*

"Can you talk to me?" he asked.

"I'm really tired, I just want to go to bed," I answered in defeat as I stumbled to my feet. He was still on his knees as I moved past him and his hand grazed mine, but it didn't stop me. My mind was solely focused on what was happening to me, but I'd have to deal with it eventually. Despite Tabor looking as defeated as I felt, I was selfishly only worried about myself.

He was behind me as I made my way up the stairs, my steps slow and heavy.

I should have washed my face.

I should have brushed my teeth.

I should have done lots of things, but I did *none* of them.

I didn't bother changing my clothes, either. Instead I climbed into bed and pulled the covers over me, waiting for sleep to return. My body tensed for a moment when I felt the bed shift as Tabor got into bed beside me.

His arm snaked across my stomach as he moved closer, pushing his chest firmly against my back. I didn't want him to hold me, and yet I needed him exactly where he was. And when he remained quiet, I was thankful. But the silence didn't last.

"What are you thinking?" Tabor whispered over my shoulder. "Talk to me."

"Like I said, a bad day," I answered.

"Do you need to talk about it?"

I shook my head and squeezed my eyes shut, willing the emotions to stay away. His concern was tearing me apart because the job situation was *my* problem, not his. And though I knew it wasn't his fault, a part of me blamed him. If I hadn't fallen in love with him, I wouldn't be where I was.

"Clearly something is wrong and you're shutting me out."

"Maybe I'm not cut out for this," I said quietly.

"For what?"

"This. Us. Football. Watching you get hit and injured, it's scary," I admitted, though it was only a ruse so I didn't have to discuss what was *actually* wrong.

It was easy to say when he couldn't look into my eyes. I knew that if he could see my face, he'd know everything I was thinking. So I kept my voice steady and convinced myself that I believed my own words.

"I'm fine, Dani. I promise. You just need to have a little faith in me."

"You know that football isn't my thing, and watching the person I love going head to head kills me. It hurts me to see you hurt. I don't know how your mom does it. She has to be one of the strongest women on the planet," I said.

"She's been watching it for a long time. Trust me, she wasn't always so cool." He laughed and it echoed against my back. He placed his hand on my shoulder and pulled me to that I was lying on my back. His weight rested on his arm and as Tabor looked into my eyes, the moonlight from outside was the only thing illuminating his face. Why did he have to look at me like that, like he could read my mind?

Tabor was beautiful, and not in the traditional sense. Every imperfect part of him, each scar and gash that marred his body, made him beautiful. The way he looked at me like I was the only thing that mattered...made him beautiful.

"I'm sorry," I confessed sadly. "I wish I were stronger, but it's so damn hard. I watched your game with my parents, and I think I spent the entire game when you were on the field holding my breath and watching through my fingers. And when you were hit, I worried that it was too much. Too hard."

"Do you trust me?"

"You know I do."

"Do you want to be with me?"

"Tabor," I started, but he cut me off.

"Answer the question," he said firmly.

"Of course," I sighed.

"Then you have to believe that I know what I'm doing and there's no way I'd let anything happen to keep me from you."

"You're not God, Tabor. You're not invincible. How many times can you get hit or do the hitting and not be hurt? I don't want anything to happen to you."

"I get what you're saying, I do. But this is what I do, it's what I signed on for, and short of getting hurt, I'll be doing it for three more years with the Quakes."

A small nod was all I was able to muster and he leaned down, kissing me until he was sure I was finished debating the issue.

I breathed a sigh of relief that I'd diverted his attention long enough that he didn't ask about work. It wasn't something I was ready to discuss anyway. But as I rolled over, guilt washed over me knowing that I was still keeping something from him. There was nothing he could do and I needed to sort out the situation so I could determine how to move forward.

My back was tucked snuggly against his chest and I liked my bubble—*our* bubble. It was typically my favorite place to be. But my worries and fears were consuming me. The outside world meant nothing to us, but it was beginning to infiltrate our lives, and he had no idea how badly.

CHAPTER 23

DANI

The sunlight was barely visible through the blinds in my room, the heat of Tabor's breath hot against my neck. I wanted so much to turn to him and tell him what had happened, but I still hadn't wrapped my mind around it.

When he'd finally fallen asleep, my stomach felt nauseous from the wine I'd consumed—or maybe it was because I knew I was keeping the truth from him. My mind was reeling from the article and the consequences that had gone along with it. It seemed unfair that the district would force me to take a break, especially considering that our school needed all the help they could get.

I was restless the entire night, and though I knew it wasn't the end of the world, it was still bad.

Tabor stirred in the bed, and I closed my eyes and pretended to still be asleep. The bed shifted when he climbed out and I heard him quietly getting dressed before he walked to my side. There was a moment where I tried to make sure my eyes remained still because I was certain he was looking at me. He leaned down and kissed my cheek, sweetly brushing my hair out of my face.

"I'll call you after work," he whispered.

It was on the tip of my tongue to tell him not to bother...that there was no job to go to, but instead, I kept my eyes closed and waited while his steps tromped downstairs. I heard the front door lock and waited until the sound of his engine revving told me it was okay to get up. But I wasn't sure I wanted to move.

I was knee-deep in my self-pity because it was my first day "off" of work and I was utterly miserable. I could stay in ratty clothes all day long, watch movies, and eat junk food all day long and no one would care.

No one except me. I *wanted* to be at work, setting up my classroom, finalizing lesson plans...all of it, because I loved my kids.

If someone had told me three years ago that I'd love being a teacher, I would have laughed in their face. Kids weren't on my radar, and standing in front of a classroom shaping minds was even further. But it turned out that it's what I was meant to do. I was a damn good teacher and my students loved me.

And one viciously awful, lie-ridden story threatened to ruin my entire career. I wanted to strangle Candayce or whoever had sold that damn story to the gossip site. How could they live with themselves knowing they were making up horrible lies and potentially ruining people's lives? Did they even care?

Still, I just kept wondering how *I* ended up on a gossip site.

I knew that being with Tabor brought a new set of issues that normal couples didn't experience. But for some reason, I had assumed that I would be boring enough that people wouldn't pay any attention to me. And I couldn't have been more wrong.

"Enough," I muttered, deciding to stop feeling sorry for myself. I was better than that, and it was up to me to make the most of the time I had. I pulled myself out of bed and managed to get dressed. It didn't matter that nothing matched and there was a pretty good chance the shirt I was wearing was dirty; at least I was up.

Coffee would be my best friend, helping me to accomplish everything—assuming there was *something* to accomplish.

Standing at the bottom of the stairs, I looked around, trying to determine *where* to start when I heard my phone ringing. It was then I realized I'd never called Millie back, and I was certain she was steamed. But when I scrambled to locate my phone, figuring it was likely her, I came up empty. I moved pillows, blankets, and a load of laundry in my attempt to find it. Just as it was ringing for the final time, I found it…under the couch.

"Hello," I answered, winded.

"Why didn't you call me back yesterday?" Millie demanded, and I winced at her tone.

"I'm sorry."

"I heard about what happened," she said, softening her voice. "Are you okay?"

"I guess everyone knows."

"And not one of them is buying that story," she consoled. "It's a load of shit."

"Thanks, Mill," I groaned, throwing myself onto the couch. "I'm just so pissed. I don't know what I'm supposed to do. I mean, I could sit here and wait it out, but what does that get me? And what about River's Kids? Who's going to run that?"

"Your best friend who loves you and believes in your vision," she said timidly.

"Millie?" I asked, choking on her name.

"Don't hate me."

"Hate you? Why would I hate you? Are you serious? You're going to take over for me?" I asked.

"Yes. I'm serious. When I saw you running out the building, I went to Lopez to see what happened, and the first thing I asked was about River's Kids. He said that the program would be put on hold if we didn't find someone to step in…so…I did."

"I love you, do you know that?" I asked as my eyes teared up. "You're the only one I'd trust to run it."

"Thanks," she said.

It was quiet, neither of us knowing what to say. My friends were always there when I needed them most, and I felt incredibly lucky to have them. But this was beyond anything I expected. The time commitment for someone, let alone a new mom, was significant. So I knew that she'd stepped in because she loved me.

"What did Tabor say?" When I didn't answer, her tone turned scolding. "Dani. You *did* tell him. Didn't you?"

"Not really?" I cringed at my own words.

"Not really?" she repeated. "Dani. You either did or didn't tell him."

"Yeah. One of those," I said noncommittally.

"You're ridiculous. Tell. Him," she demanded. "He's going to figure it out anyway. And he needs to know what people are saying."

"Does he? What good is that going to do?"

"I hate to remind you, but you're in a relationship now, which means you work it out. To-ge-ther," she lectured.

"Fine," I grumbled.

"You know I'm right."

"I know," I muttered. "I know, I know, *I know*. I'm just not sure how to tell him without sounding like the bitter woman I am."

"That man loves you…and I'm sure he still will when he sees the crazy bitch you've been hiding all this time," she teased. "Time to take off the mask, Dani."

"Gee, thanks," I laughed, my mood slightly better.

"So what's the plan while you're on *vacation*?" she asked.

"I have no idea. Maybe some cleaning? Get around to organizing my closet? Funny thing is, when I'm working I look forward to my time off, but this feels like a punishment for something I didn't do."

"So do something about it. Don't roll over and accept the hand you've been dealt. Call Lopez. Call the school board. Email Fangurl. Set the record straight."

"That's only going to make it worse. Then I go from being the jealous girlfriend to the prima donna who cries when her name is mentioned in an unflattering light."

"Then talk to Tabor and tell him. Maybe he's got a better solution."

"Yeah, maybe you're right. Thanks, Millie, for everything," I said, genuinely feeling blessed to have my best friend stand by me.

"Anytime."

***

By the end of the day, my condo was spotless. I'd cooked dinner, and even managed a shower. I felt like crap, but I didn't have to look it, so I made the most of my time. At Millie's prodding, I decided that I would tell Tabor what was going on and hoped that he would have a way of handling things.

"How was your day?" Tabor asked as he walked into the living room.

"Uneventful," I answered.

"Are you finished setting everything up for school?"

"Not exactly."

I walked into the kitchen and grabbed two water bottles from the fridge, handing him one and chugging mine in an attempt to brace myself. I had dreaded the conversation all day, and no matter how I'd told myself it would go, I knew my emotions would get me. And in my case, things never went as planned.

A *V* formed between his brows as he studied me carefully. "Did I do something wrong?"

I scoffed and my lips curved into a sad smile. "I guess you haven't seen the latest from Fangurl, have you?"

He was still watching me with curiosity, his head turned to the side. "What's going on?"

Without another word, I brought my laptop over to him and found the offending site to show him the story. He took the device from my hands and set it on his lap, looking from me and back to the computer, utterly confused. It was hard to look at him, so I took a seat on the opposite side of the couch and played with the label on my water bottle.

Tabor's eyes were scanning the screen, his face impassive. At one point he inhaled sharply and shook his head. From the corner of my eye I saw him glance at me, but I didn't meet his gaze. And when he finished, he looked angry or disappointed—I couldn't tell which. He gently set the laptop on the coffee table and moved closer to my end of the couch.

"Damnit, Dani," he grumbled. "I'm sorry, babe."

His outstretched arm offered me consolation that I wasn't sure I wanted or needed at that moment. I felt like the worst person, because I saw the hurt flash across his face when I flinched from his touch. I wanted to take it back, but I was so deep in my own misery that it was hard for me to crawl out of it.

"This isn't my fault," he reminded me. Despite my knowledge of that information, I was still upset. "And Fangurl is nothing more than a bitter, angry, lonely person who has nothing better to do."

"Trust me, I know. But that story is out there. A completely fabricated, malicious lie that has big implications."

"I wish I could fix it, but this is a side effect of being with me," he reminded me, as if I didn't know firsthand.

"This is what I was afraid of all along! The whole reason I wanted to keep *us* a secret...and now everything is ruined," I spat, before I was able to take the words back.

"It's a stupid story, Dani. Stop making a bigger deal about it than it is," he argued, standing up to move away from me. "It's like you're looking for a fight. They're words. I get you're upset, but this is ridiculous."

"Ridiculous?" I questioned, my voice rising as I stood up. "Maybe *you're* used to people being in your business and making up stories about you, but I'm not. And these lies *can* ruin people's lives."

"It's a stupid gossip rag. No one believes that shit!"

"Yeah, well, tell that to my boss, who put me on temporary leave of absence."

"What?" He took a step back. "When did this happen?"

"Yesterday."

"Why didn't you tell me?"

"Because I didn't want to talk about it. I was sent home before lunch and that's it."

"But you still have your job, right?"

"I don't know. I wasn't allowed to finish setting up my room, and the school's been hounded with inquiries for interviews. I guess I was just one hassle they don't want right now. And I get it. This is a damn circus."

"Don't you think you're being a bit dramatic?"

"No, actually, I don't. I'm the exact modicum of drama I should be, considering that I might not have a job to go back to."

"So you can get another job somewhere else," he suggested. Funny, it was as if he thought jobs just fell from the sky.

"That's not the point, Tabor. I'm good at what I do. And what about my kids? What about the after-school program that I've busted my ass to keep going? This isn't just some hobby of mine to pass the time."

"I didn't mean it like that," he said apologetically. "I'm just trying to point out it's not the end of the world."

"No, it's not. But this condo, groceries, and bills don't pay for themselves," I argued. "If by some chance they don't let me come back, I have about three months of savings that I can live off of before I'm up shit creek."

"Don't you realize I wouldn't let that happen? Jeez, Dani…I love you and I want to be there for you. Hell, you don't have to work. And if you can't pay for this place, you can just move in with me."

"Are you kidding me?" I laughed humorlessly. "Just stop."

"All I'm saying is that there are options."

"Moving in with you isn't one of them. I've been on my own since I was eighteen—I can take care of myself. And the reason I move in with my boyfriend isn't going to be because I lost my job. Don't you get it, Tabor? I love what I do and I don't want to lose it. And yet here I am, giving it all up for a guy. A guy who gets the shit beat out of him on a weekly basis."

"You're back on that again?" he asked, running his hand through his hair. "There's more to this. What are you trying to say?"

"Just…I don't know, maybe we need some time apart."

"Are you breaking up with me?"

I shook my head, my eyes filling with tears at the mere suggestion. I'd never even considered breaking up, because he was a part of me. But so were my students.

"Just a break," I answered, dropping my gaze to the floor.

"Jeez, Dani, this isn't some sitcom where time stops while you figure your shit out. A *break*?"

"Just until the season is over and the attention dies down." It sounded like a reasonable request. Nothing permanent, but a solution to a temporary issue.

"This isn't what you want. And I *know* it's not what I want," Tabor argued.

"Please, just give me a little time," I pleaded as my eyes stung with unshed tears.

"What do you want? Do you want to end this?"

"Of course not."

"Then drop this break idea of yours. Let's deal with this like any other couple would."

"But we're not any other couple. You're JT Hunter and I'm just a schoolteacher who fell in love with you."

I walked to where he stood and noticed his hands were balled into fists, his breathing heavy. He looked completely destroyed, and I realized I'd done that to him. When I reached for his face, he flinched as though my touch alone burned him, and my heart broke.

"I don't know what the answer is here, but we both have a job to do...and right now I need to focus on trying to get mine back and proving that what we have isn't going to get in the way of my commitments."

"And breaking up will prove this how?"

A glimmer of hope sprang up as an idea came to mind. "Maybe we don't have to break up," I said with a smile. "We can just 'pretend.' Let people believe we're over and still be together in secret."

Tabor pried my hands away from him and kissed my knuckles before releasing me, my smile slowly fading. He took a step back and shook his head, and I knew what he was going to say before the words came out.

"I can't do that, Dani."

"It wouldn't be forever," I said. "Just until all of this blows over."

"But that's just it," he said, leaning down to look into my eyes. "I'd never ask you to hide who we are, and the fact that you even consider this to be a good idea kills me."

"Tabor, I'm just trying to come up with a solution to get my job back and keep you."

"And who said you have to choose?" His voice sounded so pained. I did that to him. "Why is it so easy to walk away from us? It's almost like you're looking for an out."

"That's not true. You're putting words in my mouth," I said weakly.

"I don't think I've ever felt as shitty as I do right now."

He started to walk away, so I grabbed his hand and moved in front of him. "Wait. Just stop, please. Listen to me...I love you."

I leaned down and he wrapped his arms around me, hugging me against his body. My hands gripped his shirt tightly like he was my lifeline. I lifted my chin and looked at his face, his eyes reflecting his pain. He placed a chaste kiss to my lips before pulling my hands off his body.

"I love you, too, Dani. But I can't do what you're asking."

He walked toward the front door and looked back at me over his shoulder, and my heart sank.

"Tabor," I called out.

"Good luck with your job."

With that, he opened the door, and when I heard it shut behind him I collapsed to the floor and sobbed. The pain in his eyes had crushed my soul, and I prayed that I'd be able to make it right, because he didn't deserve my words. I didn't want to lose him, and yet he'd walked out the door—and it was all my fault.

CHAPTER 24

DANI

Tabor left and all the joy was sucked from my day.

He didn't call.

He didn't text.

But neither did I.

It was radio silence and I was miserable without the contact. I kept watching the sports edition of the news, hoping to catch a glimpse of him. The Quakes didn't do well in their fourth preseason game and the commentators were critical of all the players' performances—even Tabor's.

School started and I was still at home, on my couch, biding my time until I could return. I received a glimmer of hope when the latest post from Fangurl Sports was posted.

Hunter's Back in the Game

You heard us right. And we're not talking football. A source close to JT Hunter revealed last night that the football star and girlfriend Danielle Miner have called it quits. (Insert BOO-HOO here) But Fangurl is pretty excited by the news, considering we always imagined JT Hunter with someone like Candayce, or maybe even his ex, Natasha. Time will tell.

As for Miner, she's been in hiding since the breakup and has been a no-show for work. Unverified stories claim that she took a leave of absence, while others claim she was fired. Still, it seems as though the teacher-turned-football-star-girlfriend may have been the one to break up with Hunter. He's been seen around town sporting facial scruff, sunglasses, and a ball cap. Local reporter Carl Jenkins claims that he and others have been unable to interview the football player and he's only honored his commitments to the kids that he supports through various hospital charities. Maybe there's a doctor on-call to mend his broken heart.

This Fangurl person hid behind a persona that was mean-spirited, and yet had tons of followers. I knew, because I was stalking her feed. But I refused to read the comments people left. I'd made that mistake one time, and when I read people bashing me and calling me horrible names, I vowed to never do it again. With one post, she wielded the power to ruin relationships, end careers, and spread lies. And that's just what she was able to do to Tabor and me.

A week without Tabor was torture, and the only way I could see him was by watching his football games on television. His first regular season game was coming up in a few days, and I was surprised when I got a call from Marta.

"Did I catch you at a bad time?" she asked sweetly.

"No, ma'am. How are you?"

"I'd be a lot better if I knew that you and my son made up," she said with a laugh. "How are you doing, honey?"

"Honestly? I've been better," I answered. "How is he?"

"Miserable. Dani, I don't want to pry, and you can tell me to mind my own business, but what happened with you two? He won't talk about it and I'm worried about him. I don't think I've ever seen Tabor more happy than he was with you."

My heart filled with so much love and hope with her simple words. I couldn't recall a happier time for myself, and being without Tabor was like a piece of me was missing.

"I said the wrong thing," I admitted sadly. "I'd just been put on leave of absence at work because of our relationship, and I hurt him so bad. I didn't mean it."

"Do you want to be with him?"

"More than anything," I sighed. "I miss him so much and I don't know what to do about it."

"You tell him. Tabor is stubborn and sometimes he forgets that things like relationships can get crushed under the public eye. He doesn't realize that it's not the easiest life. But he's worth the effort."

"Yes. He is."

"I'm glad you see it that way," she said. "Because I have a big favor to ask."

"Okay," I said, suspicious of the question.

"I planned on going to the opening game, but Abbi has a meeting with a wedding planner and this is the only weekend she has available for a while. So would you go to the game in my place? I know it's hard for you to watch him—"

"I'll be there," I interrupted, putting her concerns at ease. "I hate watching him get hit, but I love him and I need to show him that."

"Thank you, Dani. I appreciate it." It sounded as though our conversation was coming to an end and I realized I needed something else.

"Marta?" She didn't say anything, so I continued. "Don't tell him."

Her sweet chuckle made a genuine smile appear on my face. "It's our secret."

"Thank you," I said before we hung up.

I had a renewed sense of hope that maybe I could repair the damage done. Starting with my job. I put on a bit of makeup and got dressed quickly before making the short drive to River Valley Junior High School. It was only the first week, but I wasn't going down without a fight. I deserved my job, and if they didn't want me there, they were going to have to fire me.

Linda, the secretary, spotted me as I entered the double glass doors and gave me a knowing smile.

"Is the new principal in?" I asked confidently and she nodded. "If he's not busy, may I see him?"

"Dr. Putnam, Danielle Miner is here to see you," she said over the phone.

"Now?"

"Yes, sir," she said and winked at me.

"Oh-Okay. Send her in."

"Thanks, Linda," I whispered as I walked past her desk, toward the office where my career had been paused only recently.

Dr. Putnam was a tall, thin man with graying hair and glasses that looked too big for his face. He was dressed in brown slacks and a white golf shirt, sitting behind his oversized mahogany desk. He looked less approachable than Mr. Lopez, but still smiled and greeted me as I walked in.

"Ms. Miner, please come in. It's nice to finally meet you," he said, motioning to an empty chair. "What can I do for you?"

"I'd like to talk to you about my employment status," I said.

"I understand that you've taken a leave of absence," he stated, looking confused. "Are you here to resign?"

"What? No. The opposite. I didn't take a leave of absence. I was forced," I informed him.

"I don't understand," he said. "So why haven't you been here?"

"I was told that the administration requested that I take a 'vacation' until all the hoopla around JT Hunter and me died down."

"What do you have to do with JT Hunter?" he questioned, and I wanted to hug the man on the spot. He was probably the only person around who was oblivious to the story.

"We've been dating for a few months. And when a gossip site posted a story, making unflattering and untrue claims against me, the school didn't like the light that was being shed on me or them."

Dr. Putnam sat back in his chair and swiveled it side to side like a child, his index fingers steepled over his mouth. He leaned forward and punched a few things into the computer and stared at his screen.

"Ah. I see," he said. "I'm looking over the notes in your file and this is actually quite ridiculous. I see no need for you to be disciplined over something that is out of your control, Ms. Miner."

Finally! Someone else sees it the way I do.

"So does that mean I can come back to work?"

"Let me make a few calls and I'll get back to you tomorrow?"

"Respectfully, sir, I'm not going to end things with JT because of my job. I love what I do, and I want to do it here, but I'm not willing to give up my relationship for a job."

"Noted. And I'm sure you're eager to get to your classroom and your students," he said, smiling at me.

"Thank you, Dr. Putnam. I appreciate this more than you know." I got up to leave, but turned around. "And what about River's Kids?"

"Assuming everything is approved, it's all yours."

***

Millie called me when she heard the news, and invited me to go over for dinner. It had been a while since I'd seen Nick or Colton, so I was looking forward to a quiet evening with friends.

My family was pleased when I shared the news that I had been reinstated, effective immediately. They questioned what it meant for Tabor and me, and I assured them I was not ready to give him up. I just hoped that he would be willing to hear me out and forgive my poor behavior that night.

"The best way to get over someone is to get under someone else," Millie said crassly as she enjoyed her second glass of wine after dinner.

"I'm not trying to get over him," I argued. "I don't know where things stand, but I'm not going to give up."

"But...wait. What about this one—if you love someone, let them..."

"Stop. Please," I laughed. "What are you, a fortune cookie gone lame? I don't want to get back out there. I had what I wanted and I messed it up."

"You know, Nick saw Philip again and he asked about you. He heard that you and Tabor broke up and wondered if you were up for hanging out."

I sighed heavily and rolled my eyes. "That's a hard no, thanks, Millie."

"I know you're not ready to date, but maybe seeing an old friend could cheer you up."

"I don't want to see him!"

"What's your deal? Philip was a part of your life for a year. What harm is there in coming over and having a drink?"

"Come over…as in he's coming over *here*?"

Millie nodded her head and smiled, proud that she'd pulled one over on me. But my blood was boiling and my body grew damp with sweat. If she couldn't see the absolute rage in my eyes, then she was blind.

"When?" I asked, standing up and trying to locate my purse.

"What's wrong?"

"When, Millie?" She flinched when I shouted at her, but I wasn't playing games.

"Thirty minutes or so?"

I picked up my purse and started for the door when she threw herself in front of it. "What's wrong with you?"

"You had no right!"

"Lighten up, Dani. It's a drink, not a marriage proposal," she shot back, rolling her eyes.

"Let. Me. Go," I seethed. "Now."

"Not until you tell me what's going on. Why are you so pissed?"

"Millicent DeMarco. Move."

She cowered at my use of her name, but remained still.

"I can't see him."

"You don't still have feelings for Philip, do you?"

"Yeah, actually I do. Feelings of hatred. Murderous feelings. Castration feelings. Beat the living shit out of him feelings. Do I need to go on?"

"I had no idea."

"No. But I've told you I don't want to see him, and that should be enough of a reason. I shouldn't have to explain myself to you or anyone else."

"But he was so great, and you two together were adorable."

"Yeah, we were so cute together—especially when he hit me. He was the perfect boyfriend," I said, condescension dripping from my words.

"What?"

"Just let me go."

"He hit you?" she breathed out, barely audible as she reached out to touch my arm. "When did this happen? Why didn't you tell me?"

"Because I took care of it. Look, I have to go before he gets here," I demanded urgently.

"I never would have pushed if I'd known," she defended sadly. "I'm so sorry."

"We'll talk later," I said as I began to reach for the door, but a knock sounded from the other side. "Shit!"

"I'll take care of it," she said apologetically. "Go play with Colton."

My hand was still braced on the door and I shook my head before turning to face her. I lifted my chin and took a deep breath. "No. I'll take care of it."

"This is my fault. I invited him here," she conceded. "Honestly, I've got it."

I didn't argue with her, instead pulling the door open to find Philip, the man I had once loved, standing in front of me looking as handsome as I remembered. But there was an ugliness beneath that beauty. Jealousy, control, and misogyny were always there, waiting to show through. I'd been victim to his verbal lashings more than I was willing to admit, but the physical threats were far more recent and were the reason I had stepped away when I did.

"Dani," he said with a smile, leaning forward to kiss my cheek, but I stepped away.

"Philip," I answered curtly. "I'm sorry you came all this way, but I'm afraid there's been a mistake."

"But Millie said you'd be here and were looking forward to seeing me," he stated, and I glanced at my friend, who winced at the truth.

"I believe the last time we spoke, I told you that I *never* wanted to see you again. This will be the last time I say it, so I suggest you turn around and forget that you ever knew me."

His lip curled, a sneer appearing on his face, and I knew Millie was about to witness the ugly I knew too well. Philip was a master at pretending in front of other people; it was when he got you alone that his mean side appeared. Only this time, I'd embarrassed him.

"So you go out with JT Hunter a few times and you think you're better than me? He dumped you, Dani. You'd be lucky to have me, because no one wants his sloppy seconds."

My hand connected with his cheek, the snap so loud that Nick stepped into the room to see what had happened. He looked at Millie, whose hands covered her mouth, and then to me. But when his eyes landed on Philip, who took a step toward me, Nick lunged forward and pushed his hands against Philip's chest.

"Listen, buddy, you need to go. I don't know what's going on here, but it doesn't look good."

"That bitch just slapped me," he said, pointing at me.

Nick looked at me and I shrugged.

"Bitch? Really, man? All this talk like you want to get back together and then you call her names? If that's what you do, I can see why she hit you."

Millie's hand reached for mine, my entire body shaking at the exchange. I hadn't planned to slap him, but after a year of not doing anything when he'd said and done far worse, I saw red. She squeezed my hand and pulled me toward her.

"Philip, you need to go," she said evenly. "And don't come back."

He started running his mouth, so Nick walked him outside and closed the door behind them, leaving me in the front entry with Millie. Her eyes welled with tears and she wrapped her arms around me.

"I'm so sorry, Dani. I didn't know," she cried.

"No one knew," I admitted. "Except Tabor."

"You told him?" she gasped. "You didn't even tell me."

"I know, and I'm sorry."

"No," she said. "That's not what I mean. It's just that you keep so much to yourself, and for you to open up to him...I'm just surprised, that's all."

"Why?"

"Because you don't just open up to anyone, Dani."

"But he's not just anyone. He's the person I love. I trust him with my life," I said.

Millie smirked at my admission and appeared pleased with my words. "I know you do. So what now?"

"Well, now all I have to do is convince Tabor that I didn't mean anything I said to him the other night."

Before I could elaborate, Nick walked in and stared at the two of us, his eyes wide. "What in the hell was that all about?"

"I'll explain later," Millie said.

"Damn, girl," he said, high-fiving me. "Hell of a slap."

"What?" I asked. "But you liked Philip."

"Hell, no! I just talked to him because he was your boyfriend. I never liked that guy. He was full of shit," he added. "Not like Tabor. He's good people."

"You don't have to hit me over the head with it. I get it. And trust me, I'm on it."

"Good," Nick and Millie said in unison.

"I need another glass of wine," she added, pulling me behind to join her.

CHAPTER 25

DANI

I couldn't recall a time when I had felt as nervous as I did on the night of Tabor's first regular season game. Was it the game? Or was it seeing him and hoping that we could get back on track? I couldn't be sure of either, but I was certain that I had to go and at least try.

I'd dressed in a pair of jeans and a shirt that had his jersey number—something Millie had let me borrow before I left her place. She'd warned me that if she didn't get the shirt back, she'd hunt me down, but I laughed in her face because I had no plans on returning it.

She owes me after what she pulled.

When my friends and family learned that Marta had given me two tickets, they began begging and lobbying for me to take them. My brother-in-law offered to wash my car. Grace said she'd cook me dinner for a week. Millie went for the gut and tried to use the best friend card. But in the end, it was my dad I planned on taking. I knew it the moment Marta had asked me to go, and when I asked him if he wanted to join, he practically screamed in my ear.

I had ulterior motives in bringing Dad. I'd need his encouragement to make it through the game, and he had the ability to calm me when needed. He offered to drive and I insisted on getting to the stadium early on the off chance I might see Tabor during warm-ups. I had a feeling the seats were good, because it was in Tabor's nature to take care of Marta and Abbi.

I saw the Tabor-Dani reunion playing out in my head like it was a cheesy romance chick flick.

I'd be in the club seats, hanging out with Dad, when Tabor walked onto the field. He'd look up in the stands to see his mom and sister cheering him on, only instead, he'd see me. His smile would grow wide and I would watch with bated breath as he used his super-human strength to scale the stands until he was standing in front of me, questioning what I was doing there.

He'd wait for me to speak and I'd tell him that I loved him and I'd needed him to know right away. And as I was apologizing for my behavior, he'd tell me to shut up and then he'd kiss me. The stadium would erupt in thunderous applause as we made out until we realized that people were watching—our faces plastered on the Jumbotron.

Of course he'd still have to play, but he'd have a smile on his face the whole time he was on the field because I was there. The Quakes would win the game in the end and we'd celebrate by getting back together, and live happily ever after.

But then I remembered that my life wasn't a movie, and I was hardly the heroine people would be cheering for. Fangurl Sports and the subsequent comments that went with her "articles" proved that already. I was being called stupid, idiot, gold digger, media whore, and unworthy all over that website. I'd had to stop stalking the page because it only served to anger me.

I found myself pacing while I waited for Dad to show up, because I had hours until the game started. It was torturous standing around with nothing to do but let my mind drive me insane.

"What was I thinking?" I said aloud. The answering silence was right: *Nothing*. I wasn't thinking at all.

Marta had agreed to keep quiet about my presence at his game, but the longer I stood around, it felt like nothing more than a ridiculous game. I didn't want to play games with Tabor. We deserved more than that; we deserved better.

My plan was to show up, cheer him on, and then talk after the game and tell him how wrong I was to let him go…to let him think I wanted out. But something inside me was telling me to do it now. Don't wait.

"I can't wait," I said silently.

I needed Tabor to know I was wrong. He needed to hear it from me, and sooner rather than later. I didn't want a break or a breakup or any other type of separation. The week we were apart was too much as it was. He was in my heart and soul and I had no desire to find a replacement for him. If our time apart had proved anything to me, it was that there was no replacement.

I found myself picking up my phone, dialing Tabor's number, and waiting for him to answer. Each ring, I held my breath, but I was disappointed that after the fourth ring I got his voicemail.

"Hey, Tabor, it's Dani. I was hoping you'd answer because I really want to talk to you. You're probably getting ready for the game, but still, I just needed to say I…I miss you. And you were right," I laughed softly. "You have no idea how bitter that tastes, but it's true and you need to know that. I *don't* want to hide us and I don't want a break or a breakup. I just want you. However I can have you, that's what I want…I wish you'd answered, because I hate saying all of this to your voicemail, but I love you. Please call me. I want to hear your voice before the game…Bye."

I hung up and hoped that he'd seen that I'd called. Maybe my name flashed on the screen and he rejected it. But my hope was that he would see there was a message and would at least listen to it. I needed him to hear my words, and hoped like hell he believed them. Because every word was true.

Before I could dwell on the fact that he didn't answer the call, I looked over my shoulder when I heard the knock at the door. Dad stood on the other side, dressed in his Quakes jersey and baseball cap. I opened the door and he was practically bouncing up and down.

"You ready, honey?"

"Yeah, just let me get my purse."

I was locking the door behind me, and when I turned to face him, he hadn't walked to the car.

"You okay?" I asked.

"Yeah," he answered, clearing his throat and making his voice deeper. "I'm good. Are you?"

"I'm fine." I nodded and smiled. "Dad? Should I drive?"

He laughed nervously and handed me the keys to his pickup. "I think that'd be a good idea."

I laughed and hugged him, because he was like a kid on Christmas morning.

The drive to Quakes Sportsplex was painfully slow, but you wouldn't guess by the seventy-five miles per hour I was driving on the freeway. I swore that snails were passing me up, but I convinced myself to stay the course. I was on a mission and the sooner I got to the stadium, the better. And hopefully in one piece.

When I pulled into the parking lot, the attendant took a look at my pass and pointed to a gentleman across the way that began waving at me. I wasn't sure where I was going, but the closer I got, I noticed we had to have the best location—directly in front of the entrance.

"Tabor hooks his mom up," Dad noticed appreciatively.

"Looks that way."

We both hurried out of the car, made our way to the gates, and waited in line. I took the opportunity to check my phone, but there were no calls and my heart sank. When I looked around, there were so many people that it felt like a cattle call. I waited for someone to moo, or make some other obnoxious noise. Hell, I was close to making the noise myself. I was becoming antsy because I was quickly realizing that I was one of many at the stadium. There was little to no chance of him spotting me among the hordes of fans. And as the time wore on, the chances of him calling were slim, at best.

"Any idea where we go?" Dad asked.

"Marta said we're in the club level, wherever that is," I said with a shrug.

"Club, huh? Nice."

I pulled out my phone to look again and Dad nudged my arm

with his elbow.

"Stop worrying so much. He's going to be happy you're here. And if he's not, then he's not the guy I thought he was."

My nose twitched and I had to look away. Words like that were rare from my dad, so when he said them I felt them deep in my chest. When I was able to get past the lump that formed in my throat, I looked at Dad and grinned.

"Thanks, Dad."

It took at least twenty minutes to get through the line and I wished I'd left my purse in the car. Instead, I had to get in the longer line so they could check my bag, along with the hundreds of other women who had made the same mistake.

We were directed to the second level of the stadium, where an usher opened a door, granting us entrance to an exclusive seating area. From our vantage point, we could see the entire field and the seats that were beginning to fill in.

"Can I get you anything to drink?" asked a woman dressed in a pressed white shirt and black pants. I read her nametag and smiled.

"Thanks, Robyn. I'm good. Dad?"

He was still in awe, staring at the field and admiring the view. I looked at Robyn and smiled when she commented that she'd return to check on us in a few.

"Dani, the Quakes are coming out to warm up," Dad said.

I was distracted by the enormity of the stadium and I hadn't noticed the players walking out. I turned and stood on my toes, as if that would give me a better view—but it didn't. The players were hard to make out. We were close enough to see the action, but my eyes couldn't make out the jersey numbers.

"I don't see him," I muttered to Dad, who walked over and stood next to me. "Do you?"

He studied the field and quickly pointed to the far right. "See the mascot running around down there. He's right next to him."

Following my dad's directions, I spotted him stretching and throwing a football around. My heart fell on the ground at my feet and I wanted to scream his name, run down the stadium steps, and jump into his arms.

FUMBLED

The game started off strong, Tabor making two sacks and blocking a free kick. Dad was impressed with my knowledge of the game and I admitted to him that I had read up on the terminology and the rules of the game. I was still pretty clueless, but as least I didn't sound like a complete idiot.

During the time Tabor was on the field, my eyes were glued to his form. He never looked up to the box where we watched, and I wondered if Marta had spilled the truth. Maybe he knew I was there and was pissed, refusing to look up. Perhaps that knowledge spawned his game aggression.

I pulled out my phone and texted Marta. I didn't want to be blindsided if he did know.

> **Me: Does he know I'm here?**
> **Marta: I talked to him last night. He knows I'm not there.**
> **Me: Does he know you gave the tickets away?**
> **Marta: You're fine, Dani. He'll be happy when he sees you.**
> **Me: I hope so.**

I shoved my phone back into my purse and played different scenarios about how he might react to seeing me. It ranged from ecstatic to disgusted and I had to try hard to shove the thoughts out altogether. Clearly I was too emotional to think straight. But all I could think about was Tabor.

"All right, Quakes fans," the announced yelled over the top, "let's make some noise!"

It was the beginning of the third quarter and the Quakes were winning twenty-four to thirteen. The stadium went wild and as the players jogged back onto the field, and this time I spotted Tabor instantly. He was walking onto the field, lagging behind a few players, when I saw him look to where Dad and I stood. My knees felt weak and my heart began to race at the sight of him. But there was no smile, no look of recognition. Tabor looked away and said something to his teammate before walking over to get into position.

"Look at me," I muttered, telepathically willing him to hear me.

The stadium was roaring and I could barely hear myself think. Everything was vibrating with excitement as the defense prepared to take down the opposing team. Just as the play was about to start, I noticed Tabor's head turn in my direction, as if to check to see if I was really there. I wanted him to be happy to see me, but I was hurt to think that maybe I was the last person he wanted to see. He hadn't called me. He didn't return my call. What if I'd made the wrong decision in showing up?

I tentatively lifted my hand in a wave, but my smile faltered when I saw him look away just as he returned his focus to the game.

He was squatted across from another big player, waiting for the play to start, and I was on edge. The whole thing was hard to watch. The quarterback was looking for someone to pass to when Tabor lunged to tackle the guy in front of him. At the same time, his teammate moved to hit the same guy, but missed and hit Tabor instead, and he went down.

A whistle sounded abruptly at the end of the play and a collective gasp from the crowd confirmed my suspicions. I turned my face into my dad's shoulder and waited.

"Number thirty-five, JT Hunter, is down," the announcer said over the speakers.

My body felt heavy with those words and I, like everyone else, turned to the big screen to see what had happened. Slow motion was just as painful to watch, if not worse. In the replay, just as he made contact with his target, Jameson—his teammate—hit him from the side.

"Dad?"

He wrapped an arm around my shoulder and hugged me. "He'll be fine." He didn't sound convincing.

I turned and looked down at the field, where Tabor's body remained unmoving—at least from what I could see. A small crowd of athletic trainers and doctors surrounded him, and several players lingered. There was an eerie quiet in the stadium, fans with their hands covering their mouths, the chatter a low hum.

"He's not moving," I whispered. "Why isn't he moving?"

"It looked like it was his knee, but I couldn't tell from that angle," he said.

"So it's bad."

"They're working on him," Dad said, rubbing my arm.

My phone rang and I answered it immediately. I didn't bother to see who it was, but I figured it had to be someone that saw what happened.

"Dani, what's going on? Is he okay? They cut to a commercial and Mom's freaking out," Abbi said, her own voice laced with fear.

"He's still on the field, they're working on him right now," I told her. "Stay on the phone."

"What happened?" Abbi asked, almost as if she didn't truly expect an answer.

I looked at my dad and then at the commotion that was happening on the field. "What's going on, Dad?"

His silence sent a chill down my spine and I wanted to cry, but I had Tabor's sister and mom to consider. I needed to hold it together.

"Abbi, they're putting him on a stretcher and it looks like they're going to cart him off the field," I told her cautiously.

Her soft cries made my own tears start to fall and I wished I'd never been there. Tabor would be okay if I hadn't insisted on keeping my presence a secret. His focus would have been on the game and not distracted by me.

"Mom and I are getting on the first flight we can," Abbi said. "Don't let him out of your sight."

"I promise," I said, hanging up the phone and grabbing my things.

"What are you doing?" Dad asked.

"We need to get to the hospital," I told him as I led the way up the stairs, past the concerned fans.

CHAPTER 26

DANI

"Can you tell me where I can find JT Hunter?" I asked the stunned woman at the front desk.

She was talking to an older couple at her station and paid no attention to me.

"I'm sorry," I said to the waiting strangers in front of me. I had one person on my mind and I needed to see him. I looked at the woman again. "Can you please help me?"

The older couple stepped aside and my dad stood next to me. The middle-aged blond woman peered at me over her wire-rimmed glasses and huffed.

"I'm sorry, I can't give you that information," she said.

"Please, I need to see Tabor," I begged and she softened slightly.

"And you are?"

On my way to the hospital, Marta had called, and I could hear the worry and terror in her voice. I'd wished I could put her mind at ease, but my own fear had me on edge. It was then that she reminded me what to say when I arrived. My stomach churned and took a deep breath, recalling Marta's words.

"His...sister," I said, though it wasn't even close to the truth. "I'm his sister."

The nurse eyed me speculatively and nodded once.

"One moment," she answered. Her fingers began moving across the keyboard and her eyes roved the screen.

"I'm afraid you can't see him right now, he's in with the doctor, but we'll send someone out as soon as we can," she said.

"Is he okay?" I asked, choking on the words.

"I'm sorry, ma'am, I can't tell you anything."

"Can't? Or won't?" I demanded, but my dad pulled me away before I could say more.

"You need to calm down. That woman is doing her job. She can't tell you anything if she doesn't know anything, so let's sit and wait."

Dad wasn't one to handle me; we were cut from the same cloth and I wasn't typically reactive. But the not-knowing part of it was killing me. Despite my concern, I did as he said and tried to get myself together. I needed to be poised and collected when I finally got to see him. Tabor would need me at my best.

My phone was blowing up with texts from everyone, and all that did was get me worked up.

Millie: Is he okay? Have you seen him?
Viola: Millie told me what happened. Are you okay?
Grace: I'm sure it's not as bad as it looked.
Mom: I'm saying a prayer. Let me know as soon as you hear something.

I didn't respond to any of them, and not because I was trying to be a jerk. My battery was already low and I was determined to save what was left to communicate with Abbi and Marta.

I was pacing around the waiting room with nothing to do but assume the worst. Tabor's family was scheduled to arrive by ten, but the flight had been delayed and I knew they were upset. Dad didn't leave my side except to call Mom and Grace, updating them that we were still waiting.

Dee, Wilson's wife, strolled into the emergency room and spotted me in the back corner with Dad. She rushed over and pulled me into a hug.

"How is he?" she asked.

"I don't know. They won't let me see him," I said, choking on a sob.

"Let's see what we can do about that," she said, leaving me with my dad.

"I bet she'll get answers," my dad said.

"He has to be okay, Dad."

"There's nothing you can do right now, except maybe pray. Just think good thoughts."

I closed my eyes and tried to do as he said, but when I closed them, all I saw was Tabor. The way he'd looked at me when he saw me in the stands. And the way he looked when he was hit. When I forced my eyes open, I noticed Dee walking over with a smug grin on her face.

"The doctor is going to talk to us in a second. He's briefing the sports doc right now," she said.

"It's my fault," I admitted. "I shouldn't have come to the game."

"He knew you were there," Dee admitted, but I was confused.

"His mom didn't tell him I was there," I recalled from my earlier text.

She chuckled shook her head. "Wilson told me to come to the hospital because he had a feeling you'd be here. He told me JT said that he saw you at the game."

"I thought so."

"Supposedly during halftime, he was looking around, and when Wilson asked what was wrong he said 'Dani's here. I don't know where, but she's here,' and that was it. Wilson said something changed in the locker room. He seemed more relaxed, I guess."

"I think he saw me when he was walking onto the field."

"Did you really tell that woman you were his sister?"

I shrugged. "Marta told me to tell them that."

"Do you realize how many women could show up claiming to be his *sister*?"

"You're kidding me. Why would his mom tell me to say that?"

"Because it works for his *actual* sister. You know, because she has ID to prove who she is." She smiled. "Don't worry, you're gonna see him."

"Thank you, Dee."

"What about his mom and sister?"

"I think their flight took off already. I should try calling and let them know what's going on."

"If you want, I'll call while you head back to see him."

I nodded and walked with my dad and Dee, hoping that Tabor wouldn't look as bad as I imagined.

***

When we entered through the double doors that led to the Tabor's ward, I was hit with the distinct smell of antiseptic. It was so cold that my nose started running, and I wished I had a jacket with me.

An older nurse stepped into the hallway and offered us a kind smile. "Can I help you?"

"We're looking for Hunter," Dee said. "The doctor said we could see him."

"Right this way."

We all nodded and followed her to a hallway that was away from the others. The doors were shut and no patient names were listed on the wall outside the rooms. She got to the third door on the right and pushed it open.

"Give me one minute," she said, disappearing through the door.

"You go ahead. We'll wait here," Dee said to me and I hugged her quickly, accepting the opportunity to go in first.

I was eagerly waiting to enter the room when the nurse reappeared and gave me a sad look when she saw me.

"I'm sorry, but he doesn't want to see anyone right now."

"Please, can I just have a moment?"

"I have to respect his wishes."

I nodded and felt a wave of disappointment overcome me. My dad wrapped his arms around me and I leaned into his chest.

"He's going to be taken to get an MRI in a few minutes," she said, and then lowered her voice. "And if you happen to be here when he's wheeled out, there's nothing I can do."

She squeezed my arm gently and disappeared around the corner. For the first time since I'd shown up, I felt somewhat optimistic. All I needed was a minute to see him, and everything would be okay.

"I'm going to get some coffee—do you two need anything?" Dee asked.

My dad looked between the two of us and offered to walk with her. I knew he did that to give me a moment with Tabor. A list of things to say ran through my mind, but I didn't know where or how to start. *Do I apologize? Do I tell him I love him?* Before I knew which route to go, two technicians passed me and walked into his room, with a simple knock announcing their arrival. They didn't say a word to me, but I didn't care. I needed to see one person and he was on the other side of that door.

My heart was pounding in the minutes before they reemerged pushing a bed through the opening. I saw his leg first, and then his face. And when Tabor spotted me, it wasn't the loving face I was accustomed to seeing.

"Are you okay?" I asked.

Of everything I could've asked, those were the only three words that came out. It felt insensitive given that I'd seen him driven off the field. But it was also the question that I needed answered.

"How do you think I am, Dani? I blew out my knee."

"I'm sorry, Tabor. Maybe if I wasn't there, you wouldn't be here right now. I just wanted to surprise you and show you how much I love you."

"Dani, I can't deal with this right now."

"Ma'am, we have to get him to radiology," one of the technicians said.

I nodded, though I didn't want to move. In fact, all I wanted to do was climb onto the bed and curl into his arms. This wasn't the beautiful, happy man that lit up when he saw me. This man was broken, angry, and my heart ached knowing that my presence added to it.

I reached for his hand, and even though he let me take it, there was no feeling on the other end. The calloused fingers that were familiar and had offered me more comfort that I thought possible were cold and unmoving.

"I'll be here when you get back."

Tabor removed his hand from my grasp and shook his head.

"I don't want you here."

He nodded to the men, who were trying to avoid eye contact with either of us, but were failing miserably. One of them gave me an apologetic smile as they wheeled him away.

When he was out of sight, I found a chair and sank into it as my tears rolled down my face. It wasn't the conversation I had expected, but he was angry and physically hurt. I hoped he was just lashing out and that his words weren't what he wanted from me...from us.

"What's wrong? Where are they taking him?" Dad asked as he walked up, with Dee trailing behind.

I wiped the tears from my eyes and tried to smile. "The MRI."

Dee walked over and reached for my hand, offering a friendly embrace. "He's going to be fine."

"Yeah," I whispered. "I know."

He would be okay, but I wasn't sure if *we* would be.

"You two go home. I'm going to wait here for Marta and Abbi," I said.

"I can wait with you," Dad said, but I shook my head.

"No need. He doesn't want to see me, but I need to be here to keep his family updated."

Dee gave me a hug and assured me that everything was going to be okay. My dad was not eager to leave my side, but I convinced him I was okay. And I was.

Or I would be.

CHAPTER 27

DANI

Marta and Abbi showed up and thanked me for being there for Tabor. There was no place else I could imagine being. Even if Tabor didn't want me around, I'd be there for him. A part of me hoped that he would see me and I could talk to him when he was not as angry. But the way he'd looked at me, I knew he needed space, and I had to give him that.

I wasn't the type to back off, especially when I felt I could help. So I waited while Abbi and Marta went to visit him and tried to keep myself busy. When they came out they wore matching smiles and seemed to be in better spirits after talking with him.

They suggested we take a walk to the cafeteria to get some coffee and wait while the doctors did whatever it was they needed to do.

"What happened?" I asked when we sat down with our cups of coffee.

"I don't know if he told you, but Tabor had ALC reconstruction in the past. This isn't a first. And he always knew it could happen again," Marta said.

"But he's going to be okay?"

"He'll probably never play football again," Abbi said. "There's no meniscus left to reattach it."

"I'm sorry," I said, shaking my head. "I don't understand—what you're saying is like a foreign language to me."

"The first time he tore his ACL was in high school. He had surgery and it took almost a year for him to get back on the field."

"The first time?"

"And the second, he tore his MCL. Rehab was bad and he knew then that another would end his career."

Marta reached for my hand and squeezed gently. "He's going to have surgery in a week to repair the damage, but he's not going to be able to play again."

"Will he be staying in the hospital until the surgery?"

"We're going to take him home today," Abbi said. "You might want to give him a day to stop being pissy before you visit."

"Visit?" I scoffed. "He doesn't want to see me."

"He's angry, Dani. I know my brother, and when he's like this he says things he doesn't mean."

"I went about this all wrong. I should have called him before or gone to see him," I said.

"There's nothing you could have done. He always knew this was a possibility," Marta said. "I agree with Abbi—let's give him some space and let him recoup a little."

I nodded and she winked.

"I'll talk some sense into him."

She knew her son better than anyone, so I deferred to her expertise. I didn't want to push and ruin the chance of fixing us.

We finished our coffee and talked about happier things, like Abbi's wedding. They had met with the planner and picked the venue, but were still trying to figure out the rest of the details. Marta was smiling as Abbi gushed about the wedding dress she'd found, but with the wedding months away, they were on a time crunch.

I didn't want to bother my family with picking me up, so I took a cab home, and when I was behind closed doors, I cried. They weren't ugly, sobbing tears. I was sad for Tabor and what he'd lost.

It had been a long day, so I stripped off my jeans and climbed into bed still wearing the jersey. I tried to think of a happy time Tabor was in the bed with me, and smiled, recalling the way he made me laugh. It had been too long since he was there, but I still felt his presence.

Despite my better judgment, I turned on the late night news and waited for the sports segment to come on. Kip Stanley and his overly bronzed skin sat behind the desk and started in with the lead story of the night—Tabor.

"Quakes fans were stunned when the giant went down as Hunter tried to make a tackle. Initial reports claimed that it appeared to be a neck injury, but the replay showed it was a hit to the knee. Our own Felix Matthews is outside the arena with more," Kip said.

"Thanks, Kip. Yeah, it was a nasty blow for both Hunter and the Quakes. The coach said he was treated in the locker room before being transported to the hospital for more tests. We're hearing speculation that it's an ACL injury, and if you recall, JT mentioned in the past that he'd already had his knee reconstructed once. For now, we'll just have to wait and see."

I clicked the remote and turned off the television because the reporters were pissing me off. They were talking about Tabor like he was just any other person, but he wasn't. He was the man I loved, who had given so much of himself for the game. They didn't know him or care for him like I did, because to them he was a commodity.

There was no use in staying awake, because I had a big day ahead of me. I'd see Tabor and help him through this in whatever way I could.

I went to sleep hoping to dream of happier times with me wrapped in his arms.

"You have to be okay, Tabor. I mean it. I need you. I didn't mean anything I said. I was angry and stupid and I didn't mean any of it. Just please be okay and come back to me."

I leaned over carefully and brushed my lips to his softly before sitting down again, still holding his hand.

Why is he unconscious?

"I had this plan," I told him. "I was going to somehow get your attention so you'd see that I was there. I needed to do something big to show you that I was sorry."

I wiped my tears away and stared at him in silence.

"I should have just called you days ago."

The door opened and a doctor walked in with the nurse. He glanced in my direction, so I moved out of his way to give him space to check his patient. I couldn't hear what he said to the nurse, but he made some notes and nodded his head at me.

"Are you the girlfriend?" the doctor asked.

"Long story," I said, unsure what we were anymore.

"Before we sedated him, he was asking for Dani."

"He did?"

He still loves me.

"There's a lot of swelling and we have to monitor him for a few days," the doctor said. "We have to keep him sedated until we know what's going on."

The doctor left the room and I was staring at Tabor, who looked peaceful. Too peaceful.

"I'm not sure if you got my message, but I called you. I needed to tell you I was sorry. Because I am. I'm so sorry, Tabor. I let you think that I wanted to hide what we were, but it was stupid solution to a problem that was out of our control."

I reached for his hand again and threaded our fingers the way they belonged.

"I don't remember the last time I was so miserable. I was starting to annoy myself with the woe-is-me crap. So I did something about it. I think you would've been proud. I went to the school and got reinstated, and River's Kids starts up on Monday. Isn't that great?"

I kissed his hand again and rested my cheek against it.

"I'm going to make this all up to you, I swear it."

Tabor's eyes flew open and he stared at me...all traces of love evaporated from his eyes.

"You did this, Dani. And I never want to see you again."

I woke up in a sweat, my eyes wet with tears. The images of him practically paralyzed reminded me of how serious his injury could have been. He was "lucky" it was just his knee, but I knew he didn't see it that way.

I picked up my phone and started to call him, but stopped with my finger hovering over his name. Abbi suggested that I give him time, and it was after midnight. Tabor needed his rest and I needed to back off, so I set the phone down and went back to sleep.

That time, I thought of everything I would say when I saw him the next day.

CHAPTER 28

DANI

Tabor's car was in the front of his house when I showed up the next day. I didn't second-guess myself when I decided to drive over to see him. Twenty-four hours had passed and I felt that maybe he'd be ready to see me. Though there were no phone calls or texts to tell me I was right...or wrong.

I rang the doorbell and Abbi stood on the other side with a smile as she held it open to let me in. It was as if I was a stranger in his home, and I didn't like it. Being in his place always felt comfortable and inviting, but at that moment, I felt anything but.

"Couldn't wait, huh?"

"If I need to come back, it's fine. I just had to try."

"No, come in. He's in the his room."

"How is he today?"

"He's on some pain meds so he's sleeping right now, but you can go visit him if you want."

I tried to force a smile before walking the short distance to his room that waited down the hallway. When I entered the room, the blinds were closed and a machine was making a loud noise that was hard to ignore.

Tabor was sleeping and I wondered how he was able to do so with the sounds swirling about. His leg was hoisted in a machine that, at the time, was still.

I sat down next to him on the edge of the queen-sized bed and took the opportunity to touch his face. He looked peaceful, like in my dream. Though I had an aching fear that he might wake and lash out.

His chest rose and fell with every breath, but it wasn't enough; I needed to see his eyes, I needed to hear his voice again.

"I'm sorry," I whispered, lying next to him on the bed.

Being next to him made me feel at home, and given the awful sleep I'd endured the night before, I felt my eyes grow heavy. I wanted to fight it, to stay awake, but being next to him was what I needed.

***

"Dani," a whisper called out. "Dani. Wake up."

I opened my eyes and shut them when I realized where I was. It felt like everything since our fight had been a bad dream.

"Dani," I heard again.

My eyes finally fluttered open and I tried to let them adjust to my surroundings. I'd lost all track of time. I wiped the sleep from my eyes, and sighed when I saw Tabor still asleep.

"Guess you're tired," I heard Abbi say and my head snapped in the direction of her voice. "Didn't sleep so well, huh?"

In my haste to get out of the bed, I fell to the floor, but managed to finally get to my feet.

"Tabor said you were a klutz," she teased good-naturedly.

"I didn't mean to fall asleep."

"It's okay. I just wanted to check on you. On both of you."

"Is it okay if I stay with him a little longer?"

"Yeah. Totally fine." She smiled before disappearing from the room and closing the door behind her.

I rested my head against his chest and listened to his even heartbeat. It was so peaceful and brought a smile to my face. But when I felt a hand cradle the back of my head, my heart lodged in my throat. I closed my eyes, the tears spilling out of them all over again. Tabor had broken the dam I had built up to keep all the emotions away, but I didn't care.

A feeling of dread washed over me, because I was afraid of

what I'd see if I looked into his eyes. The last time I'd seen him, those same hazel eyes had been full of pain and betrayal. I did that to him. No matter how much I wanted to take it back, I knew that what I did was something we had to face.

"What are you doing here?" he asked, his voice dry and void of all emotion.

"I know you said you didn't want to see me yesterday, but I had to try."

"You shouldn't have come."

As I sat upright, I saw the same dead look in his eyes and I wanted to shake him—anything to make *my* Tabor return.

"I had to check on you and tell you how sorry I am about everything. I was so upset about my job and…you know what, forget it, no excuses. I'm just sorry. I didn't mean any of it."

"You meant some of it," he said.

"Maybe at the time, but it's not how I feel. I took care of it."

"Took care of what?"

"I went to the school the other day and talked to the new principal. He agreed with me that I shouldn't have been forced to do anything because I did nothing wrong. River's Kids will be up and running on Monday, thanks to Millie."

"I'm happy for you, Dani." But his tone lacked anything resembling happiness or even love.

"I told Dr. Putnam that I wasn't willing to lose you for my job," I said, unable to look at him. "I mean, if you want to try to fix this."

"What game are you playing here?"

The door opened and Marta stood at the entrance with wide eyes. I looked from Marta to Tabor in shock. I heard Abbi clear her throat and whisper something to Marta, but I didn't bother asking anything of them.

"I don't understand."

"You break up with me and I don't hear anything from you. Then you show up to my game—what are you trying to pull?"

"Tabor…"

"You won, Dani," he snapped. "You hate that I play football…and if you haven't heard yet, I'm done. Is that what you wanted to hear? Does that make you happy?"

"Stop it," I argued. "You know that's not what I wanted."

"No, actually, Dani, I don't know. From the time we met, all I've heard is how much you hate football and how scared you get when you watch me get hit. Well, great news, *babe*, I'm finished."

"Jeez, T, take it easy," Abbi said, stepping forward to quiet her brother. "You don't have to be such a jerk."

His laughter was humorless and it made my skin crawl. I'd never experienced the angry side of Tabor before, and though I wasn't scared, it made me sad. Was that really what he thought of me?

I looked down at his beautiful face as tears filled my eyes, but he refused to look at me. When I reached for his hand again, he flinched at my touch but didn't pull away.

"If you don't hear anything else I'm telling you, please hear this: I love you. I don't care who you are or what you do. I'm not going anywhere. I get that you're pissed, and if you need to take it out on me, that's fine, I can handle it."

Tabor turned his face, and when his eyes met mine they lacked the love I was familiar with. He was broken and I still loved him in spite of it all.

"You can handle it, huh? I've lost the one damn thing I'm good at, and you can *handle* it? I have *nothing* left, football is who I am, and you walked away because of it. So why don't you go ahead and keep on walking."

His words ripped my heart in two, but I'd done the same to him before.

"I'll go, but we are not finished, Tabor. Understand me? Deal with your shit and then you call me when you're ready to talk. But we are *not* over."

"That's a cute speech," he said before closing his eyes. "Can everyone just leave? I wanna be alone."

"Son..."

"Mom, I just need some time. Okay?"

Abbi grabbed her mom's hand, her anger rolling off of her in waves, and led Marta out of the room. I picked up my purse and started making my way to the door, but stopped and walked back to his bedside.

"I'm going to say something else to you that you may want to think about. I was never with you because you're JT Hunter. I was with you because you stole my heart. In spite of my misgivings, I allowed myself to fall in love with the kindest, most big-hearted man I've ever met. The person who just tore into me wasn't the man I fell in love with."

His eyes gave nothing away, so I reached for his face and made him look at me.

"The man I love doesn't treat his mom and his sister, or the woman he loves, like shit."

He opened his mouth to speak, but I turned and walked out before he had a chance. I didn't want his apologies, nor did I want more of his biting words. Tabor had been delivered life-altering news, and he deserved to be angry. But it didn't mean I needed to be on the receiving end of his wrath.

I walked down the corridor and found Marta and Abbi standing together in the living room. When she spotted me, Marta walked over and folded me into her arms.

"He doesn't mean it," she excused. "He doesn't."

"I know," I answered, returning the hug. "I wish I could do the last two days all over again. If I didn't show up to that game…"

"It would have happened at the next one, or the one after that. It's not your fault, Dani. And once he calms down and talks to the doctors, he'll see things differently."

"I hope so," I said.

Abbi walked over and hugged me. "Mom's right. He doesn't mean it. Just give him some time."

"I have lots of that."

I started walking away when Marta called my name.

"Thank you."

"Anyone would have done the same thing," I said of my presence.

"No. For loving him, flaws and all."

She was right. I loved him for everything he was. I'd allowed him to believe differently when I let him walk out my door. But every strength and flaw made him the person I was supposed to love. He needed time to come to terms with that.

CHAPTER 29

TABOR

I almost stopped her from leaving the room.

When she grabbed my face to make me look at her, I had to fight the urge to pull her to me and kiss her. Dani's fingers touching my face was almost too much to bear. I heard everything she was saying to me, but I didn't *want* to listen to it.

I inhaled deeply, the remnants of her flower-scented shampoo lingering in the air. The night I'd left her place, I was all but on my knees begging her to reconsider. And yet, she showed up to the hospital and my house…and just like that, I was supposed to forget everything?

Dani told me that she would choose me over her career. But would she? Or was that something convenient to say, considering that she hadn't truly lost anything?

I had stood in front of her like an idiot, waiting for her to change her mind about me. About us. But she let me walk away and made no attempts to fix it. I had to assume that's what she wanted.

When Mom told me that she and Abbi couldn't make it to the opening game because of an appointment, I was relieved. I'd already endured countless questions about what had happened between us, and when the topic came up, I found an excuse to get off the phone. It wouldn't be as easy to do in person.

But then she was there.

I thought my eyes were playing a trick on me, because Dani wouldn't be at my football game. I saw her in the first quarter, but kept focused on the game, delivering one of the best openings of my career. When halftime arrived, I couldn't ignore the pull to look into the stands again. I didn't spot her and knew I was losing my mind. I don't recall a thing Coach said in the locker room, because I was replaying the last time I had seen Dani and wishing it had been different for us.

"I don't think I've ever been so disappointed in you," Mom chastised when she walked into the room. "Why did you talk to her like that?"

"Mom, please. Don't."

It had only been a day and a half, but I was antsy and being tethered to a machine that would do nothing to get me back on the field pissed me off.

"Don't speak to me like that," Mom warned. "First you lash out at the doctors and now Dani...I raised you better than that. You didn't have to be so rude."

"Look, she's the one who wanted to end things for *her* career. I'm just giving her what she wanted all along."

Waking up and seeing Dani by my side when my eyes opened had meant everything to me. Unfortunately, my happiness at seeing her was short-lived. I knew my words had hurt Dani, but how could I console her when I'd had everything I knew taken away? Looking at her pissed me off. It was misdirected, but I didn't care.

"You're not giving her what she wants. You're being stubborn and taking the easy way out."

"How are you going to tell me what she wants? I was there. She wanted a break."

"And have you talked to her since? No. I didn't think so. But I have."

"What?" I leaned forward, curious by the revelation. "When?"

"It doesn't matter *when*—point is I talked to her when you

didn't, and she was miserable. She went to that game to support *you* doing something *you* love, because she loves *you*. That's what someone does when they love someone else—they compromise, they sacrifice, they step out of their comfort zone."

"How was I supposed to know? I haven't heard anything from her since I left her house. Nothing."

"And did you reach out to her? Did you tell her that when you walked out of her door that night, you waited on the porch for her to come after you? Did you tell her that you regretted that you'd even walked out in the first place?"

"I don't want to talk about this. Not right now."

"Mom, can I talk to him alone?" Abbi asked.

Mom nodded and left the room and I knew I was in for another verbal lashing. Abbi waited until the door closed behind Mom and walked over, slapping my bicep.

"What was that for?" I demanded, rubbing the spot she hit.

"For being a jerk. I get that you're pissed and all, but that doesn't excuse your behavior. If you don't want to be with Dani, then you need to man up and tell her, but don't pretend that you're giving her what she wants."

"So you're her fan now? Last week, you wouldn't shut up about how selfish she was about the whole *break* thing."

"That was before she dropped everything to be by your side."

I rolled my eyes and reached for the TV remote that was on the bedside table, but Abbi snatched it from my hand and moved it away. I glared at my sister, who was supposed to have *my* back, and she looked at me with pure disappointment.

"For the last two years, I've heard every reason for you not being involved. You don't want to date 'regular' girls because you don't know what their intentions are. You don't want to date athletes because of conflicting schedules. You don't want to date celebrities like Natasha because it's all about using you for the attention. Well I hate to point it out, but Dani is perfect for you. She loves you in spite of who you are."

"Yeah. I know," I muttered.

"So what are you gonna do about it?"

"I can't deal with this right now. I just want to talk to the doctors and see what I can do, how can I get back to playing."

"And if you can't?"

"If I can't?" I thought for a moment and shook my head. "I can't think about that right now. Okay?"

***

Abbi and Mom drove me to see Doctor Reynolds, the orthopedist. He threw around a mouthful of big words that amounted to a bunch of nothing as far as I was concerned. None of them told me how I could get back on the field.

But I already knew.

The moment I heard the pop on the field, I realized my career was over. I didn't want to believe it and hoped to God I was wrong, but I knew it.

The exam room was heavy with unsaid words, and it was my fist connecting with the table that broke the silence. Mom's eyes were sad, and she walked over to console me but I shook my head shortly.

"Not right now, Mom."

"I'm sorry, honey. I wish there were something I could say or do to make this better for you."

"What about my team? What am I supposed to tell them?"

"Coach already knows," she reminded me.

Abbi was pacing back and forth when she stopped abruptly and turned to face me. "This isn't the end of the world, T. Yeah, it fucking sucks, but you can still walk and do the things you want to do."

"What else do I have, Abbi? Football has been my life since I was a kid. I don't know anything else," I argued.

Mom stood next to the table and reached for my hand. I knew she had something to say but was gauging my mood before speaking. She had a way of grounding me, without being insulting, but sometimes it was hard to hear. I knew this was one of those times before she ever opened her mouth.

"Football isn't your life. It's what you do."

"I know," I conceded. "It's not the end of the world."

Mom shook her head and smiled, her eyes wet with tears. "Do you remember why you start playing football?"

I didn't answer; we both knew why I had started playing. I

was an angry kid and fighting became my outlet because of the bullying. I was a scrawny kid that stuttered, always picked on. But they stopped picking when I punched Riley Connors square in the nose. Unfortunately my newfound strength spurred me to seek out trouble, until Dad put an end to it.

"You can't just go around picking fights every day. You will come up against someone bigger or stronger, and then what? If you like hitting so much, play football. Channel that energy into something productive," Dad challenged.

I was only eight and had never really thought about playing football, but Dad put his time into teaching me.

We spent almost every afternoon throwing the ball around, Dad coaching my form. As I got bigger our training moved to a gym, where I started lifting weights with Dad encouraging me to continue.

And then he got sick.

He wasn't able to go outside with me anymore, and trips to the gym were nonexistent. But I did everything I could to keep going, because Dad was proud of what we had accomplished.

When he died, it was the only thing I had left.

"Before your dad died, the two of you were always outside, but football was never your passion. You liked spending time with your dad," Mom said, breaking my thoughts.

"Yeah, I did."

"And he loved spending time with you. But football was *his* dream for you because it gave you something to do. Maybe it's time you figure out what it is *you* want."

I huffed and considered her words, but came up with nothing. Football had been my focus for so long that I hadn't thought of anything else until I'd started my foundation.

"Your dad would be proud of you," Mom said. "Everything you've accomplished is beyond anything we imagined for you. But the game isn't worth your health, Tabor. You'll find something else that sparks your interest, and knowing you, you'll be great at it too."

"Easy on the ego, Mom," Abbi teased. "He's not perfect."

"No, he's not. Far from it, actually," Mom said as she squeezed my hand.

"How did we go from talking about how awesome I am to how much I suck?"

"No one said you suck, honey." Mom smiled.

"Surgery," I scoffed, repeating the doctor's words. I was no stranger to the scalpel, but allowing them to do what they were suggesting would essentially end my football career.

"Any idea what you want to do with the rest of your life, T?" Abbi said.

"Well, considering I was told only an hour ago that I officially need a career change, I might need some time. Like at least a day," I deadpanned.

"Okay, well I was thinking maybe you could be a car salesman...you know, if the modeling thing doesn't work out. Or what about rodeo clown?" Abbi mocked, and I laughed.

"No rodeo-clowning, but maybe he could be a boring suit-and-tie guy. Can you imagine him sitting still all day?" Mom asked.

"He wouldn't last for more than an afternoon," Abbi snorted. "He needs something active. Like water aerobics."

Mom and Abbi kept making jokes and I welcomed the distraction. I needed their words to remind me that I had things more important than sports to keep me going.

"Football might be ending, but how many people get the chance to start over and find something they really love?" Mom asked. "Whatever comes next, I think you're going to do amazing."

"You know what you'd be really good at?" Abbi asked, all traces of humor gone from her tone. She looked at Mom, and it was as if they were having a conversation made of weird eye twitches.

"Just say it," I demanded, forcing a laugh.

She looked at Mom and raised a brow before looking at me again. "Coaching."

One word. But it held endless possibilities. In a way, I did coach already. Whether it was with my teammates or the kids that my foundation helped, it was something that came naturally to me. Mom grabbed her things and walked to the door with Abbi, leaving me to consider my options. Before she walked out, she turned to face me and flashed her knowing smile.

"We'll be waiting in the lobby," Mom said. "But I want you to think about something else."

"What's that?"

"When you picture the next phase, is Dani a part of that future or not?"

CHAPTER 30

TABOR

After four days of hobbling around on crutches to keep the weight off my knee, I was finally able to walk on my own. From the outside, I looked well enough to get back on the field and do what I did best—crush people. But inside my body was another story. When I calmed down and took stock of what was going on, I spoke with Doctor Reynolds again—first apologizing for being a jerk, and then to find out what the best option was for my situation.

My agent was hounded with requests for interviews, and the foundation had seen a huge increase in calls as well. Unfortunately, not all of them were to help the kids we served.

Mom and Abbi were waiting for me because I had a press conference that I needed to attend with Coach. The night before, I had turned on the evening news and caught Kip Stanley reporting from outside of Quakes Sportsplex where he began telling the city the latest on my condition.

"In a press conference with Coach Jackson this afternoon, he updated fans on JT Hunter's status. If you'll recall, he sustained an injury during the third quarter of the season opener."

"JT will have to undergo surgery on his knee at some point,

but right now, he's fine. Unfortunately, it means we're without a critical player," Coach Jackson said.

My teammates were supportive and offered to help in any way they could, but we knew there was nothing left. I'd have to go clean out my locker, and the plan was to go when no one was around. I wanted to see the guys and wish them luck on the rest of the season, but seeing me was a reminder of what could happen to them. I'd see them, but I'd be stronger and in better spirits because I didn't need or want their pity.

As for Dani, we hadn't spoken since she'd left my house. It was nearly a week and a half since we'd argued at her condo and four days since I was admitted to the hospital. At my request, Mom and Abbi agreed not to contact Dani. They weren't happy with me, but what happened between Dani and me was our business, and I needed to take care of it on my own. If we had any chance of fixing the mess we'd created, we needed to do it alone—with no outside input or meddling.

"You ready for this?" Abbi asked as we walked toward the door that led to the press conference.

"Let's just get this over with," I grumbled as we stepped into the room.

Several of the local news reporters were waiting to get their sound bite for the late news, and I had to face the music. Mom and Abbi stood off to the side, prepared for the onslaught.

Coach Jackson walked in and we took the two seats available while flashes were going off.

"JT, how are you feeling?" one female reporter asked, louder than the others.

"I'm doing good. Better every day." I smiled. "Thanks."

"Is it true you're out for the rest of the season?" the familiar voice of Kip Stanley asked.

"No," I answered before quickly adding, "I'm out for good. No more football for me."

There was indecipherable chatter among the reporters and the onlookers, making me feel uncomfortable.

"How do you feel about that?" Kip followed up.

"It sucks. I've enjoyed playing and the Quakes are my second family. The guys, the staff, the fans—I'm going to miss all of it."

"Coach, what are you going to do without Hunter?"

Coach patted my back and smiled for the cameras. "There's no replacing a player like this guy. He's one of a kind and his teammates are going to miss him."

"JT! Do you have anything to say to the San Diego fans?"

I looked over to see Mom and Abbi smiling proudly and I nodded my head toward them. "Playing here, in this city, has been a dream come true, and I want to thank everyone for the support and making my time here the best. Your emails and well wishes mean more than you know."

The questions continued for another ten minutes, most asking the same thing in a different way. I enjoyed it because I knew it would be my last, and I was still trying to come to terms with that reality.

Mom, Abbi, and I walked to the waiting SUV, putting a temporary end to the speculation about what had happened to JT Hunter.

I climbed into the driver's seat and started the engine, gripping the steering wheel tightly. We remained still for a bit and then I glanced in the rearview mirror, meeting Mom's eyes.

"I need to make a stop before we go home," I told them.

***

It was already seven when we got to Dani's condo, but from the light flickering off her TV, I knew she was home. An uncomfortable silence settled in the car when I turned the engine off, and for a moment I second-guessed what I was about to do.

"I'll be right back," I said to them before stepping out.

"Go," Abbi demanded with a toothy grin.

When Mom had posed the question of whether I saw Dani in my future, the immediate answer was yes. I knew it the night I'd walked out of her condo, and I knew it as soon as she'd shown up to the hospital and tried to see me. Dani belonged in my future—of that I was certain. But I needed to tell her myself when I could stand in front of her and look into her eyes. Angry and bitter while I tried to come to terms with my future was not the right time. Besides, after my shitty attitude and the way I'd lashed out when I was told I was done with football, I needed to apologize to her.

I walked up the steps and took a breath before I knocked on the door. The porch light turned on and I stepped back so I wasn't intruding on her personal space, only it wasn't a woman's figure approaching the other side of the door. When it swung open, a blond-haired man, thinner and much smaller in stature, stood in front of me.

"I should have called," I muttered, feeling like an idiot. "I was just stopping by to see Dani for a second."

The guy remained still, his jaw slack, and he didn't say anything but I could tell he recognized me. I extended my hand and he hesitated before shaking mine.

"JT," I said. "Sorry to interrupt. I just...can you tell...never mind."

I turned and started walking down the steps, but paused and looked over my shoulder at the man who was still staring at me.

"Treat her good, man. Don't let her get away. Trust me, you'll regret it if you do."

He remained frozen in place, not saying anything, but as I turned to walk to the car, I saw someone walking downstairs. The moment I spotted Dani, I knew I had to at least walk over and say hello, so I did.

"What are you doing here?" she asked as she walked toward me.

"I just got out finished with my press conference...I wanted to see you," I said.

"Yeah, I saw...How are you?" She stepped forward, looking for visible signs of injury.

There was at least five feet between us and I hated it. I wanted to hug her, to tell her everything I had thought about since she'd left my room the other day. But it wasn't fair to her because she had company.

"I'm okay, I guess. Better." I smiled and nodded my head toward the audience behind us. "I didn't mean to interrupt anything."

Anything.

The word ripped something inside of me, but I didn't have the right to be mad or jealous. In my quest to do right by her, my silence told her that I was done. What was she supposed to do?

"You're not interrupting anything, Tabor." She smiled and looked over her shoulder. "Will, get Vi, come meet Tabor."

"Will?" I repeated, recalling the names I'd heard Dani talk about before. I knew that Vi and Will lived an hour or so away, but until that moment I'd never met them.

"Yeah, his band had a gig here last night, so he and Vi stayed with me."

A surge of relief shot through me and I stepped forward, almost reaching for her hand, but I didn't want to overstep. I wasn't sure where things stood with us and it wasn't my place to be presumptuous.

"Can I talk to you, for just a minute? I won't keep you long," I promised.

"Yeah, just a second." She walked to the door and said something to her friends before meeting me at the bottom of the steps. Dani was so close, but I don't think I'd felt further from her than I did at that moment.

"I wanted to apologize. I know I was a jerk at the hospital and the other day at my house. I feel like a dick for taking it out on you—you don't deserve that. I just need to tell you in person that I didn't mean any of it. Hurting you is not something I ever wanted to do, and I just hope that maybe you can forgive me."

"I understand, Tabor. It was a lot to take in…I get it," she answered, flashing a shy smile. "I just wish things happened differently."

I reached out for her hand, and when she didn't pull it away I took it as a sign that I was free to continue. I'd stand there all night if I had to.

"I need you, Dani," I admitted.

"You don't need anyone," she revealed, no hint of bitterness in her tone.

"That's not true." I shook my head. "I need the woman I love to give me another chance. I came here to tell you that, Dani, to make sure you know that I'm a jerk and said some pretty stupid things, and I meant none of them. I took out my shit on the one person I *want* in my life."

"Tabor," she whispered as she looked at the ground. When her eyes met mine they were glassy, and I hoped it was because she felt the same way.

"Do you think that we can start over?"

She closed her eyes and took a deep breath and my hope started to vanish. "I don't want to start over," she admitted. "I want to move on."

I didn't expect her to jump into my arms or anything, but moving on wasn't on my radar either. I thought we had something worth working on, but it was clear she didn't.

"Okay." I nodded and stared at our hands before releasing hers. "I understand."

She looked up at me and shook her head with a smile on her face. "No, you don't get it…crap, I'm totally fumbling this."

"Did you just use a football reference?" I asked, unsure *where* she was going with her rambling.

"No…yes…I didn't mean to…What I'm trying to say is that I don't want to start over because it means making the same mistakes, or worse. I want to move on…*with* you."

"That was mean," I scoffed, stepping closer until she was in my arms. She was pressed firmly against my chest and I waited until she tilted her face to look into my eyes. "You did that on purpose."

"Maybe," she teased.

"I love you, Dani."

"It took you long enough." She smiled.

I moved my face down to her because I needed to feel her lips against mine. We had spent too much time apart and I had missed her more than I thought possible. Just as we were about to kiss, a horn honked, startling both of us.

"What the hell?" she shouted, looking over my shoulder.

"Abbi," I grumbled, turning to walk toward the car, but Dani reached for my hand and pulled me back.

She wrapped her arms around my neck and my hands found her hips when our mouths finally connected in a kiss. I had missed everything about Dani, and I was determined to never miss it again.

The Beginning…

EPILOGUE

The Future

The roar of the crowd was something Tabor never missed—mostly because he was only without it a short time before he was back in the game. The odds of his return were slim, but the media never gave Tabor enough credit.

Watching football eventually got easier for me...once I understood the game. But I still cringed when I heard the crack of the helmets or the someone stayed down on the ground too long. Tabor assured me that it sounded worse than it was, though I never quite believed him.

It was a warm September day and I was in the stands, my mom and dad on one side and Marta on the other. Abbi and Grace were sitting behind us with their families, which had grown over the years.

We were waiting for the team to take the field and I noticed that the stands were filling in quickly. It was rare that my parents came to a game, and Marta typically came to the season opener and maybe the last game. But this was a special occasion and I was happy to have so many family members share the day with us.

Especially my dad.

A few years after Tabor and I were married, my dad was diagnosed with early onset Alzheimer's and he was understandably devastated. Mom was amazing at helping him come to terms with what was happening. It was hard to watch, but seeing the two of them come together and grow stronger made all of us proud.

"These are good seats," Dad said to my mom, looking at the bench where the coaching staff was standing. "Who's playing?"

"Dad," I said, getting his attention and pointing to the field, "it's almost time."

"It's almost time," he repeated. He looked around, trying to figure out what I was referring to, but seeing the players running out helped him.

"Is Tabor playing today?" he asked.

"Just watch," Mom said patiently as she rubbed his arm.

We were grateful that his disease progressed slowly, though it didn't buy us as much time as we would have liked.

"Where's Tabor?" he asked again.

Before we could answer, the announcer started calling out the senior players' names as one by one they made their way onto the field. We clapped and cheered as each one made his way out, and I watched with bated breath for the final name.

"And wearing number thirty-five...DJ Hunter!"

I looked at my dad, who was wearing a confused look on his face as he stared at the field, but we gave him a moment. I knew he'd realize it soon.

"Danny's playing," Dad said, and looked at me for confirmation.

"He is," I answered, my eyes filling with tears.

"It's the championship game, Dad," I said, with so much pride I thought I was going to burst.

Dad looked around and faced Mom. "Where's Tabor?"

She smiled and pointed to the field. "He's down there coaching your grandson's team, honey."

He looked at me and wore the widest grin I'd ever seen. DJ

and my dad were close, and he was the only one who still called him Danny. And though it was hard to watch his grandfather deteriorate, my son made sure to visit him every week.

"Danny's in the college championship," Dad said as he started remembering what the day way about.

It was the first time Beachmont University had made it to the big game, and my son had helped them get there. It was a proud moment when DJ ran onto the field for the last time as a college athlete. He'd decided to forego the football draft and finish up his business degree, despite speculation he'd be a first round draft pick.

DJ and Tabor were close, but he didn't want to follow in his dad's footsteps, and we only wanted our son to be happy.

Tabor looked over his shoulder and spotted me, waving and grinning. He had taken over the head coaching position when no one else had wanted it. Many thought it was a bad move, but it kept us close to home and gave him the opportunity to do what he loved—working with kids.

He was surprised when DJ had decided to go to Beachmont so he could play football for his dad, but I wasn't. Our son idolized his father. To have the opportunity to play the sport *and* be coached by one of the best defensive ends to ever play was a chance he didn't want to miss.

The team walked over and joined the coaches for a huddle and DJ looked over at my dad, giving him his signature salute before facing Tabor. There were a few minutes before the game started, and the players were talking amongst themselves when Tabor looked at me again.

He walked toward me and my smile, which hadn't faded, grew. There was a cement wall that kept us from getting too close to the field, but it had never stopped Tabor before. He grabbed a hold of the metal attached to the wall and lifted his body as close to me as possible.

I leaned down and kissed him because it was our pregame ritual.

"Good luck," I said.

"Don't need it. I have you," he said.

"Always."

Coming Spring 2016…

The Girls of Beachmont Book 2

String Beans
by T.K. Rapp

Prologue

"I'm heading home, Alex," I told my boss as grabbed my belongings. My long brown hair was caught beneath the strap of my messenger bag and as I wrestled with setting it free, I stumbled. Fortunately, I beat out clumsiness because I caught myself before falling over completely.

"Already?"

"Yeah, just finished with Sadie," I smiled.

"How's she doing?" he asked through a laugh, keeping his eyes fixed on the drum kit he'd been working on.

"She's doing great, but then again, she's your kid," I reminded him with a grin.

I typically gave his eleven-year-old guitar lessons when a client canceled…and it was safe to say, she had been getting lots of practice time. She was a natural. Still, it would be nice if my regulars showed up. Will and I needed the extra money to help make rent.

"You and Will doing anything tonight?"

"I doubt it. He's been working nights at the club and our schedules are completely messed up."

"Marriage life, right?" he laughed again.

"Yeah," I muttered before grabbing my guitar case and waving as I headed out the front door.

The warm afternoon air greeted me and the descending sun momentarily blinded me until I slipped my sunglasses on. We had had so much rain the last week that I was beginning to think the weather might be the reason for all the cancelations.

My beat up whit Beetle was parked in the back of the historic red brick building, right next to Alex's new pickup. I was sure he freaked when he saw me pull into the spot near his new baby.

Will hated driving my car and teased me that the undercarriage was probably rusted and before long I'd be *Fred Flintstoning* my way to work. She may have been old, but she'd gotten me where I needed to go, even if it did take at least two times to get her started.

"C'mon baby," I said, trying to start the car.

I turned the key again and the engine finally turned over. I started heading home to our one bedroom studio apartment a short fifteen minutes away eager to see my husband.

We moved to Spring Park after we finished college because Will said it would be good for our careers. Granted, there wasn't much back home for music majors, but I wasn't sure Spring Park was any better.

It took me almost two months to find my job at Hodges Music Store, and while I appreciated the work, it wasn't exactly where I thought I'd end up. That's why I went to college, right? But then again, I did select music as my major. I could have gone with something practical like business, but I was practical all my life.

Despite that one leap I took, I was always practical, even in our marriage.

We were a perfect match ever since we met at Battle of the Bands in Wheeler. I was there with my roommates because they knew I was friends with a few of the groups that were competing. All the girls had a thing for musicians, but that was never my scene. I always loved music, and could appreciate someone's ability, but hooking up with talent wasn't me.

Until Will.

Two Years Earlier

The third band was playing and I didn't care for their style, so it was the perfect time to hit up the concession stand for another beer. Some guy was standing in front of me drunk off his ass and when he turned to leave with his beer it was sloshing all over the place. Will must have seen it coming because he wrapped his arm around my waist and swung me around so the beer missed me, instead sending the amber liquid all over his shirt.

He was an adorable mess. His brown hair was mussed, though I assumed that was him, not the beer. His concert tee was soaked so he pulled it over his head revealing muscular abs and a sexy smirk when he caught me looking.

"Thanks," I said, as coolly as I could muster. "Wasn't

necessary, but thanks."

"No worries," he smiled. "Having fun?"

"Yeah. What about you?" I asked, stepping up to order my beer. "Can I buy you a beer?"

"Isn't that what I'm supposed to say?" he smiled, but not offended by the offer. He looked up at the stage and nodded at the band playing. "So what you do you think of them?"

I didn't even wait to think of my response, I already had an opinion.

"They're trying too hard. It's not bad, but where's the passion? Where's their soul? I want to feel their words, but all I feel is screaming and angst...and not in the good way. They just sound soulless."

When he looked at me, his mouth was slightly agape, but he recovered and handed me my beer as he took the other.

"Don't hold back," he laughed. "So what's your name?"

"Viola, but everyone calls me Vi."

"Well, Vi, maybe I'll see you around? Talk music sometime?"

"Yeah, Sure," I said and started to walk off, but he called my name and I had to turn around.

He was holding a black sharpie in his hand. "So, does that mean I get your number then?"

I smiled at him and scrawled my name and number on his forearm, wondering if he'd be able to make any of it out through the sea of tattoos that covered skin.

The crappy band finished playing as I was joining my friends and the MC announced the fourth band would take the stage soon. My roommates were laughing and carrying on, but I was too distracted by the image of Will to participate.

It was twenty minutes later when the fourth band took the stage. I was getting settled in when the lead singer stepped to the mic. I knew he couldn't see me, but I knew he was talking to me.

"Hey everyone, I'm Will Banks and we're Sound Venom. I was just talking to a friend who said that she needs passion, so here we go."

My eyes were wide and felt my cheeks flushed, but no one knew he was talking about me.

I watched as Will strummed his guitar and began singing

lyrics to a song I'd never heard. He was so handsome up there and in his element. There were no excessive lights, no crazy on-stage dramatics, just the band and their music. It was perfect.

He called me later that night to ask what I thought and I was a little surprised that he didn't play the game. Most guys played the game, but not Will. We talked all night and met up in the morning for coffee so we could talk some more.

Three months later, we were engaged and six months later, we were in front of the justice of the peace, getting married after our last class of the day. Our parents were against it, but there was nothing they could do or say to dissuade us.

It wasn't incredibly romantic, but it was exactly what I wanted.

Will was able to bring out the fun and spontaneous of me and I tried to keep him on track. We couldn't have been more different, and I liked that.

Polar opposites.

I needed direction, a plan, something to work toward. Will liked to go with the flow and see what happened.

Unfortunately, the go-with-the-flow mentality didn't pay the bills. A six months into marriage, the going got tough...

Real tough.

We were fighting over bills and school all the time and struggling to make ends meet. It wasn't what I expected married life to be, but we had more good days than bad.

It was nearly a two years after we married that, Sound Venom broke up. Damn shame because the guys were amazing. It was hard on Will because he missed collaborating. Every once in a while, we would try to do something together, but our styles were so different that it never really meshed. He was beating himself up because he felt like a failure without his musician brothers and ended up having to get two jobs and dropped out of school.

But he limited the time he spent working because he wanted to continue making music.

Will was a dreamer. I was a realist.

***

I pulled into my parking spot and grabbed everything before I headed inside. Will worked crazy hours at The Firehouse, so we were lucky if we shared a bed for more than a couple of hours. I hoped that I could have dinner made by the time he got home so we could catch up before he left to tend bar at the club.

He made serious bank when he tended bar.

But I wasn't an idiot. I knew the reason he made such great tips was based on his sexy as hell rocker looks. I had gone to the club to listen to local bands play and I saw the way women looked at him. It always makes me laugh because he gave them a smile, or so they thought, but his eyes were always glued to mine.

They could have the dream, I had the guy.

Our apartment was on the first floor, which was a good thing. Will liked to play his music a little loud, but I figured the old lady that lived above us was probably deaf because she never complained. And the guy to our right was always too high to care. We had never had a chance to meet any of the other neighbors, but no one had told us to keep it down. A surge of excitement rolled through me when I heard the music knowing that he was already home.

Acknowledgments

First, I have to thank my husband because this book wouldn't have happened if it weren't for a simple conversation we had one night. You are my sounding board and biggest supporter. I love you. I thank God for you and for allowing me to pursue this dream.

This book was made possible by the letter "K" Kayla who kept me on track and the letter "D" for the Dunn Bros. people who kept food in my stomach. It takes a team, people!

My betas – Lisa, Erin, and Blue – your encouragement, suggestions, and notes made me laugh and meant more than I can tell you. Goose, I miss you and I'm so ready for you to get back to the world of the writing. Kari Gardner, thank you for fixing me and making sure I didn't break anything unnecessarily.

To my group of funny, inspiring, talented, and honest women. Claire Riley, A. Meredith Walters, Amy Queau, and Stacey Lynn, I appreciate all of you and the way you helped make this book a reality. Thank you for taking time out of your schedule to help me when I need it most. Kelsie Leverich, I miss your adorable face and Brittainy Cherry, I'm amazed at what you've accomplished.

Thank you to my wonderful editor Amy Jackson because you're simply the best. (And now I'm singing.) And to Penny Reid because she is so supportive and helpful…did I mention smart? Because she's crazy smart. And a special thank you to Kim Greny and Chew Brown, two of my dearest friends who are there for me when I need them. I love you both.

I am blessed to have the Tenacious Ten that supports me in so many ways. My mom and dad not only encourage my stories, but also read them. My sister is the first librarian to put any of my books in their system (It means the world to me.) My niece Joey is ready for another Barmy book and my nephew Mr. Man is waiting for me to write something he might like. A big HUGE thank you to all of my family.

Finally, to Peese and Gidget, my wonderful daughters who schedule time to let me write and make sure that I stay on task. I love you both so much that my heart might burst. I hope to make you proud.

T.K. Rapp

About the Author

T.K. Rapp is a Texas girl born and raised. She earned a B.A. in Journalism from Texas A&M and it was there that she met the love of her life. He had a contract with the U.S. Navy that would take them across both coasts, and ultimately land them back home in Texas.

Upon finally settling in Texas, T.K. worked as a graphic designer and photographer for the family business that her mom started years earlier. She was able to infuse her creativity and passion, into something she enjoyed, but something was still missing. There was a voice in the back of her head that told her to write, so write, she did. And, somewhere on an external hard drive, are several stories she started and never finished.

Now at home, raising her two daughters, T.K. has more time to do the things she loves, which includes photography and writing. When she's not doing one of those, she can be found with her family, which keeps her busy. She enjoys watching her kids in their various sporting activities (i.e. doing the soccer mom thing), having Sunday breakfast at her parent's house, singing out loud and out of key or dancing like a fool. She loves raunchy humor, gossip blogs and a good book.

Visit T.K. Rapp online:

FACEBOOK
TWITTER
GOODREADS
T.K.RAPP'S WEBSITE
MODEST VIEW BLOG

If you enjoyed this book, check out the others by T.K. Rapp:

Being There
Mine to Lose
Mine to Steal
Finding Laila (YA Novel)

www.ingramcontent.com/pod-product-compliance
Lightning Source LLC
Chambersburg PA
CBHW022158170626
46807CB00005B/2258